A Guilty 1

Mary D Curd

A Guilty Retreat

Published by Amazon KDP: https://kdp.amazon.com/en_US/

Printed by Amazon KDP

Why is Lisa in retreat at a holiday home high in a forest in Southern France? After visiting an isolated Buddhist temple, she is involved in the lives of two young women, temple guides. These lead her to the hermit, who lives mysteriously in the heights of the forest. He warns Lisa to confront her own secret past and the estrangement from her daughter, Sophie.

This is also the journey of a youthful Lisa; the flight from her family in England to the Costa del Crime, and a precarious, naive life there which is soon severed.

Must she return to England to seek family and resolution, and how can she make amends?

Dedication

This book is dedicated to my husband, Tony

Acknowledgements and thanks to…

Matt Ewens for the cover design & publishing

My inspiring manuscript readers: Margaret, Liz and Ann.

Preface

It was not long before someone found her. Feeling on edge, even as she approached the front door, she put her key in the lock, noticing the scratch marks surrounding it. Expecting the lock to be broken, she took a step back, frightened of going inside. There was no sound from within.

With a clammy grasp, she turned the key and tiptoed in, listening. Not a sound. Grabbing a bronze figure from the side table in the hallway, Lisa moved towards the open door of the kitchen. Barely breathing, she slid a knife out of the block on the work surface and grasped it in her right hand.

"Put them down and you won't get hurt." A hand clamped over her mouth. The hand was dry and tight; in some way familiar. Her first concern was for Sophie. At least her daughter was not there, but safe at school. He allowed her to turn around, and she stared at his face, then away again, confirming what she had sensed. He was the stranger they had met in the Rosengarten in Bern. The man with the red blemish like a scar or a birthmark.

He opened the drinks cabinet and poured her a whisky. Did he even know her preferences in alcohol? She sipped it as she watched him cross to the window, standing to one side of the gap in the shutters, and peering down. Did he have an accomplice? Or an enemy waiting outside?

Drinking the whisky felt wrong, yet it steadied her. He took nothing for himself, but sat down opposite her and leaned forward. "Call me Ken," he said, "when we travel tomorrow." He clasped his hands together, raised them in a thoughtful pose against his face. "What's the name on the passport you're using? I need it for the tickets."

Chapter One

France Autumn 2017

It was the wrong day. She heard the dogs baying in the distance, but coming closer. Their howl was more mournful than aggressive, and it reminded Lisa of wolves. She held tight to the steering wheel, dropped down another gear, and crawled further up the rough track full of ruts and large stones. Wednesday, mid-week and, with the weekend, a principal time for hunting the wild boar in the forest. 'It lasts from dawn to dusk,' she now remembered. Lisa had not calculated how long it would take to drive down through France, how many overnight stops she would make on her journey to the south-west *département* of the Hérault, or when she might arrive.

A hunter stood to one side with his dog and his shotgun. He looked surly and did not acknowledge her instinctive nod of the head as she edged past. The muscles of his weather-beaten face barely moved, and his eyes were on her car. The sight of him made her hands shake a little.

She had seen photos of the holiday home and kept looking at the mileage. One kilometre from the main road, follow the turn off at the bottom of the village; the place lined with plane trees.

Of course, the house was recognisable when she reached the end of the journey, and with a smile on her face, she drew up in a flurry of small gravel stones. Here at last. Modern and purpose-built, the sun was already glinting off the wall of glass comprising the first floor, reflecting the vivid blue of the sky, and the thin tendrils of drifting white clouds, like a giant painting. She sighed in relief at her arrival. At leaving behind all the pent up anxiety. Forever running away from something.

The summer visitors were long gone, and the house was hers for at least six months: peace, respite. Ready with the copy of the email giving her the coded numbers, Lisa opened the key box. It was an odd arrangement. She entered the building by the laundry room, shared with another tenant located nearby, and from there through a locked door into her own accommodation. The principal living area – kitchen, sitting space, roofed balcony – was on the elevated first floor, while they had tucked the bedrooms below on the ground floor level. That way, tenants got the most from the views over the pool and garden.

She saw wine and fresh bread on the worktop; they must have received her last-minute text to confirm her arrival today. Flowers on the coffee table, and the fridge contained milk, butter and other basics. Lisa wasted no time in unpacking; instead, she found a corkscrew and a glass. Opening wide the doors to the balcony, she sat down to take in the view. Trees rose higher and higher through the steep-sided valley of the forest, and beneath that vista lay the terraced gardens of the property, shaped in a broad arc around the pool.

For autumn the air was soft and warm. The sun danced off the water in the swimming pool in scintillating, radiant flashes, rippling across it. Lisa's gaze turned to the olive tree near the edge and to the exotic, desiccated black fruits scattered about. She drew in a deep breath to smell the resin and shrugged to relax the tension in her shoulders. The sun's rays played on her face.

******

It was Martin, the other tenant, who told Lisa about the Buddhist temple. He had joined her one afternoon, sitting by the pool which they also shared, and had introduced himself. He had known of her arrival.

"I doubt I will be here long enough to swim in it," she said. "Much too cold, I would guess, before the summer."

"You might get a chance for a dip in April. I won't be here then."

Martin worked at the temple, where he had plenty to do as a carpenter. He left the forest in the Spring because of the expensive holiday rental season. For that period, he moved the caravan he owned and which he had paid to winter in its secure shelter – this was a common enough practice. He towed it away and set it up in a camping site by a lake.

"I couldn't afford to stay in the cottage here in the forest," he said. "That's the time when the owners make a hefty profit. I earn good money, but I spend it as fast as I earn it!" She smiled at his honesty.

"The temple closes to visitors after this next weekend," he said. "It will be your last chance, and it really is something."

He was friendly and always available with information, but they soon maintained a distance, which suited them both. Lisa decided she would go that final Sunday, and he gave her details of the route.

In the beginning, the scenery and the views seemed magnificent, but the journey soon became frightening and, by the end, she hated it. A mist came down, and she had to concentrate so hard on driving; continuous climbing and spiralling, trying not to look down at sheer drops without barriers, peering through the windscreen to spot the signposts.

On arrival at the car park for visitors to the temple, a group was already milling about. Martin had told her to be prompt for two o'clock; it would be busy on the last day. Lisa joined the company of mainly young people, with large bags strapped across their backs, trainers on their feet and wearing thick padded jackets and woolly hats or hoods of all colours. Some walked with arms clasping another's waist. They chatted and smiled, anticipating the tour. It was windy, and the prayer flags on their tall poles flapped wildly. She had known it would be cold up there, so high up, and was glad she had dressed warmly. Everyone wound their way down the steep slopes, pausing to view the building, becoming larger and clearer through the mist as they approached it. At the bottom of a winding trail, she stopped for longer and the delay meant that she had to hurry, not losing sight of the other departing visitors. She caught up, and they all paused at various points down the path to look at the shrines, cascades of flowing water, and carved figures. These captured her interest, despite the damp chill. But it was difficult to read the information on the boards because strands of her hair swept across her vision, and it was too raw to linger.

Taking off her shoes with the others at the entrance to the temple, she hurried across the damp paving to the door. Chilled and already thinking of the risky return journey, she wondered why on earth she had come.

The welcoming warmth as she entered was a relief. She hugged her arms to her chest as if to gather it all up in gratitude. Her gaze drifted over the large space, the mass of colour and detailed pattern lying within, the towering gold statue of the Buddha. She gasped in surprise at the alien culture of the impressive interior.

Hushed, they all sat in rows while two guides gave an amateurish introduction with a failing microphone. Afterwards, they listened to a confusing video. Although filmed in English, it had a French voice dubbed over it. For Lisa, it made the whole thing more difficult to follow than if it had been in French. She could not understand why they had done it. The dubbing seemed to be neither an homage to the 'foreign country' of France, in which the Buddhist monastery stood, nor a gesture to the polyglot visitors, who all spoke some English.

A few tourists put questions to the two young female guides. One did most of the talking. The other woman was quiet and withdrawn. She was on a retreat there, so they were told. Perhaps that was why she looked so distant and quiet. Later, in the car park, Lisa read a notice board informing them the retreat lasted three years, three months and three days, and that it was soon ending.

How could you come back to the world after that? It was a question she would wonder about in the weeks which followed. She had felt disquiet in studying the young woman, the second guide; so silent and introverted, and not looking at peace.

The return journey was worse than Lisa had expected. The mist was all-encompassing in the fast disappearance of daylight. So frightened that she prayed, and perhaps it was answered because two cars joined her further down from a side road, and she followed them in hope of deliverance. They were local, judging by the end numbers on their registration plates. These correlations with departments and number plates were a feature which they had not yet dispensed with in France, despite all the advance notifications threatening they would. She was sure the vehicles in front of her must know the way down to the village. With a deep sigh of release, she arrived home without further incident.

The visit preoccupied her from then on. It stirred mixed emotions: the fear on the journeys, the idea of a restful retreat, but also unhappy memories of religious observance in her childhood.

On the next market day, sitting at a table outside a busy cafe, it did not surprise her when the guide approached her. It was the young woman who had done most of the talking and answered questions. She asked Lisa, in clear English with an attractive accent, if she might join her. In the introduction, she explained where she was from and remembered

Lisa from her visit. Her name was Marianne. They shook hands.

A waiter brought her a fruit juice, and the woman sat back with an air of expectation. She looked different; her hair, cut and restyled, was pretty. Her clothes were formal and businesslike.

The silence between them continued, and Lisa felt uncomfortable. She sensed the guide was expecting some questions from her. It was the way she remained still, gazing straight at her, almost in a calculated stare.

Lisa fiddled with her coffee spoon. It unnerved her. What did the woman expect of her? She hoped it would not turn into some sort of religious approach, but asked what her way of life was like now, assuming from the notice board that the retreat had finished?

Marianne said she still found time to meditate, and it was possible to keep the values, although it was very different, of course. "We get a lot of guidance about returning to the everyday world." She nodded in emphasis. Her disconcerted expression was so serious.

Giving minimum details about the reason for her own presence in the area, Lisa started telling the young woman about her decision to stay for several months. She described the beauty of the forest, especially where she was living. This went on for some time, it formed a diversion.

Perhaps she became too intense, eager to maintain that life was wonderful in her new surroundings, because she was not getting much of a response.

Before she could grind to a halt, Marianne interrupted. "You have been very ill," she said, "and you are waiting for news. It frightens you a lot."

Lisa's eyes widened in initial surprise and then disbelief. She crumpled, bowed her head; both shocked and tearful. It was all so sudden and unexpected.

"Everyone has to cry," Marianne whispered. She offered a tissue from her pocket, but Lisa rolled it into a ball in her hand and looked away in embarrassment into the street full of colourful stalls. It was an unspoken denial, and she knew it. And it worked. The tears dried. She raised her head and sat up straight.

Marianne leaned forward and spoke again in a low tone. It must be for my benefit, she thought, but doubted anyone was listening to an English conversation. Who was this woman, and why had she come here and joined her in the cafe?

"I am not recommending the temple for you, nor a retreat of any kind. You understand? That is not my purpose," Marianne said and waited, her gaze still fixed on Lisa's face. Her expression softened now, and her lips curved in an encouraging smile. Lisa nodded. At least there would not be any attempt at religious conversion.

"You must talk to someone, you know. Have you family?"

She did not want to go into that at all. She shook her head, glanced away again.

Yet Marianne bit her lip in thought and did not get up from the table to leave. There was more she wanted to say. "In the forest, there is a hermit. People go to him for advice. You should try that."

"A modern-day hermit?" Lisa almost choked as she drained the last of her coffee dregs. What was this all about? She got to her feet.

"Wait a moment, before you leave," Marianne said. "Martin will tell you how to get there. You have met him? He knows about it. Find this man who is living as a recluse."

Bemused by this linking with her neighbour in the forest, aware that she had kept thinking about the other young woman she saw at the temple, and sensing there was more, if she was ready to ask, Lisa queried, "The other guide who was with you…?"

"Oh, Barbara. She has got only a little longer. You understood that?"

"No, well, yes – perhaps," she acknowledged. For a moment more, they both stood looking at each other. "Will you let me know?" Lisa asked. Now thoroughly confused, but driven, she knew not why; Lisa took out her mobile phone, and saying nothing, the two of them exchanged numbers.

Chapter Two

Lisa was always aware of the sound of the wind in the forest, the cracking of branches and the drilling drip of water. The sudden stillness, which often then followed, was like an alert; it drew her gaze up to the skies and the clouds, trying to gauge what lay ahead. It was the effects of the autumnal equinox, Martin said. Never predictable. She must attune herself to it and take no notice.

She took regular long walks using the trackways. Martin saw her starting out the first Saturday morning. She had noticed he only worked a five-day week at the temple, although there was more paid work if he wanted it. That day, he had sounded concerned, and warned her of the wild boar which roamed everywhere. He looked pleased when she said she kept to the broadest and most well-used paths. Nevertheless, he suggested they exchange phone numbers, just in case. Lisa agreed, not wanting to appear as a helpless woman, but aware that her only other contact was Marianne. Anyone could have an accident, she told herself, trying to mollify her pride. She had come here to be alone, and it had its drawbacks.

At that awkward and confusing meeting in the cafe, she recalled Marianne's advice. She asked Martin what he knew about the hermit. He did not show surprise, no raised eyebrows. She realised why when he told her that although he had never been to see him, the monks where he worked at the temple mentioned the man.

He did not press her for a reason, but explained that as she could only reach the hermit's shelter on foot, it meant a long and arduous climb. He suggested she prepared well for it first.

It was something she already did and would continue to do so; taking regular exercise since her arrival, though with no real objective. Guided by his advice, she increased the length and difficulty of her walks. Determined not to depend on others to rescue her from a mere climb, however steep.

One sunny morning, crisp with an overnight frost, but the day already brightening, she decided to use the route Martin showed her. As she sat on the balcony, drinking her breakfast coffee, it seemed right. Today would be the day. She realised the walk would take most of the morning, but the sun was already warm on her back.

Sensibly clothed, remembering his warning it would be colder higher up, she gathered together other essentials: water, food and her phone. She picked up her rucksack and packed it with care. She had realised she must have a gift too, and settled long ago on a plaid-patterned thermal blanket, with several pairs of thick socks. They would be useful and therefore acceptable.

Soon she left behind the usual pleasant paths, had taken her last look downwards at the views of the village beneath, and instead turned to face, with some apprehension, the granite rock towering up in front of her. From there, the route narrowed, became darker, closer and more oppressive. She felt the change from the invigoration of the earlier stage of the walk and struggled with the steepness. She let her body acknowledge the difficulty, took greater control of her breathing, and allowed herself frequent brief rests. These methods were very familiar.

For the last part of the track, she had been told to look out for the marks: rectangles of paint on the bark of the trees. Orange, or perhaps saffron, she thought; the colour of the robes of the Buddhist monks, she presumed. If they talked of the hermit, it must involve him with the temple. With relief, she saw the markings. Her goal was in sight.

Bending double over the last almost vertical slope, the track curved round, and into view came a blur of curling smoke, then an igloo-shaped shelter. At last, the recluse himself.

He was stacking wood in a covered lean-to, which lay to the side of his home. Glanced up at her arrival, paused, and continued his task. Dressed in trousers and boots, he wore a jacket of some sort. On his head was a colourful woollen hat. He looked like one of the *forestiers*.

Lisa stood watching him for several minutes, getting her breath. He called out, "Have you brought something? What is it?" in clear but accented English. She removed her rucksack, dragging out the blanket and the socks. She felt foolish and wary. Were they the right gifts?

She asked him how he knew she was English. He didn't answer, just motioned to a space in front of the shelter. She walked closer and put her gifts down on the spot he indicated. He came nearer, studied her – which gave Lisa the chance to study him. Curly, long hair trailing down his neck to his shoulders from under the woollen hat. What struck her most were his eyes; huge, dark pupils looking out almost vacantly from a weather-beaten and bearded face. Not old, not her idea of some sort of yogi or guru. What was she expecting?

"Who sent you?" he asked. She told him about Marianne, a guide whom she'd met at the Tibetan monastery. He nodded before she expanded any further on that, as if to cut off an explanation.

There was a long pause. It made her feel uncomfortable. She wondered why she had come and recognised it as the same reaction as on the journey to the temple. Was this man another lost soul? Seeking enlightenment? His air of presence, something spiritual. The few people she had seen on that visit, who were not a part of the group of young tourists, struck her as religious waifs and strays. Perhaps, in coming to find the hermit, she was on the same road.

He said, "I am going to make some tea. It will warm you." Then motioned her towards the stone shelter. That seemed more encouraging. The drink was herbal, no milk, but steaming above the rim of the tin cup. She warmed

her hands on it, as did he. She looked around, barely turning her head because the rough stone building was tiny, sparse; a small stove and some bedding. She thought she could make out a few tins of dried goods against the wall at the back. Some kind of lamp, oil or paraffin, threw shadows inside, but little actual light. Only the opening, a narrow archway, allowed a streak of sunlight to penetrate within. The floor was of dry compacted earth.

They stood and sipped the tea. Lisa felt calmer, more intrigued, and less cautious, but she still wondered what to say now that she had found him. Any preconceptions, all her last-minute prepared phrases, such as they were, vanished. She could only stand there, warming her hands on a tin cup.

A frisson of fear, a trembling, almost overwhelmed her. It was strange because the emotion had nothing to do with him. Her concerns, already dispelled by the tea, the few questions. She looked out through the opening of the shelter to a gap between the trees, then up at a lowering sky. The distraction worked, and she made herself calm down. She realised that her return might be through rain and glanced down at her footwear; encouraged that they were good, strong walking boots. She would soon be on her way back. The hermit coughed, recalling her attention to him. "Face up to whatever it is," he said. "We all do in the end. However painful." His voice was firm and pitched low, but the tone was bitter.

His lips tightened against the next words he spoke. "Think of the young woman … dying, and she had no chance of life." He looked at her in a questioning manner, as if awaiting a response, until she nodded her head to show she realised who he meant.

He shook a few drops of tea onto the ground and put out his hand to take her cup. "And no secrets. Tell the truth." That resonated with her, and she glared at him, imagining for a moment that he perceived why. He stared back at her, with hard, probing, piercing eyes.

When he turned away, walked out of the shelter, avoiding anything further and returned to his stack of wood, it relieved her. It was the sign that he had finished with her.

Although tired when she got back, the journey downhill had felt less difficult. A soak in a hot bath would help, and she took a glass of wine with her. She lit the first of the thick and decorated candles she bought on a whim in a nearby town on market day. Inhaling the heavy scent which filled the bathroom, she relaxed and luxuriated in the heat.

She noticed from the crossed off days on the calendar that the letter would soon arrive; the one she dreaded and yet was impatient to receive. Throughout her treatment, she had endured without fuss and struck up deep but short friendships with others suffering in the same way. Online was easiest. Now she had come through it all, and undergone the ultimate tests in England, before she left for France. They would forward the computer-generated result to her here. Her mail arrived, and the system was working. This long-stay holiday accommodation, in a beautiful part of the world, was reserved as her reward for what, she hoped, would be the end of that troubled period in her life.

She climbed out of the bath and half-towelled herself dry, slipping her arms into the sleeves of a thick, soft bathrobe, while all the time trying to clarify what was on her mind for so long, which led her to see the hermit. When the letter arrived, she did not want to read it on her own. She needed someone there – whatever it said. The hermit told her not to keep secrets. Well, there were secrets and mysteries. This one she wanted to share. What about the others? She could not contemplate going further to answer that implied criticism about 'telling the truth'. It went too deep.

It must be the one person she could call on to help her through this last part. If the visit to the hermit did nothing else, it had made her more aware of that. She would have to contact her daughter.

Chapter Three

The phone call came in the middle of the night and it surprised Sophie. No, shocked her. It *seemed* so early. She justified her reaction after checking the actual time. Of course, she realised it came from another time zone, an hour's difference in France. "Anyway," she said aloud as she sat up in bed with her phone, "it better be important."

Dazed with sleep, surprise deepened when she recognised it was Lisa calling her. Often estranged, they made brief contact for long periods. And even during her mother's recent illness, she almost disappeared, shut herself away. At first, Sophie felt it was like talking to a stranger, not her mother. She struggled to hear the words at the other end; a muffled greeting, some urgency about a terrible connection and poor reception.

It took her back to childhood. Lisa did all the right things, of course, when Sophie was young, but she was always such a closed-in person for a mother. A parent she never knew in any depth and had to call her by her first name. Although not uncommon then, it increased the distance between them. Or so it seemed to Sophie.

Of course, she now agreed to her mother's summons. How could she not? Strange that she would want her there for the final health check. Why was Lisa so worried this time, when she had told her the results had been clear for ages?

At the airport, it was a relief to see her in the flesh, yet she looked so tiny, fragile. Thinner and older. Perhaps because of the protracted recovery from her illness. How had this little woman produced such a large, robust figure like me? Sophie wondered as she waited for a greeting.

"It's been a long time, Sophie, I know," Lisa said, and squeezed her hand.

Sophie put down her suitcase, which she had just caught from the few items on the carousel. The plane had not been full. She juggled her other bags with difficulty. Now she was ready. She rested her hands on her mother's shoulders, studied her face for a few seconds, and kissed her on both cheeks. "Doing things the French way," she said, and that made Lisa laugh.

Sophie's gesture marred because she almost tripped over the trailing strap of her bucket-shaped handbag. Her mother seized it. "Clumsy girl!" she said. They organised how to carry the luggage, and the closeness of the moment broke.

Sophie knew the holiday home was in a forest, but had not realised how isolated it was. Her mother drove with care up the long track to the house and led her indoors. The lovely views from the living area struck her on the first floor. She stood on the balcony, absorbing the setting of the house, peering into the distance as far as she could see.

She had noticed several prints on the walls by Klimt and Matisse. "Bet you were pleased to see those, Lisa. Your taste exactly." She pointed to a framed poster of 'The Kiss' on one wall. Her mother's rental of the house was for at least six months, and Sophie was certain she wanted all the furnishings and fittings to be right.

****

Sophie knew she would not sleep long that first night because of the travelling to the airport, waiting around for the flight, and then the car

21

journey to the forest. All tiring enough, but meeting her mother had been a strain, too.

When she awoke early the next morning, Sophie wanted to explore on her own. Lisa said she always took a sleeping pill and slept late, so she would not disturb her mother. She wrote a note for her mother and found a jacket amongst the incomplete unpacking of the night before. Not only to explore her new surroundings, she wanted exercise, a good, long walk. As she wandered along the first track leading away from the house and into the forest, she heard the whine of a machine tool, and the noise drew her on. She approached a slim, tall, slightly balding man bent over a work bench where he was planing wood. Sophie thought he was middle-aged, but her guesswork often proved to be wide of the mark. She glimpsed a small building a few yards behind where he was working in the clearing. His workshop? Or perhaps his cottage?

He stopped to look up. "You must be Sophie," he said, dusting a hand free of sawdust onto his jeans. "I'm Martin." They shook hands. With relief, she realised he was English; no need to summon up some schoolgirl French.

"Lisa – your mother – told me you would come to pay her a visit." They smiled at each other. He pointed to a small cherry-wood chest of drawers, with garish decorations. "I'm building some furniture – on commission. Not to my taste, though."

Perhaps he had seen her expression. She nodded, but did not comment any further on the piece, not wanting to appear rude.

He invited her into his house for coffee, and while he made it, he told her about himself. He worked at a Buddhist temple where there was plenty of carpentry work for him. This intrigued her.

"My mother mentioned something about a temple for a community of monks yesterday. High up in an isolated area," Sophie said. Though she had taken in very little then, she was curious now. "Where is it exactly? And why a Buddhist temple in this area of France?"

"The temple is about fifteen miles away. It's perched up high and the name in Occitan French is 'the place of springs'. This is your first time in this area of France?"

"Yes. I am not familiar with it at all. Just visiting my mother."

"Well, the monks chose the location because it looks like Tibet," Martin said. He toyed with a spoon against his coffee cup. "I suppose you know about Tibet and the tradition of the monks." This time Sophie could nod in agreement.

He frowned, hesitated, and shifted towards the door. "I suggested to your mother that she should go there, and not to miss it. She went on the last Sunday at the end of the season. The public only gets the chance to visit for a couple of hours on Sundays."

She edged around him in the small space and approached the door. He did not seem to want to say anything else.

As she stepped outside, he said, "I think it affected Lisa more than she imagined and not in a good way, either. I'm sorry."

He wanted to get on with his task. He told her he had to deliver the finished article to his client the following week and pointed to the trailer in which he would carry it. Puzzled by the change in his tone, Sophie thanked him and left him to it.

She strode at a pace, enjoying the exercise and scenting the pine trees in the clear air. By the time she returned to the house, the sun was gaining warmth. Her mother was stirring and Sophie told her to stay put in her bed while she cobbled together breakfast on a tray.

Sophie carried it downstairs to her bedroom and placed it on her lap.

"I don't need all that," her mother said. The coffee spilled over. She saw her mother suppress a "tut-tut" as she concentrated on mopping it up with a paper napkin.

"I met Martin earlier. He seems pleasant enough. Friendly. Do you have much to do with him?"

"Well, he's my nearest neighbour. Yes, I suppose we exchange a few words now and then." She nibbled on buttered toast.

"He mentioned your visit to the Buddhist temple. Some distance away, almost in a mountainous area. Sounds interesting. What was it like?"

Lisa wiped her lips and paid more attention to clearing her plate. Only a small portion, but at least finished and without complaint. She looked different that morning from the day before. Sophie wanted to credit the improvement to her own arrival. Perhaps her mother needed company now?

She pushed aside the tray, showing slender wrists more knobbly than Sophie remembered. Her bare collar bones outlined in sharp angularity above the scalloped shaped edge of the nightdress. But her expression was more animated.

She told the story of her visit to the temple and was more expansive than Sophie expected. Perhaps her mother was picturing the journey and what followed as she related it. It all meant something important to her. Her eyes stared ahead unfocused, almost as if she did not have a listener. Sophie did not question, nor interrupt. The strangeness of it mesmerised her. She listened and tried to work out why Martin had thought it so significant an experience for her mother. Albeit not a good one.

She began forcefully. "I went there, and I will *never* forget the journey." She clenched her fists on the thin counterpane covering the bed. "It was … tortuous."

Sophie glanced up, startled at the word. She assumed and hoped the experience had been worth it. Otherwise why continue? The journey had taken a long time, but it must have been terrible for some other reason. What was the attraction in the beginning, except for the recommendation by Martin? Her mother was not, as far as she knew, religious.

Lisa crossed her arms, hugging them close to her chest. Sophie got up and opened the blinds to let in the sun's warmth. "It's pleasant out there. I had a lovely walk," she said. "I left you a note...." Her mother was not listening, but running a finger along pursed lips.

Sophie motioned towards the orange juice, and when her mother nodded, took it from the discarded tray and put it into her outstretched hand. She sipped at the juice.

"I think it was the mist. It jolted me back remembering another time." Sophie waited, intrigued, but no longer sure this was a good idea.

"I remembered when I first got my diagnosis, all that time ago. That was a grey day, too, with a mizzle rain. Fitted my mood. I wandered for ages after they told me the bad news, walking in that horrible greyness." She shivered and pulled the bedclothes up further.

Is that it? Sophie wondered. The connection?

"It is other worldly," her mother continued, without further encouragement. "The temple itself, as well as the place. Give me my phone and that album, the one on my dressing table. It's more of a scrapbook, I suppose."

Lisa leafed through the images taken on the phone, copied texts and information leaflets – all downloaded, she assumed – until she found those from the visit. Sophie leaned over, trying to gauge what had impressed her mother. One picture showed a temple nestled in a dip in an otherwise deserted landscape. Spiky golden pinnacles topped various levels of the swooping, up-turned roofs of the temple, coloured deep red.

Her mother swiped her screen to a photograph which showed a huge gilded figure of the Buddha, anchored in the middle of a lake, surrounded by prayer flags and tall, wintry grasses. In several other images, close-ups highlighted the red, white and gold on the walls of the temple. In front, incongruously it seemed to Sophie, trimmed grass like a cultivated English lawn, provided a setting for several foreign-looking statues.

The images struck Sophie as odd. The place had no obvious resonance for her. She murmured a surprise, but said nothing.

"We didn't see the monks." Her mother was more animated. "But on our return we spotted the other buildings, houses of retreat with warning notices – for visitors to respect and keep clear of them. I remember thinking they must house the monks somewhere in those buildings, although nothing differentiated them." She sipped at the orange juice again.

"Anyway, we paused at various points down the path to the temple to look at the shrines, statues and cascades of flowing water. " Lisa abandoned the phone and the scrapbook and, raising her knees, grasped them under the covers.

"Before we entered the temple, we had to remove our shoes. I lined them up, fixed a point of identification for our return. You would know how I felt about that!" She turned to face Sophie, not antagonistic but caught up in her recollections. It was a reminder of her desire for order throughout her daughter's childhood, and Sophie smiled at the admission.

"They showed us a video which explained what it was all about. Well, it wasn't all that good, in fact." Sophie nodded. The experience must have had a lot of impact on her mother, judging by what Martin had said, but it still bemused her why it had.

"Did you make any sense of it all?"

"Well ... it was about dying, I suppose. Or, at least, how to make a peaceful death. Distancing yourself from this world: possessions, ambition, even people and relationships. It said that you cannot gain spiritual enlightenment if you cling to earthly things. Oh, and don't look back," they advised.

Sophie took Lisa's hand, which felt freezing. She let it linger there.

"Afterwards, we could examine more closely the sacred decorations of the temple."

Sophie wondered if it was only her mother who had been so absorbed and so affected. "What was everybody else doing?"

"Same as me, I suppose," she said, as though the idea had not occurred to her because she had no interest in what the others were doing. "But then they invited us to put questions to our guides. A few people moved forward to do that."

Sophie raised her eyebrows in question.

"No, not me."

"Was that it?" Sophie asked. "The end of the visit? You went back to the car park and came back here?"

"Yes, but it had taken quite a long time, the walk down to the temple, and the video followed by the questions. There was not much daylight left. The return journey was even worse; later in the day and the mist covering everything."

"Did you tell Martin about it, afterwards, the visit?" She was reluctant to reveal their own brief conversation together. Her mother would hate the idea that they had been talking about her.

"Yes, I did!" Lisa said in surprise. "But he got in first; said that some people thought the place was 'over the top'. He meant the bright colours, I think." This sounded more like her mother, Sophie thought. Ever ready to give the facts?

"The thing I heard on the video – the one we saw at the temple," her mother added as an afterthought, "is the idea that you should cultivate only positive thoughts. Perhaps it is hard to be negative with all those bright colours surrounding you. Still, I can't imagine how they do it – keep positive, I mean."

With one sudden movement, she was out of the bed. "I need to stock up on food now you've come, so let's go out," Lisa said, searching with her feet for slippers on the floor. "Won't take me long."

Sophie tilted her head, hearing distant shots somewhere higher in the forest, and her mother must have realised she was listening. "It's the mid-week hunters," Lisa said. "They hunt at the weekend, too. Wild boar." Sophie left her to get ready.

They were going to the nearest town. As they crawled down the track, small stones rattled against the car, and she saw dogs sniffing around the trees, weaving in and out, alert and full of life. In the rear-view mirror, they glimpsed the men emerge, holding shotguns, observing their departure. "Don't frown so," Lisa said. "They have enormous status in the community, the hunters here, but every year there is an accident and someone gets shot!"

Sophie blanched a bit at that, looking across at her mother's taut expression, her hands gripping the wheel more tightly than their slow progress necessitated. She had thought the caution was because of the chipping on the paintwork of the car, which had also made her flinch at first. "Why? Are they so incompetent? Don't they work as a team?"

Lisa hunched further over the wheel. "It's different here. The villagers have complicated relationships, often quarrelling – it sounds like feuding. Odd. Martin warned me."

How accidental were the accidents? Sophie wondered. Perhaps they played out their feuds and vendettas through the hunts. She shrugged. Well, they are not likely to hurt us; she thought.

"Do they hunt near the Buddhist temple?"

Lisa appeared not to have heard. It is not far away from this forest, Sophie reckoned. How would it work? The monks didn't even eat meat. What would they feel about the slaughter which she imagined the hunt involved? Or maybe, she mused, dismissing the idea of threat to them, the monks had acquired a lot of land around their mountainous retreat. Perhaps, so that they could keep it pure, unstained by the activity of the hunters.

It was a relief when they arrived in the lively town. Market day attracted a crowd. At first, the smells of spices from the stalls and coffee from the cafes overwhelmed Sophie. Tables and chairs spilled out onto the pavements, even that early in the year, when the sun had little warmth until mid-morning and then often disappeared by 4 o'clock in the afternoon. They became part of the throng of people, merging with them to buy vegetables and fruit.

Sophie suggested they had a coffee and watched the world go by. Her mother chose the place.

"Un grand crème," Sophie said to the proprietor, with confidence, when ordering her drink, having revised some phrases from a book purchased on impulse, and rolled her 'r' s. She had practised that, as well. He smiled in appreciation and returned with a steaming cup of espresso coffee with hot milk.

Four men sat at another table and passers-by stopped to greet them, men kissing men on the cheeks, touching hands, raising and pointing fingers in a gesture of approval. It all looked so foreign.

An older couple arrived and sat at the table opposite. He spent his time with a newspaper, and she kept interrupting him. All the while the slow, untidy straggle of people drifted down the cobbled street, fingering the handbags and the coloured head-scarves on the stalls in front of them.

The scene immersed Sophie, and she did not see how quiet her mother had become, until her spoon rattled against her cup, and she saw her agitated expression. "What's wrong?" she asked.

"This is where I first met Marianne. Well, spoke to her for the first time," Lisa said.

They sat over more coffee, while Lisa told Sophie about meeting the guide who had finished her retreat at the temple. She continued to tell Sophie about her visit to the hermit. The whole idea of it astonished Sophie more than all that had gone before.

"The forest used to be full of hermits in medieval times, Martin told me," her mother said. "I researched it a bit. In the following centuries, there were a lot of priories which followed an austere way; barefoot, regular fasting, no heating, no meat."

Sophie had seen an example of a shelter that morning; one that lay just outside the *domaine* of the forest. Its shape, like a rough stone-hewn igloo with just an arched opening. It intrigued her at first sight. Perhaps her mother had been thinking about it just then. Everything Lisa said seemed triggered by her deep emotions.

Chapter Four

They were waiting for the letter, although Lisa had not mentioned it again. Her forwarded mail arrived every few days. Some came directly from contacts advised of her temporary change of address to one in France.

"You will wait until I have news?" Lisa queried one morning.

Sophie agreed, providing it did not take her further than the last week of the month of November. She had not disclosed that she left her job two years before and started up on her own, with the help of a business loan. Her absence could not extend too far, and she had already foreseen sacrifices for taking of time off for the Christmas holidays. Her return ticket was open-ended, and her mother had insisted on paying all her expenses.

In the meantime, Sophie was eager to see something of the sights and what the region offered. It was preferable to watching Lisa brooding. They studied a map and decided together on several places of interest.

In Lodève, the nearest town, they attended the Remembrance Day ceremony on the eleventh of November, coming upon it just by chance. A group of school children brought wreaths to lie at the base of the large, intricate memorial. It was an emotionally moving sculpture, showing a line of ordinary civilians, with heads bowed, looking down on a fallen soldier. The Mayor gave a speech. Some adults wore the bleuet, the traditional blue flower, in contrast to the red poppies of Britain.

Sophie fell into conversation with a few English speakers and learned that the First World War was at the heart of most observances in France. Although, they told her she might see smaller, plain stone markers dotted around in villages. They had inscribed these with the names of the 'martyrs', at the places where they had died fighting in the Resistance movement during the Second World War. Also, they remembered the losses in war in Algeria, between the French and the people they had colonised.

"Of course, you don't remember your father," Lisa said, as they lunched at a restaurant, following the ceremony. Sophie was enjoying the cuisine of the south, which was more varied.

"No. I was only five when he died. He wasn't a military man, though, was he?"

She had seen photographs of him. Some showed him holding her as a baby. All of them appeared to be holiday images; from sunny beaches or hillsides, with expensive villas in the background, or by a pool outside luxurious hotels. Her mother often gazing at the two of them, father and daughter. Who had taken the photographs then? It had to have been someone else.

Seeing herself in these old pictures, Sophie felt nothing, even from the images where Lisa was holding her hand, or carried her close, tucked in her arms. She did not recognise her baby self. Did anyone relate to photos of themselves when they were so young? It was all beyond memory, she presumed, to identify yourself at such an early age.

In photographs of Sophie with her father, her mother often stood in the background, as if the focus should only be on the two of them. Though she was always expressionless herself, Sophie noticed that the petite, lithe figure of Lisa attracted the gaze of onlookers caught in the frame. She realised how strikingly attractive her youthful mother – at that youthful time in her adult life (how old would she be – twenty?), Lisa appeared. Voluptuous in a baby-doll fashion, a preferred shape of the era, but one that was still projected by famous models in Sophie's own youth. Perhaps her mother's diminutive but shapely form struck her because the contrast was so stark with her own sturdy body. She thought her awkwardness, clumsiness, stemmed from her own much more robust stature.

Her gracelessness, a point of irritation, at least, for her mother, could be helpful sometimes. She smiled at her niggling under-confidence in her own appearance. When she recalled a few advantageous moments, it was a consolation. It could be useful to be clumsy when some appealing stranger came to your rescue, or someone needed a strong pair of hands.

Sophie encouraged the ordering of a dessert, as Lisa pushed away her plate from the main course, having eaten little of it. She wanted to pursue more details of his life, and this seemed an opportunity.

"My father was a lot older than you, wasn't he? I don't remember a thing about him. I'm glad you kept some photos."

"It's only ice cream," suggested Lisa, studying the card propped on the table and ignoring the question.

Sophie persisted. "You never re-married, so I always supposed he was the great love of your life. Did you ever meet someone else, after you were widowed … I mean, even in the last few years?"

A hard question, she realised, because of the irregular contact they had with each other. But her curiosity grew now that the two of them were together and under one roof. She did not know if Lisa had indulged in many, or any, affairs. Nothing overt. As a child, she did not remember seeing other men in their household. But they had moved around so much, and it separated them for long periods when her mother sent her to a boarding school as a teenager. Of course, there had been male friends or acquaintances in social groupings, with whom she mixed and her mother had introduced them to her. To her knowledge, no one was significant. In maturity, she soon became independent, started out on her own with a job and a flat. Afterwards, she never knew what went on in her mother's world.

Lisa looked up from the restaurant menu and discarded it with a flourish. Her face flushed now, and she gave her daughter a fixed, blank glare. It reminded Sophie she had seen several of those disapproving, withdrawn expressions so far on this visit, and it meant that her mother did not want to discuss anything further.

"He was rich. That's why I married him. You do not know how important that was," she said. "He was also … kind." She shrugged and thrust the menu at Sophie. "You choose."

******

On subsequent days, when the weather was fine, although becoming colder, they toured the coast and visited various resorts. The small, quiet fishing port of Mèze on the extraordinary étang de Thau, a saltwater lagoon devoted to the cultivation of oysters, was not busy at that wintry time of year. All the restaurants were closed bar one, in which they ate a lunch in splendid isolation, feeling surprisingly welcome.

When they arrived in the heart of the city of Sète, driving along past its many deserted sandy beaches, Sophie at last heard gulls. The absence of birds in this part of France, so commonplace on the coast of England, had surprised her, and she missed hearing them. Now she picked up their mews and stood watching with delight as they circled high above her in flight over the sea.

"Perhaps when the fishing boats come in during a different season, it would be the same as in England. You would see more of them and further inland," Sophie said, but her mother was not listening. She held out a brochure with a map.

"We must go to Mont St Clair. It says here that the views of the city of Sète are wonderful from there; 'Venice of the Languedoc', they call it, for its canal network." She slid her glasses back onto the top of her head, looked up and added, "there's a penitential chapel, called La Salette."

"Why do you want to go to a church? Have you caught religion or something?"

Lisa folded the map. She gave her daughter a quick, side-long glance, her lips pursed, her hurt expression mixed with annoyance. "Never mind. I can come back and do it when you've left."

Sophie felt contrite, but did not understand how she could have offended her. Perhaps it was enough to have opposed what her mother wanted to do. She refused to fall in with her mother's plans all the time during this brief period of sightseeing. It was disturbing though – what appeared to be an additional, hard-to-manage aspect of her parent's character. Something brought on by her illness?

On another occasion, Sophie proposed they visit the beautiful *lac du Salagou*. She had read about the abandoned village of Celles, and it fascinated her. They forcibly deserted the entire place in order to construct a new dam. Not completely flooded as yet, the wrecked church and the vestiges of some other buildings remained exposed.

They found it with ease and wandered around, mapping out the former housing from the ruined site, delighting in the peace, eating a picnic lunch purchased on the way to the mysterious and deserted location. It was one of their best days. On their route out of the area, they drew in and parked up to investigate a scattering pathway of stones on either side of the narrow roadway they were travelling in order to rejoin the main road. Walkers had picked them up, they presumed, and inscribed names and messages upon them before they placed them in patterned positions on the banks.

The extraordinary sight absorbed Lisa as well. "People like to leave their mark, don't they?" She took photographs of the pebbles with as much enthusiasm as she had of the ruins at Celles itself.

"Young ones, judging by the words on them," Sophie said. It was moving reading the messages. How long had they been there? Did Jean still love Annette? Or had he found another since then?

"We moved house so often when I was younger. Did we leave any traces?" she asked. "Not like this, though." She laughed at the idea.

Lisa stood up straight, abandoning her study of the stones, and the camera strapped around her neck swayed and fell discarded onto her chest. "What do you mean, *traces*? You always had a home to return to from school, didn't you? Even if we lived in several places. You were comfortable enough, I imagine. I denied you nothing."

What on earth had brought this on? Sophie put an arm around her mother. "I didn't mean anything. Of course, you always looked after my needs. What's all this about?"

White faced and trembling, Lisa withdrew from her. "Nothing. Nothing. Let's go home now."

****

When the letter from the hospital arrived, it came with a few others – circulars and advertising.

"Shall I open it for you?" Sophie took the envelope, already slit at the top. Her mother's need to have her there for this result still puzzled her. She had made sure she knew about all the tests, kept herself informed, albeit at a distance, during the treatments. After a succession of negative results, with no troubling information, she had awaited news of them with less and less concern. On arrival in France, she had asked her mother if she was feeling unwell again, and tried to find out the reason she appeared to be so worried. Why this summons to come to her in France? All to no response.

Lisa scanned the single sheet this time and smiled before she even turned it overleaf. Just in case there was something on the reverse to counter the good news. For once, there was no need for her to say anything as Sophie watched her expression. Her mother accepted a hug and said, "We must celebrate."

They lunched out. Afterwards, Lisa bought some titbits, savouries, and hors d'oeuvre from a delicatessen with delicious odours and attractive displays. She left a note pinned to Martin's door and hoped he would share a bottle of bubbly with her and her daughter.

He came along that evening, and by the time they had toasted her mother and drunk some of the champagne, he was expansive and suggested to Sophie that she join him the following evening. He was learning to salsa. When he explained his hobby, he told her not to laugh. It was for fitness, but also as an interest. No, it was not a place he went to in order to look for a girlfriend (he used the word 'pickup', after a thoughtful pause), and in fact, the lady he partnered was now too pregnant to continue. Adding straight away, he had nothing to do with that! This salsa class was the following night. Would she like to accompany him? It would be fun.

In the end, Sophie agreed. She warned him she was no dancer, but saw it as an opportunity to quiz him about her mother. What had he gathered in the short time they had been close neighbours, sharing the pool, garden, and the laundry facilities? What did he make of her?

The following evening, Martin drove right into the centre of the colourful city of Montpelier. She enjoyed the journey and the sight of the lively nightlife; the lights, the bustle, and the razzmatazz of the dance hall dazzled her. The dancing was another matter; energetic and tiring. She had no rhythm as she repeatedly advised him, shouting above the sound of the music, which was the only element she appreciated.

It seemed an exotic and exciting experience. Returning to the forest in the early hours of the morning, stimulated and tired after all the exercise and excitement, it was a pleasant note on which to end her stay; she thought, before she tumbled into bed. Though in that, she was wrong.

Chapter Five

For the day of her return flight, her mother urged Sophie to be ready in good time. She flapped her hands to shoo her off to bed for an early night. Awake at the crack of dawn, or so it seemed to her, Sophie listened to the disturbing banging of cupboard doors. It came from the kitchen on the first floor, above the bedroom in which she slept. She found it hard to go back into a dreamless, cosy sleep. Though she snuggled down, within a few minutes she gave up the struggle and got up.

"What on earth are you doing up at this hour, Lisa?" she asked her mother as she reached the top of the stairs and the opening to the vast windowed room of the first floor. Rubbing her eyes, securing the tie of a fluffy dressing gown against her waist, Sophie peered at the wall clock in the kitchen area, just in case she had got the time wrong. No, it was that early.

The dressing gown was too short and gaped open. She had borrowed it, of necessity, because she was unprepared for the drastic drop in temperature, which she now realised meant that winter was on its way.

"I thought southern France was hot in summer and temperate in winter?" Sophie said, framing it as a question, but an accusing one, and yawning all the while.

Her mother was looking for something on the worktop. She moved to the fridge, opened and closed its door, but still looked at a loss. She raised her head. "You better have a substantial breakfast."

So that was what she was up to. This offering, which sounded so maternal, made her smile. It was so unexpected. She took a mug out of the cupboard and filled the kettle with water. "Have you had a coffee yet? Want another?" Her mother pointed to the empty cafetière. Sophie busied herself at the sink, draining off the cold dregs. Lisa told her she must have a cooked breakfast and itemised various options. Sophie selected a few of them; it was easier than a complete refusal, and she wanted her departure to be a harmonious one with no sign of the rancour of previous times. I hope my mother will not try to supervise my packing, she thought, suppressing a laugh.

It was a mid-day flight, and at this hour, it appeared to be cold and overcast in the early morning light. The house was high in the forest, and Sophie knew it would be warmer when they reached a lower level in the valley. Even more so on the route from there to the airport. Vistas of vineyards and the dew on the grapes came into her mind. Those were images she would hold and cherish of the surrounding landscape, and she must get her mother to email some photos of their time together. During the visit, she had been glad to neglect her own phone. She had switched it off for long periods and had taken very few pictures herself.

Sophie had wanted to buy something to eat at the airport, but with a full stomach, there would be even less to do while waiting for boarding. She sighed and resolved to be calm and cheerful and eat her breakfast. Though she was looking forward to getting back to her work and her own home in England, some good had come out of this visit. Of course, there was the relief of sharing the last negative test result with Lisa. Nothing must spoil this point they had reached in their relationship. She would leave her mother with a favourable impression, and hope it remained permanent. They sat opposite each other on high stools at the breakfast bar, and Sophie attempted to eat. Her mother appeared to be watching her. "I think you have my eyes," Lisa said.

Sophie smiled. In reality, she did not consider they looked like mother and daughter; too many basic differences. She was tall and sturdy. Lisa was fair, whereas she was dark. Perhaps there was something about their eyes, or the shape of the jaw, which came to a point in a long curve. Sophie did not know what to make of the sudden comparison. Nor of her laughter. Lisa was changing – had been ever since her arrival, and although Sophie felt she floundered a little in her company, not sure how to respond, it suggested possibilities of them drawing even closer.

They were just about to leave, having checked that Sophie had left nothing in the bathroom, when Lisa heard the ring tones of a phone. Sophie followed her up the stairs to where it lay on the coffee table. Her mother picked it up with a quizzical look, as she did not often use it and received few if any calls. Who would contact her out here?

Lisa read the text message, swayed, and as Sophie moved forward to support her, collapsed onto the sofa. She gasped, made a strange noise in her throat. Tears streamed down her face.

"Mum, what on earth …?" Sophie cried, and took her mother in her arms, rocking her in a complete reversal of roles. She took tissues out of the box on the coffee table, and dabbed away at her mother's face, until Lisa cleaned up for herself, her sobs subsiding. She breathed hard to calm herself and allowed her daughter to pick up the mobile and read the text, which had so distressed her.

'*Light your candle. There is one thing I did not say, the hermit, he is the brother of Barbara.*'

Sophie scrolled down and found a name: *Marianne.*

"What does it *mean*? Marianne is the woman you met, the guide from the temple?"

"Yes. I don't want to talk about it. Not now." Lisa blew her nose.

41

"I'm alright. It's nothing. A shock, that's all." She would say no more and got up, bustled about without purpose.

She would not allow Sophie to miss her flight, although she still looked upset. "You must have things to do – your job. You can't keep extending your stay, and the return flight is all arranged," she argued as Sophie tried to reason with her. They had plenty of time, Lisa insisted. Their journey would not take long.

In the end, Sophie agreed, thinking it could offer a distraction. If she would not let her drive – which was most likely – Lisa would have something else to concentrate on. Perhaps she might even refer to the alarming text message on route. When she had calmed down more. She always had to come to terms with crises on her own, she imagined. But when they arrived, Sophie had to hurry through the check-in and she had learned nothing. "Phone me this evening. Promise?" she called back to her mother as the staff hurried her through to board the plane.

****

Lisa sent her daughter a text when she returned home to the forest from the airport. She was feeling much better and would contact her within the next couple of days. Not to worry. Then she turned off her phone.

She was *not* feeling better. The text received from Marianne, those few words, signified Barbara had died. When she read it, she could not bear to speak to her daughter about the strange and powerful influence which she needed to come to terms with. She did not want to talk about the young woman, the effect she had produced, the concern Lisa had experienced. How to explain to Sophie her request to be informed? Least of all, would she reveal her sudden wish, expressed to Marianne, that she

42

would light a candle for her. Now it hurt even more to learn of her ignorance of Barbara's relationship to the hermit. What the man had said to her on that visit to his 'cell', on her journey which seemed to be a pilgrimage, and his visceral 'advice'. How much more attention she might have given to it if she had made the link between him and his dying sister?

The full significance of it preoccupied her after Sophie's departure. The finality of the news she had not wanted to hear sobered her. Her emotional outburst, which Sophie witnessed, to the message sent by text, had passed. In a childish way, she told herself; she had been waiting for a miracle. And why? She did not know Barbara. But the quiet, pallid woman was so young and now, she realised, so struck by tragedy. How could it not affect you?

That night, she lay awake wondering why the two siblings turned to such extremes for solace. Or were their lives so extreme? Barbara had been on a retreat in a Buddhist temple, and the hermit was in some kind of limbo. Living for however long, during the severe winter months that would come, in a tiny stone shelter, open to the elements, at the highest possible level on the forested side of the valley. How else could you describe their choices?

When she had met Marianne in the cafe for the first time, and enquired about the *other* young guide, the one she had also seen at the temple, she had sensed that Barbara was very ill. She asked Marianne to let her know when it was 'over' – a euphemism – wanting to light a candle for her friend. It was not just a gesture. Alerted by Lisa's request, Marianne sensed something in return, and had referred to Lisa's own health and state of mind.

She remembered querying Marianne's return to normal life at the end of her retreat and also found out about Barbara's ordeal. At first, Barbara thought she must fight the disease, Marianne had said. But the young woman grew calmer thereafter, and the place of sanctuary and withdrawal helped her. She was a local girl, and intended to stay with her family afterwards, for whatever time remained to her. Was her death peaceful? Lisa hoped her suffering soon ended. How difficult for her family, too. Not least her brother.

Lisa was determined to fulfil what she promised she would do. It seemed like a vow which she made to herself. There were many tracks in the forest and the next morning, she took a less familiar route; found during her earlier explorations. It wound upwards on the eastern edge, and afforded views of the valley and the villages below. Lisa looked down at the distant houses and identified some of the wild plants nearby. She established a slow and thoughtful progress, drawing comfort from her attention to the euphorbia, thistles, the moss-covered grey rocks and the drying grasses which lined the path. She listened to the birdsong, caught sight of small creatures who attracted her in the rustling of their escape into the undergrowth at her passing, or darted up the low stone-walled terraces for cover, in order to hide in the cypress trees amongst the pines. Even this late in the year, she noted all the different shades of green, and let her mind wander, contemplating all the natural features. The sun was gathering strength by mid-day. It back-lit a few pink-roofed houses perched on granite heights. Who lived there? Locals? Or were they holiday homes, like the one she rented?

The path opened out before she reached the hamlet. She approached the ancient chapel, which she had discovered on an earlier day, when her heart was not heavy, but filled with curiosity about the forest and all its surprises.

She paused, drawn to the sight of the bell poised above the roof over the entrance. Silent, muted in the still air, an open stone arch enclosed the bell. The door was ajar as before. Lisa doubted they ever locked it.

Once inside, she sat down at the back on one of the new wooden pews. She gazed up at the contrasting old timbers of the vault. Someone must look after this place and ensured it did not fall into ruin. Above the stone altar, a few rays of coloured light, from a tiny, broken, stained-glass window, patterned the floor. On top of the altar, a line of stubby candles set in metal holders showed further evidence that the church was in use.

To the left of the altar, in a niche on the side wall of the nave, stood a statue of the Virgin. Freshly painted, all in white. Who used this isolated shrine? She wondered. Perhaps it was on a pilgrim route during Easter and the summer months, but she could not imagine services taking place at any other times of the year. Lisa breathed in the musty, comforting, ancient smell of the interior. It reminded her of her youth. She got up, took a candle out of her bag and a box of matches. She lit it and placed it in one of the metal holders. Spent a few minutes remembering words from long ago, letting them pass through her mind, and looking up at the altar. Memories of her childhood flooded in.

Chapter Six

Childhood

"Where's your school beret, Lisa?"

Lisa turned her back on her mother and pointed from behind, with one hand, to indicate the right position on her head. At least, it was the place she pinned the beret to her hair; folded small, perched low down, in such a way that you could not see it from the front.

"You'll never get away with that," her mother said. She bent to remove a sticky hand from her skirt. "Where's your sister, Brenda, to play with? Go and find Brenda!" she told the toddler at her knee, wiping away food from the child's mouth with the cloth she already had in her grasp. She arched her back in a painful spasm as she stood upright and waved Lisa out of the door. It grated shut, loose on its hinges, and because of a splintered gap at the bottom, it also caused icy blasts to enter the hallway and sweep up the staircase.

Lisa hurried to the bus stop, clutching the free bus pass in her pocket, making sure she had it with her. It had arrived in time for the new term. No embarrassment to worry about in boarding the bus. Not that her family was the only one which qualified for the concession, but for her it was a balancing act; a brazen one, covering up her awareness of how easily sympathy, even acceptance of her family's condition by other girls, could turn into something nasty. She valued her opportunity to gain qualifications at the Grammar School. She wanted a good job. And despite her rebellious exterior, she worked hard. But she never felt at ease in a social setting.

The chatter that morning on the bus was all about the summer holidays; where other girls had been, what they had seen, clothes and food. Of course, the lies came, too. She was certain most of them were. Boys they had met and kissed, whispered confidences of other things they had done, albeit only because of the particular boy's persuasion. Lisa was adept at avoiding joining in these conversations, keeping herself in the background. It was enough that she wore various items of her uniform 'creatively' – to just within the acceptable limits – for the others to admire. She had other methods, but it was often by 'a sharp tongue', as her mother called it, and she used that less now. She stooped to push her ankle socks further down into her shoes, so that they were invisible now, and as she straightened up, she checked for the respect, envy, or mild disapproval on the other girls' faces. They all had to wear complete school uniform, even travelling back and forth from home, and everyone hated looking like a schoolgirl.

That morning's assembly, the first one of the Michaelmas term, was much longer than usual. Lisa liked the orderliness, the filing in to the hush, followed by the demanded complete silence. She hoped to be chosen for the school choir and looked forward to singing the morning hymn. It was easy to remember the words, with so much repetition from week to week as they sang their way through the school hymn book. She blanked out the ruder words and phrases, which a few older girls standing in the lines at the back of the hall often inserted. Although, at first, they had made her smile.

She had looked forward to the return to school, but it crushed her expectations when they called out her name, amongst others, from various year groups. She discovered she had to move to the top academic class in this new year. At one level, she felt delight at her achievement, but a throbbing of the pulse in her neck and a flush of heat followed in a nervous reaction of dismay. All her hard-won friendships, the easy-going approval she had built up, would disappear with her increased status and removal to a higher level. Losing her present companions, she would have it all to do again.

When she returned home from school on the last day of that first week, her mother was abrupt, her voice high-pitched, ordering her about in the chores which Lisa always completed without fuss.

She shook in alarm. Her mother had a bruise on her cheek, and her manner was different, unapproachable and preoccupied. Her parents often argued, but her father had never hit her mother before, nor any of the children. Lisa suspected that something awful had happened, but kept quiet and waited, not daring to ask questions. Her father was not there the next morning, nor had she heard him come in late from his shift work the previous night.

Life became more of a struggle afterwards. Her mother left the younger siblings in Lisa's care while she worked an evening shift at the local electronics factory. Lisa found a Saturday morning job, and in the summer holidays worked in a small guest house, peeling potatoes and waiting on guests at tables. She never saw her father again. Home life was hard, but she felt less anxious.

By gaining important qualifications, she knew she could avoid the worst employment prospects: factories, laundries, reception desk, apprentice to a hairdresser, and shop work. These required long hours, were often demanding physically, and the pay was always poor, with little hope of advancement. These options she had always dreaded.

"You could do a secretarial course, instead," the headmistress advised her when reporting to her office for careers advice, during her final year. Daunted as she was, Lisa had summoned up the courage to admit she could not stay on in the sixth form in order to try for a college course or university place; she needed to work and earn money to contribute to her fatherless family. For a moment, Lisa's heartbeat had quickened, and her hopes had risen, despite the humiliation she felt standing in front of this large powerful figure, clothed in a black university gown, her swollen ankles splaying out over the heels of the utilitarian black-laced shoes. A remote and stern figure who throughout had made it clear she demanded high levels of morality, dutifulness, and submission to society's expectations from them all. But a woman who also promoted careers for girls. She had seemed to hold out the hope of an escape for Lisa from the drudgery and penny-pinching of her mother's life.

"Would I get a grant?" she ventured, her thoughts racing. Perhaps that would help compensate for the lack of earnings, and she could always find weekend employment to contribute to the family income.

The headmistress sat down behind her desk and shuffled some papers. She looked up, her thick eyebrows pulling downwards, her mouth tight at the corners. "Yes. Well, you might for books … in the circumstances," she offered.

Lisa nodded. That would never be enough. She murmured her thanks and left the headmistress's office, with her dreams dashed.

During that last year at school, the girls were learning 'Country Dancing' on certain time-tabled afternoons, offered to them in order to fill a few private study periods. At first, it had been a time of great enjoyment, with little dedication to the 'calls' or instructions for the steps, much boisterous exuberance, collisions, and laughter. Even the teacher who tried to instruct them appeared to be satisfied with their enthusiasm, only imposing, now and then, more discipline, or a reprimand, to counter their loud, high-pitched squeals. The teacher was young and pretty and the girls liked her.

Everything changed in the second term. The dance teacher announced that some members of the sixth form in the boys' Grammar school will join them for sessions. It would thus provide them with male partners. An astonished silence fell. It was the end of that session and, for once, the girls left in restrained order as she dismissed them from the hall. Afterwards, it was difficult to ignore their renewed effort and dedication to learning the dances. The sessions grew quieter, the movements more refined. They practised harder, taking turns at being boys or girls, no longer squabbling, and changing partners without hesitation in order to gain confidence.

****

That's where it started, Lisa thought, getting up from the bench in the chapel in the French forest. She was stiff with sitting, and it surprised her when she looked at her watch. It had been peaceful, contemplating her surroundings, wondering how long the chapel had stood there. It looked ancient. What sort of French local community could it serve?

She had wandered this far before and investigated further down the track into the hamlet beyond the outskirts of which the chapel lay, and could count the number of houses she saw then on one hand. An old woman had watched her with suspicion from the front step of her cottage. She was still watching Lisa when she returned from a brief foray to an even greater distance. There had been no other sign of life.

The chapel could never have had much of a congregation. She stood in the doorway for a few moments, noticing some bat droppings on one side of the new pews. Someone must attend to all this; she thought. As she turned her back on the chapel, her mind focused again on the young girl, Barbara – an image of her on that day at the Buddhist temple, quiet and looking wan. She was drawn to that face. Now she was gone.

Barbara could not have been much older than I was when I made my first mistake; Lisa thought. I had choices, and I made a bad one, though it did not feel like a choice.

She rounded a curve in the track and realised she was almost home. She was returning to her holiday house at a much faster pace than when she set out because it was time to do what she promised and speak to her daughter. Before she made herself a cup of tea or could change her mind, Lisa sent a text to say she would contact Sophie that evening. Later that day, after her meal, a brief affair of not much substance, she sat down with a glass of wine and worked out what to say.

In the event, Sophie's concern was all for her mother's reaction to the message from Marianne, which had arrived just before her departure, and how upset she had seemed because of it. Lisa tried to make light of that at first, although she explained who the text referred to, and what it meant happened to Barbara.

"Why did it matter so much to you?" Sophie insisted. "It's sad, of course, but you say you never even spoke to this young girl – Barbara? Lighting a candle, Lisa, in a chapel in a forest, that doesn't sound like you."

"You know little of my childhood, nor my youth," Lisa countered, and regretted at once her acerbic tone. There was no need to be so abrupt. What she divulged to her daughter remained within her control. But her response to the question made her recognise how vulnerable she still was; her moods, her defensiveness – they only made her sound angry – while acknowledging the pressure to explain to her daughter. The hermit had told her to stop hiding from the truth. Is that what he meant she had to do now?

"I think it's something to do with Barbara's youth. It reminded me of myself at that age, although … my disasters were of my making."

There was a silence at the other end, then Sophie said, "Go on. What disasters? I have never known much about our family history. Daddy died before I even had any actual memory of him, and we moved around so much."

Lisa baulked at revealing the whole truth, but something compelled her to answer with less evasiveness. "My early life was not great. We were poor, I've told you that before. *My* mother was on her own with three children, and struggling. From the beginning, I didn't want a life like that, and I thought I saw a solution, even if it did not remove me from that environment and such a limited, hopeless existence."

"Yes, I know, you've always said daddy was rich and kind. I can understand why you married him, too. That wasn't a disaster, though, was it?"

"No, not at all. He saved me!" Lisa's voice wavered, and what she added came out as a croak, "You don't understand. I was married before I met your father." A silence followed that admission. It had just slipped out somehow.

"There was another marriage? Daddy was *not* your first husband?"

Chapter Seven

Lisa did not take sleeping pills that night. She had too much she wanted to work through. Sleep would come in the end and without the otherwise drugged heaviness for the following morning. The conversation with Sophie had almost finished with recriminations; they had been at cross purposes. Lisa did not want them to be estranged again. She had ended the call with promises of further disclosures and followed that by pleading tiredness. She wished she had not revealed as much as she had. It was all so wearying. Had she simply made matters worse?

While she lay in bed that night, working through what they had said brought no resolution, and her dreams when they came troubled her. In the early hours approaching dawn when the dim light in her bedroom had not yet awoken her, she sat up, perspiring, and full of fear. Had she heard a noise outside? Or was that just the dream? Not a wild boar scenting her out? Martin had warned her about them. She was awake now and sat up. What time was it? This was the night Martin went to the dance class in Montpelier. Was it the sound of his car on the track which had awoken her? Had he come home this late?

She swung her legs out of the bed and recoiled as her feet touched the cold tiles of the floor. At that moment, she wished her daughter was still there. She crossed to the window and opened the slats of the blind a fraction. In the dimness, she thought she heard a muted cry, not quite animal; she was already accustomed to the sound of a vixen, the screech of an owl. Lisa picked up her dressing gown, fumbled with slippers and crept up the stairs.

From the floor above, she could see much further out over the pool, the garden, and the steep sides of the valley, which were all bathed in the low dawn light. She was sure she had spotted Martin's car in the distance, parked in the usual place, tucked away under some trees. It was unlikely he had just arrived because there were no lights in his house. He must be in bed.

She heard a noise again and saw movement down by the pool. She peered out of the window, moved the blind to one side. Though it seemed improbable, it looked as though a person was struggling to get out of the leaf-strewn water. No one had drained it nor would give it much attention until spring and the holiday season. She realised she must go outside to make sure it wasn't an animal, or simply a trick of the light. It was impossible to ignore that last cry; it sounded like someone in trouble. She picked up her mobile and phoned Martin. It went to voicemail. Disappointed and with a sinking feeling, she left an urgent text message.

The night was freezing, and if it was a person who had been in the pool, who now appeared to be lying by the side of it, they needed help.

She had to do something. A wise move or not, she switched on the outside light. Almost at once, she saw the figure move, and one arm beckoned towards the house.

Lisa rushed out, pausing only to grab a hefty torch kept by the front door, aware it was not only to gain more light, but to use it if necessary as a weapon.

It was a man. At least, the rush of adrenalin made her feel less cold and shivery when she knelt by his side. His injured face turned towards her in appeal. Of course, he was soaking wet from the pool. He tried to sit up, groaning with difficulty, and flinched as he touched his leg. Lifting his head to tug at a knotted scarf tied around his head – he must have manoeuvred it down past his chin – now he clawed it further away. "Have they gone?" he croaked, and it alarmed her to hear his voice. She stood up and shone the light of the torch all around, including, in sudden inspiration, over the distant windows of Martin's house.

"I can't see anyone." She knelt down beside him. "Are you badly hurt? What happened?" He motioned for the torch, swept the beam around for himself before he handed it back to her. "Can you get up? I'll help you." But when he placed a hand on one shoulder of her slight frame, she toppled over herself, and they both were aware she could not take his weight.

To her surprise, he continued to speak in English. "No. It is not possible. Get help." She realised then who it was. He was shivering, not only from the cold but also in shock, she realised, because his teeth were chattering so hard.

"I will get blankets. Tell me who to call. It's difficult to get anyone up here in the forest. But there must be a way…?" The words drifted from her as she turned back to the house.

Lisa stripped all the spare blankets out of the cupboard in the utility area, which she shared with her neighbour, Martin. Gathering them up in her arms, she hurried outside again. The man was sitting up and welcomed the covers. By now it was fully light and she could see a little healthy colour flushing his cheeks, though his injuries showed clearly: a bruised eye, cut lip, and one leg stretched out while the other was at an awkward angle.

She did not know what to do next and felt chilled herself. Did he need an ambulance, a hospital, or was it not as bad as that? "Did someone do this to you?" she asked. He nodded.

At that moment, she heard another voice. "Lisa, it's me! What's the emergency? It was you with the light?"

With immense relief, she recognised Martin, and let out the breath she had been holding until that moment. "I am so glad you are here! Someone attacked this man and threw him in the pool, I think." Of course, he would not know who the injured man was. He had never met him, she remembered. Martin was already examining the damage. "It's the hermit. The one I went to see," she explained. Martin looked up, his eyes widening in astonishment as he stared back at her. He turned back to the man and asked him about his leg. "He speaks English," she interrupted, but there was no need; Martin's French was good. She watched and listened as he attempted to find out the extent of the man's injuries. It became a little heated, although she did not know why, unless he was describing who had done what to him.

"I'll take him to my place," Martin said. "He can't walk on that leg and … I'll explain later, Lisa. Let's get him inside in the warm and dry."

Lisa helped to put the hermit into bed in Martin's house. She made tea and took the soggy clothes away to put them in the washing machine. She returned to her house and came back with some simple painkillers, and wondered what to do next.

"You look so tired," Martin said. They were sitting with a hot drink. The hermit was already sound asleep. "I'll take it from here, Lisa. Perhaps you can cook me a late breakfast, if you like. I'll come over." She nodded agreement and left.

She remembered it was Sunday. Martin would not be going to work at the temple. She would make sure that he and the man had an excellent meal.

****

They had a cooked breakfast together, although it was nearly mid day. Martin ate heartily, but Lisa could only pick at it. She was not used to starting with a hot meal, and only the coffee was welcome. In his house, Martin had fed the hermit some soup and bread. A bit of a 'mush', he called it, but the man's mouth was sore with the cut lip and it was all he could manage. "I'll take him in my car to the clinic – not far," he told Lisa.

She raised an eyebrow. "How can you do that? It's a Sunday. I thought the French were not very good at weekends."

"I got hold of someone and they *will* see him. I mentioned something about the Buddhist Temple. Maybe I implied he worked there instead of me. A muddled conversation!" He grinned.

She helped him to more coffee. "How bad are his injuries?"

"I don't think the leg is broken, which is one good thing. "His name is Liam, by the way."

"His sister is ... was Barbara," Lisa said. "She died recently." Martin nodded, and she changed the subject. "I didn't know they held the temple in so much respect at the clinic. As you got such a quick response, I mean."

"Nothing around here is simple. I try not to get too involved."

Despite his reluctance, she learned a little more. Three men had attacked Liam. The reason, in part at least, was because he rescued hunting dogs. He saw how they kept the bitches chained up in the forest, under-nourished and bred to exhaustion. So he set them free and took them to a secret animal refuge centre. Except that this last time, they saw him. On that day, the hunters had chased and lost him. It made them furious. They had warned him off before, but the tactic had not deterred him, and so they must have taken revenge this night.

Their cruelty to the dogs appalled but did not surprise Lisa. She knew hunters regarded pet cats as vermin, and someone had already advised her if she brought one with her to the holiday house, she must keep it indoors all day when they were about. As to taking their 'revenge', Martin had already hinted at 'accidental' shootings amongst the group, so a beating for treating their warning with contempt seemed minor in comparison.

"What will he do now?" she asked. Liam could stay with him for a few days, Martin told her, if his injuries were not too bad. He could not live in the shelter for the worst months of the winter; it was much too cold. He had to move out of the forest and find somewhere else at this time of the year.

She still could not understand why they had taken Liam to the pool and thrown him in there. Martin said he thought it was because she had gone to see the hermit. It connected her to him, especially as she was foreign and therefore, not very welcome in the place, which they deemed to be their sole preserve. The hunters barely accepted the seasonal holiday-makers, but those people did not stay for long; a week or two at a time; so the ill-feeling did not build up with them.

"You mean, they know I visited Liam in his shelter on that day?" She asked, totally taken aback.

"It's their territory, Lisa."

Seeing her expression, he assured her they would never attack her, and she must not take it to heart.

"What do the hunters think about the Buddhist temple, then? Both you and Liam have contact with it."

"Liam has nothing to do with the temple itself, as far as I know. The monks have helped him with supplies. His sister, Barbara, was on retreat there, too. Who knows what they thought?"

He did not really convince her she was safe. Perhaps he wished he had not told her as much as he had. He finished the discussion by saying there were other matters between Liam and some of the community. Not necessarily just the hunters, and it was not only the dogs. These things were nothing to do with her, and she must not worry they would harm her.

He could not have done more to increase her apprehension.

Chapter Eight

Lisa locked the downstairs bedroom windows and the door connecting her accommodation to the shared laundry room. She had not felt the need before. Who would try to gain access in this remote corner of the forest and at this time of the year? There was no one to distrust or threaten her. But Martin had left with Liam for the clinic, and she was on her own.

It was not a bright morning, but she stood in front of the blinds on the glass-walled frontage, overlooking the pool and garden, and only at the last moment pulled her hand back and away from the lever to close the blinds and block out the scene. Instead, she walked out onto the wide balcony, drawing in a deep breath of the resin-permeated air, but still looked around before returning inside and engaging the lock.

What am I doing? In sheer frustration, she sat down on the leather sofa, clasping her face in her hands. Should they have reported the incident to the police? Would the clinic insist on it when they saw Liam's injuries? No one could imagine they were accidental, least of all professional clinicians. Would Martin have to make a statement and would it involve her as well?

It was not cold indoors. She checked the automatic dial on the heating. It had switched on as usual; she had only recently adjusted the setting to a more winter friendly level. As a shiver coursed through her body, she looked down at goosebumps on her bare arms. Mixed sensations overwhelmed her, but most of it was fear. Flight or fight, they said, didn't they? The incident in the early hours of that recent morning was bound to make her feel anxious.

She scraped off congealed remnants from the breakfast dishes – more like a 'brunch', she thought, after glancing at the clock – and loaded the dishwater. Having turned on the radio station, but clicked it off again almost at once, she listened for any sounds outside.

Was she going into hiding, then? Despite the years that had passed, it always seemed the same as the first time. Trying to shrug off the unwanted memories of her youth, which had drawn her into that initial disaster, was never effective. Acknowledge what happened, she told herself, and remember not to regret everything. It was almost a mantra; she had used it so often.

Nevertheless, her memories took hold again. Ted dancing with her in the heady teenage period at the end of her schooldays. So attracted, one to the other. Awakened, in fact, because they were so young. Clammy hands and long, fixed gazes. They dared to hold that wide-eyed look, when her face turned up to meet his, and he drew her closer to him; it gave away so much on both sides. A delicious sense of danger under the watchful eyes of their supervising teachers. Now she needed to snatch at those innocent moments of first love, rather than the chaos which followed.

Her mother had recognised the change; suspicious of her daughter's half-smiles into the distance, the rush to eat her tea and get out, happiness bubbling up into laughter, and frequent flushes of her neck. Of course, her mother had demanded answers and enforced restrictions, which soon tied Lisa to the house. The breakthrough came when she realised Ted's family had status; they did not live in the back-to-back terraces. In Lisa's favour, his family knew that her mother struggled, but led a respectable life. Regular attendance at the same church also helped. We have nothing to hide, her mother had said.

On a memorable day, granting him acceptance, "Ted has lovely manners. I'll give him that," her mother remarked, after he joined them for an afternoon cup of tea and a freshly baked batch of scones. She probed his aspirations and learned that he had already secured an apprenticeship as a printer.

Jolted back into the present, Lisa jumped at the sound of a shot reverberating down the valley. She rushed to the window, wrapping her arms around her chest, then released them with a sigh of relief when she remembered it was Sunday. Of course, another hunt day. They would not dare to approach her holiday home again today?

****

Marianne met Lisa as planned outside the cathedral church in Lodève. Lisa stood and looked up with appreciation at its pinnacle: Gothic, majestic and austere. When she arrived, they entered by the decorated portal, and if Lisa had been hoping for warmth on this wintry Saturday afternoon, she was disappointed. She had been inside the cathedral before, attending an organ recital. Profiting from that experience; she wore knee-length boots today. This time, the performance was some sort of carol service for the festive season with a female choir.

After the performance, spartan with dreary music and lacking any notion of cheerfulness, they went to a cafe for a hot chocolate to warm up.

"Did you enjoy it?" the French woman asked, cradling a bowl of the creamy drink, her hands covered by fingerless gloves.

"It was not what I thought it would be. Well attended, though," Lisa replied.

She had been in contact with Marianne, who told her she had found somewhere for Liam to stay. He had recovered from the assault, but could not winter in the forest because the conditions were too harsh. This Lisa already knew from Martin. The young woman dismissed further talk on the subject and seemed more concerned about Lisa spending Christmas on her own.

"Martin has his girlfriend staying for a couple of days. He has invited me to join them at his place. She will cook a typical English lunch for us," Lisa said with a wry smile.

"You have accepted?"

"I don't want to spoil their fun. So I will get away and return to my own place by the late afternoon. Family phone calls to make, perhaps, as an excuse?"

Marianne nodded. She looked distracted, and Lisa could understand why. She and Liam were so close.

Lisa surprised herself by the sudden introduction of what occupied her own thoughts. "I have been thinking about my childhood. Well, teenage years. And first love." It was unlike her to volunteer personal information. She avoided giving any opportunity for people to question or probe her early life.

Marianne sighed, which was not the reaction she had been expecting. "I'm sorry, Lisa. It's just all this with Liam. Everything is getting so entangled now."

"What do you mean?"

"I don't know if I should tell you anything at all. But after that physical attack, and nearly drowning in the pool right outside your holiday home, the situation changed. You are involved, too, which is not right. An unfortunate co-incidence of association. You are English, of course, and with Martin, you almost form a little *enclave* of foreigners, as well as giving Liam much needed help. I do not mean to be disrespectful."

"I thought the attack was over the hunting dogs. Liam set them free."

"No. Much more than that as they see it." She looked at her watch. "I have to go now. I will talk to Martin first. He knows the story of the hermit and his sister. It's a tragic one."

"Wait a moment, Marianne," she said. "Is this to do with why Liam is a hermit? I can understand Barbara undertaking the retreat in the Tibetan monastery when she was terminally ill, but her brother – living in a cave, like a total recluse?"

The young woman's face was expressionless, but she gripped the top of the chair, her knuckles whitening. Lisa knew she wanted to leave and realised she was holding her back. "The motive? Can't you guess?" Marianne's tone was harsh and accusatory. "It is the most obvious one.

"Startled, Lisa grappled with the idea. Moral questions were not a novelty to her. The youthful days of confession were not completely erased.

"Atonement? Something he has to undo to make it right?"

"He cannot put it right. It is over now." She sighed and unclasped her hands from the chair. Her face softened again as her mouth relaxed. It was the friendly and concerned Marianne again.

"I'm sorry. I cannot expect you to understand. But if you recognise the feeling that well, you must also have a tale to tell, Lisa."

****

Light snow fell on New Year's Day. Lisa did not stay awake long enough to welcome it in. At home in England, even if not invited somewhere, she would have opened the doors and windows, letting out the old and welcoming in the new. Though she knew it was mere superstition.

Sophie phoned, and after a brief exchange of greetings with little genuine news on either side, Lisa pulled on boots, a fleece-lined baker's boy cap and draped a thick, colourful shawl around her shoulders – from where had she acquired it? She wondered, as she dressed for a walk.

Somewhere near Granada in the mountains in Spain? Of course, they had wintered there one year, retreating from the coastal resort, she remembered. No longer holidaymakers by then, but living in Spain and eager to avoid questions from her neighbours about her private affairs; where had she lived in England, what she was doing living on her own with her child in a foreign country?

Sophie had attended a school for bilingual children and gained a good working knowledge of Spanish. That would be beneficial in later life, and her mother was proud of it. What was Sophie doing now to earn a living? She had resisted asking her when they spoke on the phone. Lisa did not want to pry because if she did, it could work both ways.

How easy it was to arouse curiosity with anyone. Especially with someone as intuitive as Marianne. She recalled their previous meeting in the church at Lodève, and the conversation over hot chocolate, with dismay. Especially Marianne's comment about Lisa having a story to tell.

She glanced up at the cloudless blue sky and looked forward to starting the walk. The forest was pretty, with the covering of sparkling silver crystals in the sunlight. Martin had warned her of the change in the weather, but told her to enjoy it because it would not last for long.

****

She reflected on her youthful ambition, which had driven her along on a disastrous course. It had been dank and dreary, so early in that year, long ago, when she married Ted. The church freezing, having to wear the thin white wedding dress her mother-in-law had fashioned in expensive material and accessories. She was bone-chilled by the end of the marriage service, but glad to have accomplished the 'tying of the knot'. No going back, she had thought, remembering how she secured her mother's permission for the marriage by saying that she was pregnant.

Only seventeen years old. After the first shock and recriminations, Lisa's mother had thought it through and agreed to say nothing to Ted's parents about her daughter 'getting caught'. Not even to promote a hasty wedding. *His* mother would have parted them, shaming Lisa for leading him on, or raised some other typical excuse for shunning her and undermining the marriage. The case Lisa put forward herself, in advance, warning her mother to secrecy, was to avoid that humiliation from Ted's parents. It convinced her mother, and all went well on both sides afterwards.

The main reason Lisa had lied about a pregnancy was because she wanted to get away from home. Tired of the endless care of her younger siblings during the evenings, when her mother worked the shift from six to ten at the factory, after Lisa had already completed the day shift in the same workplace. The firm produced electrical circuitry and paid well. Her mother enjoyed the chat and the laughter as they tested circuit boards on an assembly line, and the task required little concentration after a while. She told Lisa it was almost a social evening with the other women and her life improved because of it. The family had greater security. It enabled them to enjoy more of the basics and to pay the rent of the small terraced back-to-back. After all, she had no husband, the children, no father, to bring in a proper wage to support them all. Lisa had moped, bored and trapped.

The marriage could have worked if Ted had not shown such impatience and restlessness. He soon gave up his printing apprenticeship; wages were low and the older men taunted him, played tricks on him; the usual initiation practices most youngsters faced. But Ted had a temper, and he reacted badly. He came from a social background which was not so inhibited by poverty. Attracted to the opening for a job on the ferry, he said he would only be away for a few weeks at a time. Which pal down the pub had first dangled that opportunity in front of him? Lisa wondered. Of course, his parents either had no influence over his decision, or ... well, they did not like Lisa, and she knew it.

Chapter Nine

Marianne sounded distraught; muddling her words when her English was normally so good, her voice hoarse. "Can I come to see you in your house in the forest? No, not now. Tomorrow morning after breakfast?" She would explain everything then.

Lisa had just finished her evening meal. She put the phone down, shaking her head. Marianne had cut off the call as soon as she had given her assent to the request. What was it all about? Something to do with Liam. She had mentioned his name.

She closed the blinds and glanced at the kitchen clock. The evenings were longer now spring had arrived. She had been contemplating a return home to England, feeling bored and lonely because Martin had left. On the day he towed his caravan and all his possessions away to the campsite by the lake, she had helped him. He had erected a large enclosed awning and with that it gave him almost adequate space for all his belongings. Another tenant had not yet replaced him in the forest and she missed Martin; his presence had been comforting but never intrusive.

Marianne arrived after breakfast, bringing flowers. She offered to arrange the blooms, although it was unnecessary considering the beauty of the arrangement of the florist's bouquet. Lisa found a vase. The young woman looked wan and sad. Her eyes were so red-rimmed that no cosmetics could cover her distress. With Lisa's back towards her at the sink as she filled the vase, Marianne blurted out why she had come. Liam had disappeared. No one could find him. He had left no message, no note. When Lisa turned her head and encouraged her to continue, Marianne added some further details, but they amounted to little.

Lisa's immediate suspicion was that the hunters had attacked him again. She trembled at the thought, and dismissed the worst possibilities, without suggesting them, swearing under her breath. Yet it was Marianne's desperation which puzzled her. Her connection with Liam, she had always imagined, was because of her close friendship with his sister, Barbara. They were both guides at the temple and on a retreat. Wasn't it possible, and not unusual, for the hermit to take off and wander about sometimes?

"Did he return to his place in the forest?" Lisa asked. It was all she could think of. "Is he recovered now, and where has he been living?" There was an enormous gap here, a fault in her understanding of the relationship between the two of them.

"That is why I came here. I do not know where Liam lived in that hermitage you visited. He did not want me there, and now Martin is gone and I cannot ask him where it is. Can you take me there? I know you saw him. She looked behind and stumbled back onto the sofa, breathing in rasps.

"Of course I will," said Lisa.

She gave her a glass of water, sat down next to her, and put an arm around her shoulders.

****

They left within the hour, at Lisa's insistence, having sorted out rucksacks, drinks and sensible boots and clothing. At the last minute, she added bread and fruit lying on the worktop. Lisa remembered the first part of the way and realised the signs were clear enough to mark the rest. To begin, it was a straight and open track, and then it climbed gently. By the time they started the hardest section, she had no breath for speaking; needed it for their rests and to drink and eat something. She now knew how much Marianne cared for Liam, though he had pushed her away and did not want to see her. She was candid with her own feelings. Their relationship became harder to understand, more complicated afterwards because it involved the 'secret' of Liam's behaviour, which Lisa had once sensed was for atonement. Perhaps he had already experienced a leaning towards religion and the death of his sister had strengthened it? Meanwhile, what had gone wrong for Marianne? Had she and Liam become lovers, but were now estranged, or was that just the young woman's hope for the future?

They reached the abandoned shelter long after mid-day. The sun had made the journey arduous because of its strength, compared to Lisa's last trek through the forest to reach this point, and they were perspiring and panting by the time the igloo-shaped stone retreat came into sight. Marianne cupped her hands to call his name several times, a half-smile of hope on her lips. The silence, except for birdsong and the rustle of leaves in the breeze, soon disheartened her. She stepped back; her face drained of colour. Lisa realised that she hesitated to move forward and go inside because it could only confirm Liam's absence.

"I'll go in first," Lisa said. She grabbed a torch from the front pocket of her rucksack and went ahead. The woodpile, she had noted, was still in place, but as she drew closer, she saw it was untouched. It had the look of abandonment. What might she find within?

She flicked on the torch and stepped inside. The only sign of habitation were a few tinned goods on the shelves at the back, a stove of sorts, and some fuel cans. No clothes, tools, or any other sign of Liam. "It's OK. You can come in now," Lisa called out in relief. Wherever he was, Liam was not lying dead in there.

****

They returned to Lisa's house in a thoughtful silence, which she was unwilling to break. She still did not know the reason Liam had been undertaking some form of atonement by becoming a hermit. However, thinking about it had triggered further memories of her own. These thoughts occupied her as the two women trailed back.

When Ted had left the job on a ferry, taking up another as a steward on short cruises, it created a gap, almost the suspension of their married life. The periods of absence lengthened, until if he continued to embark on home shores when he returned, he did not come back to her. She received a few letters with weak excuses, which made her cry until her head and chest ached. Had he got another woman somewhere? Had he settled with someone far away, perhaps in a different country? Why wasn't her marriage a success?

After her wedding, she had continued to work full time on the day shift at the electronics factory, even taking on overtime. Ted had stopped sending any money, so Lisa had needed to take a few shifts at bar work in the evenings. She also worked on weekends at the pub when it was very busy.

One morning in the early summer of that year, she crawled out of bed, drew back the curtains and let the sunlight flood in. Looking down to the street below, and aware it was Friday, her spirits sank rather than lifted at thoughts of the weekend to come. Instead, she would have to work in another job for a full day and an evening to follow. In the smoke-filled bar where so many of the men drank away their wages. She was still so tired and rubbed her eyes to make them focus. On what? A featureless grey length of back-to-backs below her. Although she was living in another part of town, they were all the same and her environment had not changed. She had escaped the family home and the restrictions of life with her mother, but was this any different? The flatlet comprised two rooms, and the one which provided the cramped living space had what amounted to a small alcove for a kitchen. She had to share an unheated bathroom, on the landing below, with two more tenants. The other residents included a couple with children, who screamed in wild tantrums whenever their father left the house. She saw him in the pub, too.

Was she working two jobs, all those hours, just to pay the rent on this almost unfurnished, meagre accommodation? Lisa wondered.

In a fit of pique, she opened the wardrobe, fierce anger flushing her neck, and pulled her wedding dress off the hanger. She looked around the bedroom and saw what she sought, picked up a pair of scissors from the table. It had a crazed mirror on the top of it, angled against the wall to hold it upright, to serve as a dressing table. How she hated it at that moment. She tore away at the ridiculous flounces and netting of the dress with her hands, and then savagely cut the white mass of it into small pieces.

The fury created by these last reminiscences, as they walked along the track, had not lessened by the time she and Marianne reached her holiday house in the forest. She forced herself to slow her breathing as she turned the key.

"Come on in, Marianne, let's have a drink. One would be alright, I'm sure." Lisa raised her eyebrows in query. and for once, Marianne accepted. She did not know if the young woman drank alcohol, and smiled at her in gratitude for what she assumed might be an unusual concession.

"I was thinking about when I was first married, " Lisa said. They were more relaxed now, sitting on the sofa. Lisa stretched out her legs with her second, large glass of wine in one hand, and the fingers of the other twirling a twist of her hair. A habit from her teenage years which seemed to have returned, she noted.

Marianne gulped her wine and made a face. Too heavy a red? The French knew about wines. Or did she not drink? For whatever reason, she set the glass down again.

"How old were you when you married?" Marianne asked.

"Well, we met at school. Childhood sweethearts, you would say."

Marianne repeated the phrase, rolling her tongue around the words. She sighed and looked better than when they had first arrived. The walk had tired her, as indeed it had Lisa, but there was colour in her cheeks and perhaps the exercise had helped.

"Barbara and Liam were young, too. And innocent," Marianne said, nodding her head in emphasis.

"Can't you explain what it is all about? This – atonement? What has he done?"

Marianne sat up straight and hunched forward, her hands clasped in her lap. She flashed one look at Lisa and waved a finger at her.

"What I say you must never repeat," she said. "Promise me!"

Lisa nodded, but could not imagine to whom she could relay anything spoken in confidence. Unless Marianne meant Martin. Apart from him, she knew no-one.

Marianne paused, and the rest of it came out in a rush. The brother and sister were both orphaned as infants; a road accident, a dreadful collision in a remote village in the mountains. Someone in the locality of a nearby town adopted Barbara. Eventually, another couple took Liam, but his adoption took place much later, after a period spent in a children's home. As babies and because there was only a year between them, different social agencies had offered them to childless couples who knew nothing of each other, of course. It was a mismanaged affair.

She explained the complications which had led to the two siblings meeting as adults, though they knew nothing of their relationship. Liam grew up far away in another département, but as an adult, he found out where he was born, and he returned to find his birth mother. Then he met Barbara. The Hérault was home territory for her, of course.

As adults, and with changes in the law, they both became involved in searching for their natural parents. They did not know they were related. With modern methods – they provided DNA samples – they discovered, to their horror, their relationship, but by then it was too late. Their mother had been a single parent and of ill-repute, and did not record the father's name for either birth. At the time of the disaster which killed her, the two babies – there was just a year between them – had no living relatives. No-one had documented that they were siblings. It was all because of an 'oversight' by the various social agencies involved when they settled the babies in different families in regions far apart.

"They were attracted to each other when they met. Do you understand? It is not uncommon in siblings when they reunite," Marianne explained. This was the crux of the tragedy, and what Marianne had laboured to reveal.

There were tears on her cheeks, and she took Lisa's hand in hers, gripped it hard. "They didn't know. They were both searching for what they thought were their individual, natural mothers, not the same woman!

Now it was all uncovered. It was horrible and Liam was so disgusted. He could not believe what they had felt for each other.

"I am so sorry, Marianne. I don't know what to say. Would you like some water? I can see you don't want the wine." She poured her a glass. Another idea occurred to her.

"And the hunters here in the forest, Marianne. Do they know about all of this?"

"They know *everything*. They hated Liam because several times he took away their dogs to rescue them. You knew about that?"

Lisa nodded. "Martin told me about it."

"Once you search local records ….," Marianne said. "You understand? Of course, the forestiers are important men to the Mayor and everyone in the town hall." She wiped tears away with her sleeve. "So they found out about the brother and sister relationship, and then they behaved even worse, wrecking Liam's stores in the shelter when he wasn't there, shouting abuse at him in the forest."

Is this the knowledge that made them so vicious when they attacked him? Lisa wondered. Made even worse, perhaps, by the death of Barbara, a local girl and from a respectable family. She was young and dying. Did they view that as caused by sinful behaviour? These men came from old-style 'hellfire' Catholic families, so she had gathered. Why else was Barbara in retreat at the Buddhist temple, if she was not trying to atone, do penance and find peace, but felt unable to be seen to do it in the church of her own upbringing? Lisa's early life offered these explanations, though she did not think she had ever believed in the rigid, traditional dogma of her faith. Liam took the full force of the forestiers' reaction, she assumed, because *they* did.

Marianne accepted a tissue from Lisa and blew her nose. She turned

75

towards her, calmer now, and finished the tale. "They diagnosed Barbara with a terminal illness at around that time. Liam still thinks that's why she did the retreat, because she convinced herself it was the reason for her suffering. She always denied it, but Barbara was devout, you know. So, Liam's response, from the first, was to isolate as a hermit. It is also a punishment for him. But it isn't his fault!"

Chapter Ten

Marianne could not believe that Liam was dead. The hunters would not have gone that far, she argued, and he had no other enemies. It was the lack of a note, any communication before he disappeared, which distressed her.

Meeting in Lodève the following day, Lisa accompanied her to the Buddhist Temple to talk to a monk. They knew about Liam's assault, and the English woman, Lisa, who helped him, and so they agreed to see both women, even though the temple was closed to outsiders. That Marianne had recently been on a retreat there also contributed to their goodwill; Lisa thought.

The journey this time was in sunshine, the treacherous winding road empty of cars, and the drive almost pleasant if it were not for the reason they were undertaking it. Lisa seemed comforted by the different conditions and, as they rose higher, with the windows opened, she breathed in the clear, reviving air. She would be more optimistic if only for the sake of the young woman whose worried expression never wavered as she drove along. What was Marianne thinking or hoping? Did she believe they would get useful information, even a clue to where Liam might be?

There were no gates and nothing barring their way at the entrance. They parked in the empty visitors' car-park and stretched in relief as they got out of the car. They stood admiring the view down to the colourful shrines and the temple before descending the path. Marianne had been told where to go and who they would see.

A young female with a close-cropped, almost shaven head appeared.

She wore the traditional saffron, full-length, sleeved robe and a warm modern jacket over the top. She carried a long string of prayer beads in her folded hands and recognised Marianne at once, simply saying 'Hello' before smiling at her. They pressed palms together in front of their chests, bowed, and exchanged the customary greeting – *Namo Buddhaya:* a bow to the Buddha – before following her into one of the modest retreat houses. A monk awaited them. After brief further introductions, they sat on cushions on the floor to question him.

He said very little and Lisa felt disappointed after a few minutes, even though she had not expected to follow their conversation in French. But Marianne seemed a different person and ignored her. There were long silent pauses which, by the calmness of her expression, Lisa guessed were valuable, absorbing, and restful for Marianne. For Lisa, the whole interview agitated her as she turned from one to the other, understanding nothing.

Afterwards, Marianne left her standing outside, in order to follow the female Buddhist to the temple to place an offering. She refused the offer to eat while they were there. It was too early, she said, and she felt too emotional in returning to the place of retreat. When she rejoined Lisa in the car-park her manner and mood did not change. Marianne was silent, faraway, and she did not speak until they had covered half of the return journey.

"I am sorry," she said eventually, gripping the wheel to round a curve. "You understand how to respect silence there, and I expect I seemed rude to you and unkind."

"I admit it was strange. But did you learn anything?"

She sighed and licked dry lips. "They have not seen him, and there was only brief contact previously. The monks used to give him supplies, which he collected. After the assault, he did not come for them. They thought he must lodge somewhere in the town for the winter and obtained sufficient resources there."

"No idea of where he might have gone? His state of mind?" Lisa had been reluctant to add the latter, but it seemed important.

"When you converse with them, it is different. Direct questions, supposition …," she shook her head. "Monks are not judgmental. Male or female, they say nothing which is untrue, unhelpful or unkind."

They drove on in silence until approaching the town. It was a beautiful afternoon and, to Lisa, everything in the landscape seemed burnished and touched with gold. She sensed she was more alive, as though awake now and with an energy missing for a long time.

Marianne, aroused from her deep, private reverie on the outskirts of the village, said, "I will take you to where you left your car."

Lisa nodded. "You gained nothing at all? No suggestions?"

"From the monk, no. But he mentioned Liam seemed troubled. Otherwise, why become a hermit? It was not, he was certain, a vocation or calling drawing him into a religious life."

"Perhaps we could ask Martin. He must have talked to Liam when he took him in that night and arranged for the clinic to attend to his injuries. I know they kept up a contact."

Marianne faced her with a sudden interest. "He may know something?"

"I know where Martin is living by the lake. I helped him to set up his caravan as a temporary home there," Lisa added.

"Yes, I heard about the move. He does it every year. I will come with you." She smiled in anticipation. "But everything changed when Liam's sister died. We must not be too hopeful. None of us can understand what

79

he is suffering wherever he is."

****

They chose a time in the late afternoon when Martin returned to the lakeside from his work at the temple. Lisa had texted him and said they wanted to talk to him about Liam. The caravan and camping sight at *Lac Salagou,* a few miles south of Lodève, was already busy with tourists, and she stopped to take her bearings, uncertain of her former impression of the layout. It looked so different. On that previous day when he was setting up his summer season home, there were only a few tourers. Now, in the height of the season, holidaymakers covered the site almost to full capacity.

As visitors, they parked and notified reception. It was confusing walking through the tracks between the multiple rows of mobile homes, touring caravans and chalets. Children dodged in play, in and out between every form of encampment and shelter, with no care. The edges of the lake, along the entire extent, were filled with the noise of dogs and people.

Lisa thought about how different the atmosphere was now. She had arrived in this part of France in the middle of Autumn, and now it was the beginning of Spring.

In fact, Martin had moved his caravan from where he first positioned it, and waved to get their attention. When this failed, he hollered their names, and they caught sight of him.

"You can see why I moved to a quieter spot," he said, after exchanging greetings when they arrived. "A cold drink?"

They remained outside the caravan's awning, which was too

uncomfortable to sit under because of the day's build-up of heat. This time in the late afternoon was often the hottest part of the day, he told them. Martin unfolded two small camping chairs for Lisa and Marianne and sat on the grass in front of them with a chilled glass of beer in his hand. He looked very sunburnt, relaxed and happy.

Lisa reflected that his mode of living and working exchanging one place for another, according to the seasons, suited him. Or perhaps it was the sunshine and the lack of responsibility. He had already told her he spent his money as soon as he earned it. His girlfriends came and went. No responsibilities there. He was fortunate, she decided, if he could achieve that most difficult of all aims: to live in the moment. The settled routine and the peace of the monks during his working hours must have influenced him, too. How striking to be so at peace.

She was not listening to Marianne's account of her concerns for Liam. The holiday atmosphere of the site felt pleasant and normal, and the liveliness of all around her reassured her. Too much had happened, she decided. It was exhausting. Besides, she had nothing to add to Marianne's account.

Marianne explained to Martin that Liam had disappeared, and no one knew where he went. In Lodève, he had cleared all his things from the hostel he moved into. Their visit to his shelter in the forest had shown no trace of him there. Martin nodded. What she continued to relate about their trip to the Buddhist temple did not surprise him, nor did the lack of any information from the monks there. Liam never lived in the community nor took part in the life, he told them.

"Have you any ideas, Martin? Somewhere else we can look ?" Lisa asked.

Martin shook his head. "None," he said.

Marianne glanced up at his last remark, but was silent. While listening with a bowed head, she had given up making suggestions. She set her glass down on the ground and pulled at wisps of grass – already browning like straw in the sunshine, and flattened by many feet – and wound them around her fingers.

They discounted the possibility of contacting Liam's parents, as they did not know where the family was located and doubted anyone else did. They were aware only of his adoption in another region, and that he had lived most of his life much further north.

****

It was almost two weeks later when Lisa received an urgent text from Marianne. Liam had sent her a postcard. He was somewhere in Spain. Could they meet somewhere the following day?

Lisa was in the middle of sorting clothes. She intended to return to England by the end of the month. The new tenants replacing Martin, a couple with a young baby, spent most of their time in and around the pool, and the irritation they caused from the squalling of the infant – was it colic or teething? – accompanied by a sense of selfishness in her reaction, often drove her out of her house. She was due to leave, her contract expired, and ready to go. Let the influx of short-stay holidaymakers enjoy the complex; she thought. They will find the experience no trouble.

Marianne's need to see Lisa did not include any desire to come to the forest, a place from which she wanted to distance herself; Lisa gathered. She was busy tying up the loose ends in negotiating leave from her employment. Lisa guessed what that decision was all about – she was going to follow Liam.

They met in the usual cafe in Lodève, where so many of their conversations had led to strange and emotional revelations. As she sipped a coffee, while Marianne wiped a fruit juice drink from the corners of her mouth, Lisa remembered the text message from Marianne which drove her to the chapel to light a candle for Barbara. How long ago that emotional time seemed when her daughter Sophie had been staying with her. A time when her close involvement in the lives of the young woman now sitting opposite her, and that of Liam, had first begun, although she had not known it then. Marianne and Liam, she was certain, were now linked in some sort of unfulfilled relationship.

Today, Marianne's expression was relaxed. Liam was on his way to Santiago de Compostela in Spain, she informed Lisa, with a tremulous, nervous smile. She placed a postcard on the table and pointed to the route depicted on it. It showed two walkers in shorts and boots with rucksacks and holding the traditional staff on a rough path. This postcard was a precious item to her, and she returned it to a zipped pocket in her handbag.

"He is on a pilgrimage. It is long, hundreds of kilometres. I know where he was on a particular date, and I can work out where he will be. At least, I have some idea of how many weeks...." She sipped her drink.

She did not show Lisa the reverse side of the postcard. He must have dated his message, or was there a postmark she could decipher? Had he written a message? Something personal? Or was it just 'greetings' and non-committal?

Marianne was not going to let her see any message, but it relieved Lisa to see that she was no longer in limbo, distraught, and fearful. He was alive and unharmed. Although Martin had said he was sure Liam was safe, he had not convinced Marianne.

"I think and I hope he will accomplish this journey and then return, so I will see him again, although I am considering joining him. No, I will not walk the whole route," she added, seeing Lisa's look of alarm. "I can take some leave and pick up the trail near the end. The destination is the Cathedral of St James de Compostela. of course. There are several alternative paths." She smiled in anticipation, and Lisa realised she must have researched the route in detail.

"It is the feast day of St. James on July 25th. Liam will want to stay for that. It is a famous pilgrimage." Marianne sat back, crossed her legs, and smiled. She seemed excited and Lisa felt her own spirits lifting at the news.

"Compostela," Lisa murmured. "Field of stars."

"You know about this place?" Marianne asked, her face lighting up. "I did not know the name, Compostela, meant anything. You surprise me. Do you speak Spanish?"

"Yes, I lived there once. Many years ago."

Lisa dreamed about her first plane flight to Spain that night. She felt again the marvellous heat as she stepped off the plane. How could you not thrill to the warmth, the brilliance of the light, and a cloudless blue sky? Ray took her arm by the elbow and guided her down as they disembarked onto the runway of Malaga airport. She was nineteen years old and carrying Sophie in a travelling cot.

Chapter Eleven

PART TWO

England 1977

Lisa did not see Ted again. She had torn and cut up her wedding dress, and by the end of that summer decided to leave. More than that – to vanish, even from her family. She sealed an envelope with money for the rent and packed her few personal belongings. When she left their tawdry marital accommodation, for the last time, she did not look back. The building society cleared her savings account, handing over the cash while asking more than once if she was sure. Perhaps they thought she was taking her custom elsewhere.

There was an autumnal feel to the morning. Her long terraced street stretched out in its usual mean greyness but, perhaps coming from somewhere better, greener, she watched a few desiccated leaves, swept along by the wind, which caught her downward gaze by their pretty colours, and her mood lightened as she approached the bus station. She was going to the coast hoping to find work at a pub in the harbour area. She had experience of the work, did not care about the hours, and would find somewhere to lodge or board. Anything was better than a factory, and she knew she was skilful in talking to people as she poured beer, calculated totals for the orders of large groups, and made herself popular with a cheerful face and a readiness to laugh, even at off colour jokes. That was why she held a good open reference of the 'to whom it may concern' type.

Removing her wedding ring as she settled into her seat, she noticed with relief that it left no actual mark, no discoloured skin, as yet. She saw herself as a serious-faced but reasonably attractive young woman, decent in her dress and with a reference – it was difficult to explain why she needed it, without giving away her real aim – and had no ties. She must be an attractive applicant, and bars always needed staff.

Her suitcase was light, but she left it in a locker, finding the information desk at the bus station when she arrived. After a long journey, trudging around with it weighing her down, when she was now tired and more dispirited, it was not a good impression to give. She drank a cup of tea and refreshed her lipstick, smoothed her skirt from the creases of sitting for so long, and asked where she might find a list of lodging houses, adding as the clerk studied her with renewed interest, if there was any bar work available in a *respectable* area of the harbour? It was where she knew the busiest trade would be.

She was lucky. The clerk, a spindly youth with dirty collar and cuffs, told her that the Sailing Club was looking for a young woman. The hours were long – a private association, with members sometimes drinking until three or four in the morning. He watched her reaction, stroking his stubbled chin. They would help her with accommodation, too. The club's run down espresso bar 'could do with someone attractive like you', he said. When he asked if she would come for a drink later, if they fixed her up, she promised him she would return and let him know. It was pointless to do otherwise, though she did not intend to keep the promise. At least for a while, he would also think he had got lucky.

The first bars along the quayside were not appealing; squalid, smokey, with men who threw her a sideways glance up and down and stopped their desultory conversations. Perhaps they assumed she was a prostitute? A streetwalker, tart? Whatever name they gave it in this part.

At first, it seemed worth a try, but a barman just showed her the door. In the next pub, he called the owner, but warned her he was asleep and they needed no more staff. He looked annoyed, as though he thought she was trying to take his job, and a few minutes later came back to announce to everyone in nasal tones that the 'boss' wasn't interested. His words and the smirk which accompanied it generated some lively, indecent comments from the men leaning on the bar before she could reach the exit.

She stood outside and blinked away tears. When she raised her head from gazing at the dried stains of a seaside pavement, a tap on the shoulder drew her attention. Flinching with the impulse of a threatened assault, she stepped back, and heard a soft, accented voice say, "Try the Sailing Club, love. That'd suit thee better."

It was the second time someone had recommended it to her, and she listened to the directions.

****

They did not leave her on the streets that night. The Sailing Club proved successful. Not only did they agree to give her a trial, but found her lodging in a nearby boarding house. Though down at heel, it was safe, the man who interviewed her said, and told her to mention that he sent her.

She trod so as not to catch her heels in the threadbare carpet in the hall and ignored the unswept wooden staircase which led to her room at the top of the building in the boarding house. At least it had a window which opened and she made sure it aired before she returned for the night. They provided breakfast, and considering her youth and good manners, the male proprietor – perhaps prompted by his wife? – came to the front door to point out the direction of a nearby 'chippy' to get her tea. She was free the next day until six o'clock in the evening.

They gave her a key with instructions not to lose it, whatever she did. They knew she would return in the early hours each morning and instructed her to 'creep' in and not to rouse other boarders in the house – who, the woman advised, with a sniff, worked more regular hours. Lisa felt uncomfortable with that last remark. Her job was decent enough, and the money was good.

She learned fast to adapt her welcoming remarks, and longer conversations, to the mixed backgrounds of the clients who she served at the bar. Most of them were male, but wives appeared in the early evenings. The ones who lingered longer at the club were the heavy drinkers. Though none were troublesome.

The original 'Yacht Club' had changed and developed in recent years into the new two-storey building, which was the present clubhouse, and so had the mix of 'clientele'. It was seen as a social club in the late evenings. But some business matters also took place in the relaxed surroundings. Membership was by subscription, and although intended for the 'middling sort' in the setting out of the association's aims, it included men who owned yachts rather than dinghies.

She enjoyed the work and her independence. One late, squally evening when the bar was quiet, and she had little to do, the Manager whispered to her she could talk to Raymond if she liked. "Take the weight off your feet for a while," he winked in encouragement. She blushed with a surge of embarrassing excitement because she knew who he meant,

She looked across the room to the windowed side which faced onto the harbour, the sandy, deserted beach, and a starlit sky as the wind dropped. Raymond waved to her from a table and pointed to the wine chilling in an ice bucket.

The wine was champagne, and he steadied her hand as she took a fluted, bubbling glass from him. They held each other's gaze. It was not the first time she shared a drink with him, but always at the bar, where he often remained to chat in between the serving of customers, waiting for her free moments. He often plied her with tastings of various spirits and arranged for her to try cocktails prepared by another member of staff at weekends. His presence in the club had grown until he was there most evenings, even if only for a short period. The Manager had warned her he was important, but why, except for wealth, she did not know. Was he married? He was older than her by at least a decade; she reckoned. She noticed that the time he spent with her influenced the other members; they treated her with more respect, intervened less in buying drinks when he was talking to her at the bar, and the more unwelcome remarks and jokes faded away.

Raymond's interest and the way others greeted and spoke to him thrilled her; sometimes as great friends, shaking his hand, touching his shoulder, and always deferential. His dress was stylish; often he wore a suit, and the expensive cufflinks and rings set him apart from others. His face was clean shaven, tanned, and his fingernails manicured, his hair well cut.

"Do you like the cinema?" he asked as he filled her glass again on that occasion. He leaned forward and brushed the tip of her high-heeled shoe with his foot.

With bubbles tickling her nose and restraining a sneeze, she nodded her head.

"What do you like to eat? Have you been to any of the places here?" He waved his hand along the view.

She had not noticed a restaurant along this part of the harbour, and it was not a place she could afford to eat. A cafe was more her inevitable choice, but the 'greasy spoons' she had soon spotted and ruled out. There was a Lyon's which she used and a tea shop which offered a snack lunch. She wondered whether to be honest or evasive, but the words came out spontaneously: "I've always wanted to go somewhere a bit 'posh' and try something different."

He laughed and in such a way that she gave in and joined him. He took her hand across the table. "You're free tomorrow? Your day off?"

Chapter Twelve

It all happened with amazing speed and, although he did not rush her further than she wanted to go, after a few nights out, some kisses and cuddles, they became lovers. He took her to his penthouse flat, high in status and position, in a modern building which was much admired for its bold and light architecture. She did not stay the night, nor move in with him. He was emphatic about guarding her reputation as far as possible.

She revealed little personal information; only that she had left behind her family in search of independence. Making clear the poverty, even though it was humiliating to reveal, helped her to feel she was being honest, if evasive.

It was not a problem. He disclosed almost nothing about himself either, except to assure her he was unmarried. He had secreted away no wife or children in the background. What did he do for a living? Unless it was inherited or accrued wealth, there was nothing for her to speculate about because he gave her no clues. Lisa had never had connections with anything resembling *his* social circles, and now these included herself, although they remained limited as members of the Sailing Club.

During one amorous evening in his penthouse, before he phoned for a taxi to take her back to her lodgings (it was always the same discreet driver), sleepy and happy, curled up in his bed with her head on his chest, he asked her if she could think about marrying him. Taken by surprise, and without further thought, she agreed. He questioned her about her faith and she delighted him further by the admission that she was a Roman Catholic, though lapsed. He delayed her return to the boarding house that night and they drank champagne in celebration until the early hours.

The next morning, when she awoke late in her lodgings, yawned, and stretched out on her narrow bed, she glanced at the light pouring through the closed curtain covering the tiny window between the eaves. Mid-day? She checked her watch.

The realisation came at that precise moment, and her stomach churned with bile from the alcohol of the night before, which rose in its bitterness in her throat. How could she marry him? She was already married to Ted!

The following weeks passed in an intoxicating frenzy. He took her to London for a few days' holiday and directed her shopping. The expensive stores and their sophisticated assistants overawed her. He led her towards the simple, stylish clothes and asked her what she favoured. He did not need to tell her to touch the silky fabrics to appreciate their quality. There was no visible price tag.

"A stronger colour? And not too short," he told the assistant who had attached herself to them. Dressed in the classical black worn as almost a uniform, the assistant nodded and walked away. He followed and caught up with her, and Lisa pretended not to hear him say, "Nothing tarty, but fashionable and – something to give her a little more maturity?" The saleswoman turned back to look at Lisa and smiled.

During this exciting time in the city, they stayed in hotels and dined in exotic restaurants with special dishes from varied cuisines. She looked like a high-class woman of the world. When people watched her, what did they think about her relationship with Ray? She doubted they could imagine how lucky she was because they always sounded natural together, and her humble background was no longer evident, she told herself. They did not look so incongruous together. The boarding house and the job behind the bar at the Sailing Club were already forgotten. Yet everywhere they went, she held out her hand to catch the light on the diamond ring. It reassured her. They could not assume she was a trollop; a young girl with an older man, because she already wore an engagement ring. Just the one item of jewellery on the third finger, but a large and beautiful symbol of respectability and security.

They extended their stay because of her obvious delight. The theatre enthralled her and the boat trips on the river – from where it was best to view the city lights at night, Ray said, – became a favourite activity. She cupped a brandy glass to keep out the chill as they sat on the wooden benches of the boat, his arm around her shoulder, pulling her in close, and she thought it was not just physical, or an illusion of warmth; she was less nervous with the drink, and any fears were more distanced.

There were other days when she met his business friends and sometimes their wives in different situations. Smokey basement clubs with card games, and cash stacked high in the middle of sticky tables covered in empty glasses. A discreet waiter hovered to take further orders. Sometimes Ray joined them for a short period. Poker, he told her. Ray's tones changed too, as did his accent as he played. His voice rasped. He cursed, and she pretended not to notice. He seemed to adopt an alternative language with these men. The switch did not surprise her so much, on reflection, because she recognised how she had used it herself in order to fit in at the Sailing Club. But seeing how he negotiated the change, and his altered behaviour, she felt unsettled. She was observing a different side of him.

He took her to exclusive houses, with long drives, in the suburbs where they drank cocktails in high-ceilinged draughty reception rooms. But he never left her alone with the glamorous women who partnered the other men there. Lisa smiled at the thought that her mother would call them no good 'fancy' pieces. Not at all respectable. She pushed aside an image of her family and extended her hand a little to flash the diamond ring under the overhead lights.

At the next opportunity, she bought some postcards of London, which came with the stamps. It amused Ray to watch her choose and collect them, and he did not question her impulsive interest as she sorted through the views and famous photographs. Perhaps he thought it was a new hobby. He did not see the message she later scrawled on one of them, and she took care to post it in a central box on a corner of a street, unnoticed by him as they strolled along on a bright but cold morning.

I am safe and happy. Never coming back. Don't worry about me.
Lisa

****

Ray asked her for her birth certificate, and for a moment she panicked. She looked at him with a wide-eyed, blanched face.

"What's the matter? Have you lied to me about your age?" he said, and hugged her close. "You silly girl."

"No, of course not. I just hope I've got my certificate. Haven't lost it, I mean. I must look for it now. What is it for, Ray?"

"Something you will like. I'll tell you in a minute."

He let her go, looking puzzled, which alarmed her still more. The birth certificate was in an envelope she brought with her. It proved that she was nineteen and able to marry without the need for anyone's consent. The battered brown envelope was unsealed and held a few other documents. She sighed as she removed the incriminating marriage certificate to Ted, and folded it up, with damp and shaking hands, into a tiny rectangle to hide it elsewhere.

She scanned the document recording her birth. It gave few details of her parentage and the address was, of course, where her mother and father lived at that time. It stated her father's occupation as a labourer. Her mother was only a housewife. Though Lisa was born and had always lived in the one town, it was a large place, and it would not be easy for anyone to find her family. She slapped the side of the head with her hand. Why was she worrying about this? It all dated to the period before Ted! Nothing recorded here could betray her secret. She had only ever used her maiden name since leaving her mother and siblings for a new life and never that of Ted's surname, which she had taken on marriage.

Ray's indulgence knew no bounds. When she returned with the birth certificate, he told her she needed it to get a passport because they were going on honeymoon abroad. She was excited. He talked of countries on the continent, the south of France, Switzerland – you would love Bern, he told her, but that's for the Winter – and there's the sunshine of Spain. He had crewed yachts when a teenager she remembered that, and now he said he intended to buy – he paused and rubbed his chin – a modest one of his own.

"I will take you sailing. Following the coast of the Med, and we will drink champagne in every harbour!" He caught her about the waist, lifted her in the air and whirled her around. Now she was laughing and nothing else mattered.

****

They married so soon afterwards that she wondered if the priest thought she was pregnant. Not that it would have been important, nor unusual, if she was. Times were changing. Ray welcomed the changes, which he discussed with her because of the marriage vows, yet he was never regular in his own religious observance nor his attendance at a church.

It all helped her to pretend an indifference to the illegality of what she was doing, which was in total opposition to the rule of law. She also told herself that none of that religious childhood reverence and discipline applied to her any more. She was an adult and could make her own choices. The church in which she would marry Ray was a modern building, which again seemed to emphasise that rules and regulations must have moved on. How different it all was to that freezing morning in the musty, damp old parish chapel with Ted. That was the past. Her future was now.

Ray settled everything with the priest. They attended minimal pre-ceremony advice; a course they followed to prepare them for a lifetime together, and to bring their offspring up educated in the faith. The thought of children appealed. She could make her own family!

She had kept her certificates for Baptism and First Communion, which were a basic requirement for the church wedding, but she was not free to marry again. In her heart, in nightmarish moments when she woke with a start in the dark, she knew it would be both bigamous and, she believed, a mortal sin.

Yet, as with everything else, Ray smoothed the path and never attempted to question her. Why would he? Nothing could restrain her, but she shook as she signed official papers before the wedding. Ray explained away her behaviour to himself as well as others, she suspected, because she was young and nervous. He was protective and light-hearted, joyful and proud of her.

After the ceremony, followed by a short afternoon buffet celebration in a renowned hotel, Lisa received compliments and congratulations from some familiar faces she had seen at the gaming tables. These people were important in Ray's life.

They toured France and Italy for two months as an extended honeymoon. It was another wonderful summer that year and during this time, Ray rented villas for short periods, in between staying at hotels to see city sights and to shop. He disappeared on brief trips back to London sometimes for business, but he did not want her with him. He said he could deal with the urgent meetings faster without the distraction of her presence, kissed away her disappointment, and rewarded her with expensive presents to dissuade her from further argument.

She was careless about contraception, blissful and enraptured both with her husband and the lifestyle. When she soon fell pregnant, they agreed she would return to England for the last months and the birth. By this means, the child would have dual nationality because Ray intended they would live in Spain.

Chapter Thirteen

The stay in England while awaiting the birth of her child, Sophie, marked the start of Lisa's interest in expensive, fast cars. Ray inspired it because of his excitement at the prospect of seeing the British Grand Prix at Brands Hatch. He planned for a weekend away, but would not let her accompany him, fearing she could go into labour. He promised he would take her to a motor race another time.

When he told her why he would be away for the entire weekend, he had reminded her of her embarrassment during the new musical called 'Evita', which they saw in a matinee performance at The Prince Edward theatre. She had been so uncomfortable, thinking her waters were breaking. How much worse it would be if she were amid a dense crowd at a race!

Although he was serious about it, at first she laughed at the idea; everything was going well regarding her pregnancy. But it was close to her time, and the idea of needing an ambulance, or other form of emergency transport, in the middle of the crowded spectacle, did not appeal to her either. In the end, she admitted that and agreed.

For Ray, the race was not to be missed because it was in England and the publicity was everywhere, producing nationwide enthusiasm. No-one could be unaware of it. She also realised that Ray looked forward to meeting his various contacts at Brands Hatch. He had talked of that, and how they would make it even more enjoyable.

She realised and accepted that for her the thrill of live motor sport would have to wait, and consoled herself by imagining the heat of Spain in the middle of July. In another month, it would be almost unbearable.

London was a far better place to have her child. For those few months living in England waiting for the birth, Ray had found a central London apartment, which was chosen for its proximity to a private maternity clinic.

The return to England had not unsettled Lisa because she knew it was temporary, and she felt happy and relaxed about the birth. As far as she was aware, her mother experienced no difficulties in childbirth, either for her or her younger siblings. Compared to her mother's circumstances, especially for the last child, when Lisa's father's violence resulted in him leaving for good, Lisa was in a much more secure situation.

Sometimes she wavered a little about the total severance of connections with her family. Perhaps her pregnancy and the imminent birth increased this sense of regret, but she dismissed it. It was better to look forward to having a prosperous, stable future with her husband. He never mentioned her family, and she guessed he realised it was what she preferred. She knew nothing of his family.

Ray often left her on her own in the London apartment. To rest, he said, but gave her numbers to call regarding his whereabouts at his business meetings. He phoned her to make sure she was alright and checked she knew what to do; how to summon help if needed.

Nothing untoward happened on his weekend away. He returned full of the highs and lows of the race, explaining that James Hunt crashed out on the eighth lap. Ray said that he aimed one day to have a Ferrari like the Argentinian winner of the race.

After the birth of Sophie, the recovery period was short and Lisa looked forward to moving to Spain. The recent interest in cars remained, and she wanted to see the top of the range sports-cars for herself. Stimulated by her continued enthusiasm, they looked at them in several showrooms. Lisa studied the glossy brochures and the motoring magazines with reviews of various models. Of course, they also revealed the prices. She was sure the Ferrari would have to wait, but did not know for how long.

Perhaps he did not want to spoil the appreciation and delight she expressed in the prospect of him buying such a prestigious car for them at some future date. He offered her a new goal; she must learn to drive, and he assured her she would enjoy it.

****

When they arrived in Spain, the Ford agent met them at Malaga airport with their car, a black Ford Granada, not a Ferrari. Lisa admired the gleaming exterior as soon as she saw it. She handed the travelling cot to Ray, and walked around, opened a rear door, and patted the seats of the spacious interior with a broad smile. Her eyes were bright with delight at the splendour of the vehicle.

Since the birth of Sophie, she felt so well and knew she looked more attractive. It was not just the clothes and the lifestyle. Having a child did not mean drudgery and care, and she had recovered her lithe figure. She would not have to endure her mother's poverty and limitations.

Yet, as she admired the car, one recurring thought jolted her again and marred her pleasure. It had distressed her soon after the birth. The sudden realisation that the church would regard her daughter, her vulnerable young baby, as a bastard. At one time, it had hit her like a physical blow. Her child was born out of wedlock, born out of fornication. These strictures from her childhood, aroused by Ray's commitment to the faith at the time of their marriage, would not go away.

Her marriage to Ray was not legal, was it?

"It's a family car," he said, "but suitable for business, too. As I told you."

"Looks good. I love it already." She smiled at him and dismissed the guilty feeling.

"I'd better sit in the back with the baby, though." She placed the cot on the seat next to her and gripped the handles to begin with. Sophie was asleep, she noted, and hoped that would last during the journey. She tried to comfort herself with the thought of the probability that Ted would have established another relationship, too.

Ray said that with the increased traffic of package holidaymakers, they would have to clear the city before picking up any speed. The route out of the airport, which he said had opened a second passenger terminal a few years before because of the numbers, looked choked with vehicles and people.

With nothing to do for Sophie, whom she had fed, nappy changed, and who was sleepy; she was watching cars in the rear-view mirror. Was it a preparation for driving lessons? The prospect excited her. In London, she had busied herself in studying the Highway Code because Ray told her signs were international and it was useful to learn it now.

Ray weaved about, in and out of the traffic lanes, and soon they left the airport congestion further back. She watched what he did, aware of how well he drove the car, and felt safe with him and proud of his skill and experience But just as she was ready to close her eyes, lulled by her sense of security and good fortune, what seemed to be his excessive manoeuvring, although not at speed, roused her. She clutched the handles of the carry cot again. Was Ray annoyed by the vehicle behind them? Perhaps it was too close and intimidating.

"That car behind Ray. It's been tailing us for the last ten minutes. Do you recognise it? It pulled in, but only for a moment, a while ago." She continued to watch and to comment. "He overtook twice on the route out of Malaga, and then slowed again, and rejoined our lane a bit later. He's really moving when he wants to."

Ray put his foot down then to see what would happen. As she knew the airport journey well, she was aware of how little traffic there should be at this point. The car was a Seat, the most common model they saw since they had moved to Spain. Nothing unusual about that. But this was a supercharged vehicle, a 'souped' up number, as Ray described them.

She had asked Ray before why there were so many of the cars, as they did not seem to be anything special about them. He told her it was all to do with what happened after Franco's death. Radical changes included the new government establishing special links with the Fiat company. Spain wanted to build up its own motor industry, he had said, and that was why she noticed so many with the Seat symbol.

Perhaps, because of the car tailing them, she remembered talking to another English expat about the Seats. Favourites of 'low-level criminals', she was told with a laugh. But when she asked what crimes, the woman's expression had changed. Blank and no longer smiling, she had turned away and closed the conversation.

It reminded Lisa that there had been so many times when she knew she was treading on dangerous ground. They mixed little and she lacked women friends. The reason for that, Ray said, was because the women were not like her, and he preferred it that way. Though pleased at the time at what seemed to be a compliment; it had not removed a sense of apprehension. Their life in Spain was complicated, and Ray kept her in the dark about his business and his associates.

At last he lost the car worrying him. In the town he knew so well, and which was the last reasonable size urbanised area before they reached their villa in the hills, he had waited for the moment.

"Hold on to the cot!" he called out to her as he swerved. They swung back and forth as he cornered with squealing wheels and entered a maze of old houses. They were in shadowed streets, which narrowed like corridors. Lisa trembled and her heart was beating too fast for comfort as she pulled the cot close to her. Sophie cried. Where was her dummy? Lisa licked her little finger to cleanse it, and then inserted it into the infant's mouth. As the baby sucked, soothed and quiet, she calmed down herself. They would soon be home. Their secluded villa offered safety.

Her mind wandered off again as they approached the villa. Count your blessings, she told herself. The neighbours comprised several English expats. Amongst them was an inner group with whom Ray had business connections. They were closer to these few and, although he did not encourage her to mix, he said she could turn to them if desperate. At her expression of alarm, he said that he only meant if she needed something and he was away.

Later she saw other, much more palatial villas, but their home amazed and overwhelmed her. She had a swimming pool; a tremendous luxury. The single-storey villa had five bedrooms. A maid cleaned for them, and cooked some meals whenever they wanted her to, and this was an especial benefit as Lisa was not fond of cooking. Too long living on the basics as a child, she decided, to take an interest in food. Although the Spanish cuisine attracted her.

Ray liked to eat at small tavernas and restaurants whose proprietors and clientele did not recognise him, but which were recommended. He did not flaunt his wealth, and they often changed venues. Lisa's appearance remained 'classy' but modest, as guided by him at first, yet soon becoming natural and preferred. Not for her the heavy gold bracelets, designer watches, and jewelled earrings of some of their neighbours. They did not attract attention.

By the time they drove up the slow, unadopted, gravelled road to their house, Lisa had dismissed her worries and gazed with pride at Sophie's beautiful little face. Her eyelids closed, and she delighted in the delicacy of her skin, almost transparent, and her baby smell.

The full heat of the Spanish day struck her as she opened the car door, and she wanted to hurry inside and out of it. A long cool drink should be available in the fridge. The maid would have made everything ready for their homecoming. Ray told her to wait outside while he turned on the air-conditioning. There were units in several rooms, but the maid, who was more used to the temperatures, might not have thought of it. They could sit outside on the covered verandah until areas had cooled down.

More time passed, and she looked at her watch in irritation. Perspiring, she picked up the cot placed in the shade of a palm tree and went on ahead, regardless.

"What on earth have you been doing? We're sizzling out here, Ray." She called out when she caught sight of him around the side of the villa.

He dusted off his blackened hands as he walked towards her, and they entered through the open doors leading onto the tiled patio. "There's a mess out the back," he said. "A few broken windows, but no other damage. Watch out for shards of glass."

****

After that incident, she saw more of Carlos, the security guard Ray employed, than her husband himself during the latter part of that year. The incident had alarmed her. Ray said it was just some envious youth who had thrown stones at the glass. He had removed it and tidied up some jagged pieces outside while she waited to come in. There was no evidence of theft, from what they could remember of their possessions, and no valuables missing; the culprit had not found the wall safe either. No signs of a planned, nor accomplished break-in. However, it was more serious than that; she thought, if that was all he attributed it to, otherwise he would not have engaged Carlos.

When she had queried, with raised eyebrows, the necessity for a security guard, he said it was only because they kept valuables in a safe. He told her the expats sometimes had to take measures against minor theft and that sort of thing. Later, she commented on other security figures in the area who looked far more threatening. He explained that away; some had bodyguards, but that was because their activities were not altogether legal. He had looked awkward and expanded no further, so she had to accept it.

Carlos spoke some English. He was a muscular Spaniard, although not tall, with a mop of wavy coal-black hair. He never smiled, but was always courteous to her. Like a real chauffeur, he opened and closed the car door. He seemed to take special care not to appear without announcing his presence, greeting her from a distance whenever he saw her. It was so that he did not alarm her; she guessed.

His role was to keep a vigilant eye on the house and the surrounding area. He always reminded her how to secure the property when Ray was away. It had an alarm system, which she set. Although, she wondered who would come to the noisy summons of it in the dead of night? Their neighbours did not have villas that close. Often, Carlos set the devices when he finished for the day. Sometimes he stayed longer, patrolling around late into the evening with a powerful torch, which he flashed now *e* then. For a while, until she had learned to drive, he also acted as a chauffeur.

His introduction into their life kept her on edge rather than making her relax. It was the reason for it, as Ray saw it, that worried her, and that it also came at a period when he spent several days at a time away from her on business.

Lisa wanted to learn Spanish. It would give her something to do. Ray's suggestion of conversations in Spanish with one or two of the other expats in a casual social meeting soon proved insufficient. Many of the women did not bother to even attempt a few words of Spanish and refused to take a serious attitude. Instead, Carlos drove her to a conversation class in the city, which was not too academic in approach, but offered the basics she needed. She enjoyed it and made remarkable progress.

The initial endeavour to engage with her nearest neighbours, of which there were few, had brought her closer to one woman, Marjorie – she preferred to be called Madge – who was older than most of the women. While Lisa went to the Spanish classes and, not long afterwards, spent time in driving lessons, Madge smiled with delight in looking after Sophie. She was a grandmother and adored the placid infant. Madge also offered adult companionship to Lisa.

During the late summer months, the number of young girls who posed around the villas' swimming pools throughout the last part of the season arrived. Wives and their infants predominated in the few villas Lisa had been inside, and she presumed they were on holiday for weeks at a time, enjoying the sunshine. Now it was later in the year. Some families returned to England because the children went back to school. Many houses closed and remained uninhabited until the following Spring. There were others, crowded, noisy, and to be avoided, Ray told her.

"Where do they all go? And why do only some stay later in the year?" she asked Madge one afternoon, when Sophie was asleep beside them, and she did not expect Ray to come home until the next day. The two women were sitting with a half-depleted jug of an over-sweet, but otherwise pleasant, alcoholic Sangria. Lisa had learned about the drink in her Spanish class. To Madge's amusement, she explained it dated back to Roman times, when they added wine to water to kill off the bacteria. Later, they used herbs and spices to make it more palatable because the inferior quality wine had a poor taste.

Madge raised an eyebrow, but showed little interest in the history, though she enjoyed the Sangria. She leaned back on the sofa, and her shoulder length hair, from bleaching and the sun, was like straw in both colour and texture. It fell forward, and she thrust it back in a habitual gesture. Her skirt covered her knees, but she raised her bottom and tugged it down further.

"You don't realise much about what goes on here, do you?" Madge put down her empty glass on a side table and sighed. "It's better that way," and with a glance backward at the sleeping infant, she got to her feet.

"Stay longer, please. I don't know if I'm asking *wrong* questions when I never get answers."

Madge hesitated and sat down again, perching on the edge of the sofa. "Ray keeps you very isolated, but he isn't … violent to you, is he? Does he smack you around? I've never seen a mark on you."

Lisa was astonished. "Of course not. Is that what everyone thinks?"

"That doesn't matter, Lisa. Not here. You wouldn't want to know about a lot of them. It is a good thing you don't mix. As for answers, the wives keep out of the way, return home with the kids, turn a blind eye to the prossies –that's what those young girls are, love. It's all about money, what you can buy, and there's plenty of both."

Madge stood up. "Have to go," she said and patted Lisa on the shoulder before she bent down to speak, almost in a whisper, whilst studying her face. "Ill-got gains, Lisa, and hiding out here, or elsewhere, in foreign places where no-one can find them. That's the men. And sometimes the families move out here, too. Do you understand now?"

Lisa's mouth opened in surprise, but she clamped it closed again. Did she want to know? She looked down at her finger nails; she had bitten them again. An old childhood habit.

Madge shook her head and turned away. "The stones breaking your window were a warning for Ray. You need to ask him more about it, but *don't* tell him I said so. OK?"

Lisa nodded, and watched speechless as her neighbour left, while locking her hands together, now trembling, and held them tight in her lap.

After a while, breathing more evenly, she tipped the rest of the Sangria down the sink and opened a cupboard, reached to the back for the bottle of brandy. A stiff one or two of that would help.

Chapter Fourteen

At first, while travelling all around Europe for almost a year, Lisa delighted in the novelty. They stayed for several weeks in either a hotel or an apartment, or for months in a villa. With little to do except to enjoy herself, she learned a lot about the continent. Travel was stimulating, and it increased her independence; finding her way about by negotiating languages, tackling the different transport offices to buy tickets to take her to this museum or that picturesque viewpoint in the cities. It made her feel self-reliant.

In the Spring, they flew to Switzerland, but not for the skiing. She held the toddler on her lap and Sophie slept without trouble. The flight was pleasant, even exciting. This was her first time in Switzerland. Everything was first class, and the pictures of the hotel, which was in the heart of the old part of Bern, added to her expectations.

"We have a complete suite to ourselves," Ray told her, squeezing her hand as they arrived. While the taxi driver unloaded their modest amount of luggage in the entrance of the Bellevue Palace Hotel, they stood looking up at the impressive building. Lisa had peered out of the window at the delightful architecture in the centre of the city, and longed to take some photographs.

A doorman welcomed them inside and afterwards accompanied them to the lift and their accommodation. Registration was quick, and the Manager spoke to Ray in welcome. Someone would bring up their suitcases without delay, he assured them. The young man who delivered their luggage said his few words in such good English that she listened hard for an accent, but detected the merest hint. Like attendants everywhere they travelled, he knew a smattering of several European languages; enough to do his job.

The streets of the city, lined in trees covered in candyfloss pink cherry blossom, and the trams weaving about, had added charm to the warmth of the sunshine as they journeyed from the airport, and now she was full of more admiration for their suite. "Spacious, luxurious, and … artistic. In three words," Lisa said and laughed. She put Sophie down on the thick carpet and watched her crawl away, exploring and mumbling something to herself. The child already showed she was forming intelligible speech, and it fascinated Lisa how fast she developed. Her own younger siblings, whom she cared for from an early age, had not been so quick as far as she could remember. But that was all so long ago, and she did not want to recall any of that part of her life.

Ray was trying to get her attention. He needed to see someone and would return in time for aperitifs in the bar before the evening meal. He left her alone for business meetings and sometimes returned tense and preoccupied. But this time it seemed unusual; they had only just arrived. What could be that important? She knew that to question or probe him was futile, so accepted his kiss.

"I'll unpack and settle Sophie down," she said. Her mood changing with his imminent departure. There was not much to hang in the wardrobes. Ray always insisted she shop for new clothes wherever they stayed. That way, he explained, you dress in the fashion and styles of your surroundings. Of a certain class, he added, by which he meant elegant but restrained. He liked them both to blend in and hated anything conspicuous, not only in their appearance but also any public display of disagreement. Perhaps it was a deliberate part of his personality, the relaxed bonhomie, which gave away nothing of their purpose, or of their lives and led her to think it was, to a degree, calculated.

"You don't need to worry too much about Sophie, darling. There's a nursemaid I've arranged for her during our stay. A competent, experienced young woman who can look after her when we go down to dinner, and at any other time. It will give us more freedom to do the sights." Lisa's eyes widened in surprise, but he turned away and, though she hurried to the open door to call him back, he disappeared into the lift. The idea of pre-arranged care for their daughter did not appeal.

****

Ray devoted his time to Lisa and the child for the next two days and dispelled some of her earlier concerns. She wanted to see the historic centre and looked through the hotel brochure, choosing the Rosengarten. She read the description of the park and the wonderful views from it over the entire old medieval part of the city.

Although she kept Sophie in a fold-up pram to begin with, she had every intention of encouraging her to walk in reins at some point. This recent development indoors seemed sensible to take further. If the toddler was tired, and the pushchair unattractive, the routine was for her to demand to be carried by her father, and he willingly obliged.

The flowers were sumptuous in their full glory and their scent. The varied colours of the azaleas, rhododendrons and irises reminded her of the strong shades of the colours in the garden created around the villa in Spain. Different plants, of course, and here they appeared softer, not striving so hard against the heat.

She found her camera and soon approached a passer-by to take a photo of them, posing with a long, flower-bordered path stretching out behind. Ray smiled in amusement at the way she cajoled strangers to do this for her family album. Sophie chuckled in her father's arms. The woman who took the photograph accepted their gratitude with nods as she returned the camera. In the middle of the brief exchange, Lisa caught the expression of alarm on her husband's face, and turned away to see what he was looking at down the other end of the path. A man was coming straight towards them.

Ray looked down, scuffed his shoes on the gravel. It was as though he did not want to meet him, but recognised him and was prepared to wait.

The man wore a dark suit, despite the warmth of the day. It contrasted with Ray's casual and expensive beige safari suit. Before the man reached them and stopped, Ray passed Sophie to Lisa. She took her in her arms, ready for a wail of frustration, which did not come. Instead, the child studied the stranger, while she put her finger in her mouth and sucked it.

"Raymond, isn't it? What are you doing here in Bern?" After this greeting, the man gazed at Lisa and the infant, and added, "Business or pleasure?"

He moved around closer towards them and she saw an angry red birthmark, or scar, on the lower part of his face.

"Definitely pleasure," Ray said, and stepped back, distancing himself.

"Your lady wife, too. A family photo for the album?" He put out his hand, and Lisa took it in surprise. A firm grip, but he held on a little too long for comfort. How long had he been watching them? She wondered.

"Well, no doubt we will catch up some time." With one last look at Lisa and the child, he nodded his head at Ray and walked back the way he had come.

"Someone you dislike?" she said, stating the obvious as soon as the man was out of hearing.

"Not anyone you would appreciate, either." He unfolded a plan of the gardens. "I think there's a refreshment place near here."

They drank tea and ate strawberry cake, in preference to the traditional heavy chocolate Swiss gateau. He was quiet, preoccupied. Lisa fed the child morsels and took a drinking cup from the pocket of the pushchair. Sophie was hot and thirsty. She removed the cotton sun hat and ran her hands through the child's damp hair to cool her head.

"Are we *only* on holiday, Ray? You've already dashed off to meetings. As soon as we arrived. Is that why we are here in Bern?" He did not respond, and Lisa felt irritable and anxious. It was too warm, and she seemed tired now. Her sense that something was wrong disturbed her more than ever. There was no one sitting close to them, but she lowered her voice. No point in annoying him further. "It's always like this. I enjoy the travelling, seeing the world, but we never settle. I thought we were to live in Spain."

He leaned forward and took Sophie's hand, letting her curl her tiny fingers around his. "Let's go back to the hotel. Tomorrow we could continue to the *Bärengraben*, the bear pit. It is another popular tourist site. Sophie might like to see the cubs."

"Or they might terrify her! I know about the place. I read about it. It's part of a zoo, of sorts."

"Maria at the hotel would take care of her, if you prefer. It would be best anyway. I need you to come to the bank in the morning."

****

They ate a continental breakfast in their suite because he did not want to linger and delay the appointment. Maria took care of Sophie without fuss. The child seemed to like her. Ray did not explain why they were going to the bank, although he described the visit as a security measure for her future, and it troubled Lisa. They left the hotel in silence.

When they arrived, she soon realised by their reception that he had set the whole thing in motion days before, and she signed various papers without doing much more than scanning the English translation. The principal tongue in this part of Switzerland was German, but the documents were also in French by default. It was possible to arrange any other language as long as they gave prior notification. Ray had mentioned this aspect, but the senior clerk repeated it as they sat in his office. An expressionless man, he was grave as he detailed the procedures, followed by reference to all the legalities involved in holding a safe deposit box. Everything was in her maiden name, and she presumed her husband must have decided that.

Two members of staff, conforming to the bank's regulations, led them down to the basement where there were two keys for each box; one for the client and the other for the bank. They knew Ray well, and he had already produced his key on arrival, but everything for her was new. For the moment, she had nothing to deposit in hers. Left alone in the vault, Ray took various items and placed them in front of her. While she examined them in confusion, she heard him shuffling through his own contents before he locked them away. The items he removed were now her property. Lisa picked up the jewellery, wrapped in cloth, let it fall through her fingers, and looked at him for guidance.

"Am I to wear these, Ray?" It comprised sets of clunky necklaces, rings and bracelets, but nothing attractive.

"No, but they are valuable and you could sell them one day." She touched tight clips of new Swiss banknotes, and some, which she did not examine further, were in other currencies. "Look at these documents, although you don't need to read them now, but remember them as stocks and share certificates." Ray unrolled a bundle of papers for her to see and said, "The deeds of some property we own." She saw wax seals, and decorative headings on sheets so thick they were like fabric. "All of this is a treasure store for the future," he told her, his expression serious.

She locked her own box and pushed it away, feeling alarmed and repelled, and unable to work out why. Taking the key from her, he tucked it in a pocket with his own.

"We will find a place which is secure for both of them," he said, before an official took away the boxes and they left the bank.

Lisa looked at her watch; it was mid-morning. "Can we go somewhere for a coffee now, and I would like something stronger, too?" If he had foreseen pleasure, that the experience at the bank would thrill, perhaps overwhelm her, she felt she disappointed him, and he would see the radical change in her mood even if he did not understand it. They returned to the hotel to collect Sophie.

The tour of the bear pit did not improve the experience of the morning. Such poor conditions in which they held the animals upset her. She expected better as she had been an inactive, but still a supporter of Animal Rights in England. Why had Ray brought her and Sophie here to see these pathetic creatures?

Linked to the main enclosure by a small expanded area built for the cubs, was a tunnel which he pointed out to her and tried to draw to Sophie's attention. This offered more than the original arrangement, at least in terms of space, but not much, as it looked medieval and reminded her of history lessons at school when they set dogs upon chained bears just for public entertainment.

She learned the zoo had changed location several times to different areas in the city. Why then had they not made any substantial improvements in the last 50 years? That it was even a bear pit at all caused complaints; she overheard other tourists expressing disapproval, which matched her own angry thoughts. Was it only that which influenced her mood, or only a part of her overall concern about the visit to the bank, which still felt uncomfortable? What did it mean having so much money and valuables secreted away?

It would be simpler to go somewhere else, she decided, and because Sophie did not like the bears, it was reason enough to convince Ray. Perhaps the display was just a remnant of tradition in the Swiss culture from its original time: they built it in the mid-nineteenth century.

It was a fine afternoon as they strolled along the banks of the River Aar and admired the old bridges. She calmed down, and Ray made her laugh at his antics, holding the reins for Sophie and getting them tangled in his own legs, so that he fell down, while the child stood looking at him, her expression puzzled. It was the wrong way round; she did the falling over, the child's reaction seemed to convey.

When they returned to the hotel, the clerk had a message for Ray, delivered by hand after lunch. He read it while Lisa struggled with bags and took the child out of the pushchair. The receptionist hurried to help her fold it up, then summoned a lift. Lisa heard Ray scrunch up the single sheet and watched him thrust the paper into his pocket.

Chapter Fifteen

Spain was cold and the wind icy when they returned. Even in the south that year in the early months, and before the first signs of Spring. The local Spanish said they were freezing to death. The prevailing mood was gloomy and both Ray and Lisa were preoccupied and distant with each other. He took several flights to London and left her with Carlos in place again for her protection, and the maid to help with Sophie so that it allowed Lisa to continue with her activities.

"We could go with you this time," she suggested, as he packed the slim leather holdall for the second flight that month. Why are his business meetings so frequent and he does not tell me anything about them? She wondered.

"Why do you want to go with me, darling? What for? It is just as cold and dreary there, and I will be back in three or four days." He ignored the clean, folded shirt she held out. "If I need any more, I'll buy them over there."

She sat down on the bed with her face in her hands. He heard her gasping sobs and came over to her, clasped her to him. They both knew that this, too, was not unusual now. He waited until she calmed down again, let go of her, and picked up a box of tissues. He had asked her once if she was pregnant, as neither of them had contemplated another child yet, but she assured him she was not.

"It's OK. Just finish your packing. I'm alright, Ray."

He sighed, and she fled from the bedroom before he could say anything more. She put on coffee and, when the aroma was wafting around, took the brandy out of the cupboard and gulped down a large measure. Only a pick-me-up, she thought. She sipped at the black espresso, holding the cup between her hands, and tucked the brandy glass under the worktop, out of sight. Lisa glanced at the clock. Not even lunch time yet. Perhaps another small one.

Carlos walked past the French windows and averted his gaze. He was always unobtrusive but, with a sense of shame, she knew he had spotted the drinking. She refused to hide behind blinds and in shuttered rooms in her own home on every occasion she needed a drink. Besides, Ray had left.

After the visit to Switzerland, they had drifted apart because he was so secretive. He promised they would spend a few weeks on a yacht in the summer. Perhaps he offered it to improve their relationship because it was what he had talked about a long time ago; to sail along the Mediterranean coastline, mooring at ports for the restaurants, the night life and the lights.

She looked forward to the planned trip if it materialised, but she was also thinking about England. Her mother was a grandmother, although she did not know it, and that fact was raw in its implications, affecting her low moods and unease. Was it was too late to have a rapprochement with her family? How could she explain to her mother about her marriage to Ray? What if Ted was still around and her siblings remained stuck in the same environment, envying her escape and wealthy lifestyle? It was all too difficult.

They did not receive any mail at the villa. Ray collected it from the town. He said it was a poor service; that post often arrived late and torn, or they lost items. It seemed a common practice amongst the ex-pats to use a private box of some sort for collection at a Post Office. Madge had suggested that it was easier not to have a personal delivery.

Lisa saw no letters, but sometimes advertising material found its way into the community. She had never written to her family since that postcard sent in England after meeting Ray.

One afternoon, while he was absent on his business trip, she wrote a brief letter and enclosed a photograph from the Swiss 'holiday' of all three of them. Perhaps her mother would want to make contact. She gave her address and felt comforted by the idea.

****

Ray kept his promise, and they followed his plans, travelling for two months that summer. First, Ray hired a luxurious villa, and they took a flight to the Cote d'Azur. A fortnight of total relaxation. Lisa turned a deep golden brown, and they both fussed and played with Sophie during the day, only leaving her in the evenings to dine and take part at the casino tables. The child slept, and the young woman, Sabrina, whom the agency supplied as a nursery maid, grew fond of her. Lisa enjoyed a new activity, too. She learned to play at the gaming tables. Overawed by the glamour to begin with, she soon looked forward to every evening with girlish glee, favouring the roulette wheel in the elegant halls of the French Riviera.

"It's the speed of it," she told Ray. "The idea that it all changes so fast. Bad luck and good fortune. I want to watch the way some people are so tight-lipped about it. I can't be like that, though, and I could never play poker."

Ray made her gamble within a small, calculated stake, which he set for her each time, only increasing it in increments. Her excitement grew with the pile of chips. When they ran out, he pulled her away. She noted his own placing of bets was cautious, although he seemed at ease, win or lose. As always, he seemed to fit into the environment, however its raw newness or unfamiliarity affected her.

She noticed how little alcohol he drank on these nights, and she was more careful in filling her own glass. Whereas once she used spirits as a comforter, now it helped her to relax. One evening, as they left, he grabbed her arm because she tottered down the broad steps of the entrance onto the palm-tree lined drive.

"It's only the sudden change from light to dark," she insisted, holding him and checking the thin straps of her sparkling, flimsy sandals. "These are ridiculously high heels," she giggled.

He knew how much she enjoyed fashion, and he laughed with her over the absurdity of that trend. "We make an attractive couple," he said. "Everyone admires you and I see how they look at you. Very glamorous, but only up to a point. We agreed on that?" She nodded, knowing what he meant; he did not want to cause any intrusive curiosity or speculation. It was why they did not strike up friendships, took part in the minimum of polite, casual conversations. "We're only on holiday; here today and gone tomorrow," he reminded her.

One morning, Ray mentioned he had chartered a yacht and was thinking of further plans. He described the yacht as large, but not monstrous; a new hybrid with sails and power. He wanted Lisa's approval to sound out the agency and see if the young woman, Sabrina, would like to accompany them on a sailing trip. She would have a paid holiday with some duties; care of the toddler in the evenings, and preparing simple meals. Later, he enquired about the availability for two crew. Sabrina had already accepted their proposal and was engaged to go with them.

Ray arranged for them to sail from Toulon on the French coast; a port city with sandy beaches and shingle coves, fishing boats and ferries, as well as a naval base for submarines and warships. In another life, he had explored the area. He intended to go where they could enjoy themselves, avoiding the inevitable tourists and crowds of the high season. It would be much quieter than the haunts of the seriously wealthy on the Cote d'Azur.

Meanwhile, they registered their stay at a hotel in order to see the sights. They took the cable car up to Mont Faron to see the city spread out below in a memorable panoramic view. The trip in the red cable car was short, and despite its vertiginous precariousness, not disturbing. She caught her breath at the vista.

At the peak, he drew her towards the memorial dedicated to the Allied landings in Provence and the Liberation of Toulon in 1944. He read the inscription.

"My father was part of this," he said. "You are too young to know anything about the war, and I was only a toddler, like Sophie, when he returned home to us afterwards." He turned away, took her hand, and pulled her with him, both laughing as they descended the slope.

It was the first time he had told her something about his family. Until then, he always seemed as reticent as she. She understood he must have been at the top of the mountain before and came to this spot now in remembrance. From the touring days of their honeymoon, she knew he had a working knowledge of French, and realised how far he had travelled the world before he met her.

His experience of a world unknown to her, and his familiarity with this area in particular, sparked a sudden interest and desire to travel more herself. In Spain, she had wanted to settle in one place. Was this constant change making her more adventurous, because he did not leave her on her own in a foreign place, as before, and she could rely on him all the time? It enabled her to take bolder steps with strangers, taking advantage of the holiday atmosphere. She said little to anyone, but held her head high and spoke with deliberate assurance when she did. It was still difficult to shake off her own humble beginnings; the narrowness of her world before Ray. But with money came confidence, and their lifestyle expressed their wealth. She need never feel insecure again. Perhaps it was unnecessary to concern herself any further about Ray's background.

After a week at the hotel, Sabrina joined them and they set sail. She was young and good company. At first, Lisa cast a worrying glance at her as she sunbathed on the deck in a tiny bikini. But Ray did not pay Sabrina any attention, other than to remind her to watch Sophie. He often warned her that a yacht was a hazardous environment for a child. Lisa knew Sabrina was not far off her own age, and her English was more than adequate, so she found her easy to talk to. Ray also encouraged her to revive her schoolgirl French with Sabrina. It was not long before she suggested they should take Sabrina with them sometimes for an evening when they moored overnight, so that Sabrina could also dine well. They found a secure 24 hour creche and made arrangements. At the first shopping opportunity, Lisa bought her a charming dress with a jacket and shoes. Now Sabrina could feel at ease, too.

They docked in Marseilles for several days. The variety of the cuisine, especially the Moroccan influences, attracted them, and the sea air on the voyage enhanced Lisa's appetite. She remembered how often alcohol had replaced a meal when Ray was not at home with her. He commented on her healthier look and said it was not just because of a deep sun tan. She appeared to have 'filled out a bit,' he said. Lisa was more animated, energised, and showed her fascination in the variety of people she saw thronging shops, thoroughfares and markets, and in all the sights the old port offered.

When they left Marseilles, Custom Police stopped them out at sea, ordering them to hove to. At first, alarmed, Ray assured her that the agency from whom he chartered the yacht scrutinised the employment details of the two crew members. For what, she wondered? At least it did not involve herself and Ray. Sabrina's explanation was ready: drug smuggling.

The 'search' was slight, routine, after they looked at all the paperwork for chartering the vessel, and acknowledged the unquestionable authenticity of the personal documents of all on board. It was random, Ray suggested. If the customs men received a tip-off, it would be a different matter, much more thorough.

The rest of the holiday passed in an agreeable blur, which Lisa later recalled only with happiness. Sabrina left them to return to her University course, but by that time they did not need her; a comprehensive routine was ingrained regarding Sophie and her safety. The child thrived, laughed and played in safe pools wherever they went, and was already swimming with floats. She babbled away in a mix of Spanish and English, and because of Sabrina had learned some words in French.

Lisa fell in love with the sea and sailing, especially snorkelling in clear waters. They spent an entire week exploring Malta and talked about buying a property in Valletta. She told Ray she wanted to learn to scuba dive and vowed that someday she would revisit the island.

"I have become very lazy, Ray," she said, yawning widely, on a fine morning, during the much swifter journey to reach the coast of southern

Spain and return home. They did not idle with sail now. Their progress was fast and exhilarating.

"It suits you, my love. You look well. Rested."

She had been thinking about her mother and siblings, and the letter she sent to them. She recollected Ray's unexpected and encouraging reference to his father during the Second World War when they were on Mont Faron. Was this the right time? Now that Sabrina had gone back and they were alone, perhaps she should mention it. The suspense agitated her as they drew nearer home; a glow of anticipation if a letter in reply awaited her in the villa, mixed with the certainty of deep disappointment if it did not.

She brought mugs of coffee up from the galley and they sat on deck propped against the side, sheltered from spray. She raised her head to enjoy the sun on her face and closed her eyes before she told Ray about the letter and her hope for a reply on their return.

"You did *what*?"

His tone was so abrupt that her mug tipped, splashing most of her coffee onto the boards of the deck. When she saw his grim expression and his lips set in a tight line, it made her heart pound.

"You gave your mother our address in Spain?"

He stood up and looked down at her in bewilderment. "I told you I collected our post from a numbered box. That has always been the case. What on earth possessed you, Lisa?"

Chapter Sixteen

There was no reply awaiting her. She could not decide whether it was a relief after Ray's reaction. After questioning Carlos about any visitors or enquiries at the villa, and checking *la oficina de correos* in the town for his box number collections, Ray suggested her mother and her siblings could have moved house. He did not discuss the subject any further, and she was grateful that he let it drop. What was the point if the letter had gone astray? If it had reached her mother, she obviously did not want to see her daughter any more. That saddened her, and she hid away with her tears for a while. She hoped the letter had arrived with the photo, and her mother was curious to see her grandchild and would make contact later. Harder to understand was Ray's reaction to the idea of her mother knowing where they lived. What did that matter?

They resumed the pattern of their everyday life, except Lisa was keen to find somewhere for Sophie to meet other children. She chattered all the time and, when they looked at picture book stories together, Sophie's words were in both Spanish and English. She could name and ask for what she wanted, but had not fully sorted out which language to use with different people.

Though they did not live in the heart of it, the English community lacked children. Many villas and apartments closed at the beginning of the autumn. The holiday season was over, families returned home to schools for the start of the academic year. Not that Lisa and Sophie had mixed much with the families. She did not understand their arrangements. Several of the older men lived in Spain permanently, and this separation puzzled Lisa. Was it to do with business, whatever that might be, and she suspected much of it was illegal? Sabrina's mention of drug smuggling suggested Spanish coastal areas, as well as southern France, could be involved. Although living in the hills away from the coast and summer holidaymakers, the men could still be involved in that. The people living near to her were wealthy, with London or northern accents. They had houses in cities in England. That was all she had ever gathered from the brief contact Ray made with them.

Marjorie was a valued neighbour. Widowed and older than most, she had few friends, although she said that the climate outweighed other considerations. Soon after the return home from their travels, Lisa invited her company once more. She wanted advice about a nursery for Sophie, so that she met other children to play with.

Madge sat back in the cane seat lined with cushions, and sipped at the gin and tonic Lisa had prepared. It was late afternoon and the French windows were open to the swimming pool and the coolness of a slight breeze. Both women were almost nut brown and Lisa had decided she would spend less time in the sun, keep more to the shade. Madge's skin was dry, a dark shade broken by lighter lines in the seams of the wrinkles on her arms and chest, and it seemed leathery, unattractive.

Lisa related some highlights of their travels; the exciting parts first, but then she mentioned the customs police boarding the yacht after they left Marseilles. Was it drugs they were looking for? Her speech gathered speed and so much urgency that Madge sat up, leaned forward, and stared at her in surprise.

Lisa wanted answers. "How do the men here get all their money, and why do they stay behind when their families return home?" she asked bluntly. She touched her neck in embarrassment, feeling the flush of heat from her anger rise upwards. "I often wonder, what exactly does Ray do?"

Madge took a deep breath, drained her glass, and put it down on the table between them. "I might need another one of those in a minute," she said.

"You must have seen some of the English newspapers and the headlines, Lisa?"

Lisa had not. Ray never brought papers into the villa and she never thought to buy them. In that moment, she realised how he protected her from the news by never discussing what was happening in England. Yet, he visited London often, and a few other European cities sometimes. He said it was 'business and 'boring' and she would not understand it. So that she remained in ignorance of what was going on in the world.

"The train robbery in sixty-three? Ronnie Biggs?"

When Lisa shook her head once more, the older woman added, "Probably before your time," and tried again. "This place here, well all along this coast, is where people on the wrong side of the law need to escape to, from time to time."

There was no help for it. Marjorie had to explain further. Though they lived in the hills; an isolated, rural area of the southern part of Spain, some called the expanse of the immediate Spanish coastline the 'Costa del Crime.'

"Oh God," said Lisa. "I kept feeling there was something rotten in all this." Her mind raced with the questions she did not ask, or Ray avoided.

"When the extradition treaty between the UK and this country ran out in 1978, and they did not renew it, criminals flooded here. They took the opportunity of safety from arrest and trial in England. In this place, we are not right on the coast, and they always took less notice of us. We're not the worst of them, anyway." Madge looked thoughtful for a moment.

"In any case, my dear," she said to Lisa, patting her knee, "the men are safe from arrest and courts. Although, not necessarily from each other," she muttered under her breath."

"What about Ray?" Lisa asked in a whisper and her hands shook.

****

"Soon we must move house again," Ray told her as she helped Sophie spoon boiled egg into her mouth. The child could almost feed herself unaided.

She looked up at Ray. "Why must we do that? What's happened now?"

"We can talk about it tonight. I have to meet someone this morning." He bent to kiss her and patted Sophie on the head. "You're too mucky for me," he told his daughter.

He waved goodbye with the usual rapid opening and closing of his fingers over the palm of his raised hand, and the child responded in the same way. "Bye, bye, Dada," she babbled and smiled. Another mixed combination, Lisa thought, of *Papa* and *Daddy,* and she resolved once more to settle Sophie in a group with other children.

She felt even more apprehensive. The consequences of their life in Spain seemed all too apparent in these last few weeks. Madge had given her some idea of Ray's 'business' activities. Slowly, she had put together, from the vague further pointers Madge gave, and her own determination to unravel them, that it involved him in money laundering and a 'bit of theft.' It made Lisa think of Switzerland and the bank, although she gathered that was not the only outlet for money laundering. Madge had calmed Lisa's immediate dismay by the reassurance that Ray had nothing to do with the prostitution or drugs rackets.

"He's not a bad guy," Madge had said. "In fact, you're lucky, you know." Then she bound her to secrecy about their conversations.

Yet, Lisa now knew for certain that there was no other source of their income other than an illegal one. It had not taken long to work it out. Acceptance was the difficulty. She wondered whether if she had ever pressed Ray hard enough, he would have 'come clean', given more encouragement?

If she was honest with herself, she had guessed long since what lay behind their lifestyle. Would the earlier knowledge have changed her mind? So that she stayed in England, went back to that two-room slum, with Ted absent, and scraped through a lonely life on her own? That was the alternative.

In recent weeks, Ray had also shown her the secret safe in the villa. She had not known they had one. He arrived one day in a convertible sports car and threw her the keys. "All yours, babe. Enjoy it!"

Had Madge said something to Ray? Or was it the other way around? Madge had agreed to find out for him how much, or little, Lisa guessed? The men did not discuss matters with their wives or girlfriends, and to appear unaware was the norm. Madge was older, a neighbour and a friend. She had opened Lisa's eyes to it all and warned her to keep it to herself. Ray could know nothing of her revelations.

That evening, Lisa and Ray sat close together. She sipped a brandy in the last of the sunshine and stretched out her legs on the tiled mosaic pattern of the patio beneath her feet. Ray put an arm around her shoulder and pulled her close against him. "Sophie tucked up? Asleep?"

She nodded dreamily. "So we can have Christmas here, before we move, Ray?"

"Yes, and don't mention anything about the move. Not to anyone. Understood?"

"What could we get Sophie for a present? She's talking a lot now and I must also find somewhere; a crèche, or a kindergarten sort of place for her. Like they had in Switzerland and elsewhere, too, I noticed on our travels. She would benefit from it. Promise me, when we move, that you will make it a priority."

"I thought they started education later here, in Switzerland and France, too?"

"Formal school, that would be. I am hoping we can find a bi-lingual set-up in Spain. Especially if we find a place in a large city in the north, as you suggested. What about Barcelona? You see, I have been looking at the map."

"We are agreed then." Ray kissed her. "Tell me again. You remember the combination for the home safe? And where we put the keys for the Swiss deposit boxes?"

Chapter Seventeen

She woke at dawn and rolled over, stretched out an arm to the other side of the enormous bed and realised it was empty. It was not unusual for Ray to fail to return overnight when he had a meeting. She sighed, listened for any sound of Sophie sleeping on her own now in the next room. Nothing, only the repetitive trill of a bird outside. Others would soon join it. She tried to go back to sleep. Later, she gave up and forced herself to start the day.

Sophie was difficult that morning; not happy with the fresh clothes Lisa chose for her to wear, wanting the ones in the laundry basket from yesterday. Though annoyed with her wriggling and cries, she noted how observant the child was in noticing where her favourite items now were. Signs of intelligence. But all mothers thought that, she reminded herself. At breakfast, Sophie refused the scrambled egg and grasped a fruit topped *ensaimada*, a sweet bread normally offered to her as a following on treat. She tried to cram the whole pastry into her mouth, picked another one from the plate and would not let it go, wailing and half-choking in the ensuing tussle.

"Whatever is wrong with you this morning, Sophie? For goodness' sake!" Lisa picked her up from the highchair and patted her back, suddenly aware of the drumming on the glass of the kitchen door. She saw the anxious face of Madge and, as she opened up, a uniformed police woman a few metres behind her. Her smile disappeared at the sight.

She could not understand at first. They made her go inside and she stood holding onto the worktop, already fearful. Madge took the child into her arms and Lisa's legs gave way. They settled her curled up on a sofa. She heard the police woman's accented English coming and going in phrases without meaning. Ray was dead. A car accident. He had ploughed straight into a tree.

****

Lisa tried to express her gratitude as Madge held her icy hands between her own and gazed sadly at Lisa's red-rimmed eyes because of the lack of sleep and the tears. She looked drawn and ill. Was she eating? They sat in the living area with blinds half-shut against the weak sunlight. Lisa said it hurt her eyes. Carlos was somewhere there in the background, and the maid was helping look after Sophie, she assured Madge.

Funerals took place soon after the event in Spain, Madge told her. It would all be over before she knew. Lisa looked blank. Madge explained what she had arranged; which was everything. Her brother, Brian, had flown out to help them. Lisa acknowledged her gratitude, but was unable to find the words to express it. She registered only an overwhelming numbness.

She wanted to run away with Sophie. Go somewhere quiet to mourn. It was the repeated request she made to Madge and Brian.

"That's what you soon can do," Madge assured her. "First, we have to get this out of the way and … I must make you understand our advice, Lisa."

What was there to understand? Ray was dead. Never coming back, and she did not know what to do next. Nothing practical, no plans, just the desire to think about him.

It was Brian who made headway with her in the end. Perhaps

Madge's life before widowhood had not been as innocent as Lisa had thought. He referred to the English community in different terms, and he appeared to have considerable knowledge of what lay behind the lifestyle in the free-for-all violence and vice of sunny Spain. Even if not involved in anything criminal himself, not now, nor in the past, perhaps Madge's husband had been, and Brian was much more forthcoming than his sister. He helped Lisa to consider each step. First, get through the funeral. Madge fitted her out with a simple black dress and jacket, and advised her to add a tiny hat with a frontal veil. Nothing conspicuous.

"The Spanish wear them anyway," she assured Lisa. "You're a Catholic, aren't you?" Lisa looked baffled and questioned the need for it. Madge turned to Brian, who mentioned photographs and explained, with an encouraging nod from his sister, that there would be at least one person taking photographs at the funeral. It was an English funeral and there was a certain notoriety about those who would attend, which would draw attention to it. It was better to remain anonymous, without a picture of her for others to gawp at later.

Which others? Why later? She wondered for a moment, but agreed.

She saw Ray in the open coffin before they sealed it down. Just the once, and after persuasion. She had dreaded it as too final. Tidied up but identifiable, he had not looked real, though she kissed his effigy goodbye. The cold, clinical, chemical smell permeating the funeral parlour, despite the hothouse flowers, would never leave her. There was worse to come, but at that point, she felt unable to take any more.

She recognised that Madge and Brian were protecting her. Acting as a barrier, dealing with the worst pressures of the paperwork and officialdom. She had never faced such bureaucracy before because Ray dealt with it all.

The commiserations of the remaining English community soon followed. Older men unknown to her, to whom she spoke a few words of thanks. She did not have the energy or the will to concentrate on names, or to work out who they were, whether they were business colleagues or acquaintances. Although they were a rough lot in speech, they all wore smart dark suits, which looked new, as they expressed their condolences in identical short phrases at the villa's door. They left flowers and wreaths and departed in sleek and expensive cars. As they went away, money appeared in thick bundles on an ornamental dish in the hallway, and she watched Madge take it on her behalf, tuck it out of sight somewhere else.

After the funeral, the two of them devoted each evening to sitting with her. She had Sophie as an obvious distraction during the day, and the maid maintained a sensitive presence, keeping in the background, but ready to take over when Lisa, too exhausted, did not even get dressed for the day.

Madge and Brian worked hard to make her understand the necessity of disappearing from the Spanish scene, while not alarming her further. They gave suggestions of places where she might like to live. Talked of travel and Sophie's schooling. A drip, drip approach.

On one occasion, she surprised them by showing the courage, enough strength of will, to talk about Ray's death. How had it happened and why? Perhaps they saw it as an encouraging step forward.

"He was an excellent driver. He was not drunk," Lisa said. "The inquest stated that. So how did he hit a tree? I don't understand it. The weather that night. It was dark, but conditions were fine...." She shook her head and looked at them both, waiting for an answer.

"They recorded the death as a road accident," Madge said firmly, and grasped Brian's arm.

"I know that. What else could it be? No other car was involved." She got no response. Madge looked at Brian as if for guidance.

"Are you hiding things from me?"

"Sever all connections with your life down here." Madge said, before Brian could interrupt.

This was the constant repetition of the advice she drummed into Lisa's head. It brought Lisa no relief, no answers. It was practical, and Madge stressed, for her future safety. What did that mean? She was alone now, and that was difficult enough. What did she have to fear?

"Give her something to hold on to. It's cruel otherwise," Brian muttered. "Do you want Lisa to think he *killed himself?* To have that as a last memory of Ray?"

Madge glared at her brother, then averted her gaze as a flush of anger rose, and stared down at her hands twisting together in her lap.

"That is the only alternative, and she knows it."

"He didn't kill himself!" Lisa said. "He would never do that! Why would he when we were moving away? We had plans. We were going to find a place where Sophie could mix with other children and lead a normal life. I hated it here. I wanted to go!"

"Calm down, love." Brian got up and sat down beside Lisa on the sofa, put an arm around her shoulders, waited for the tears to stop.

There was another explanation, although Lisa gained no comfort from it when they offered it to her. Ray had stopped most of his illegal activity about a year ago, a gradual process, determined to live on what he had made. That was the rumour going around, which he had confirmed. It was not unusual, Brian told her. Many of the men spent all their 'ill-got gains' within a short period, and could not afford to stop what they did. If they loved the lifestyle, which most did, they must continue to finance it. They had to add more pay-offs to their depleted capital and resources. Even if they sometimes talked of the appeal of finishing with their activities, leaving it all behind them, the alternative of returning to England was far too dangerous.

Ray's forte was money laundering. He had learned how to continue to increase his assets without squandering them too much. Though Lisa widened her eyes in astonishment at hearing this confirmation of his illegal practices, the explanation, if not laudable, was not as bad as others might have been. Brian persuaded her to see the sense of that. It helped her in that it fitted with everything she appreciated in Ray's character; he was not violent, not a swindler, but he took calculated risks.

Madge, encouraged by Brian's openness, also revealed other loose talk which, although she said it was not true, had forced their hand in telling Lisa to move away from any involvement in it all. Some people in the community had suggested that Ray was a 'nark'. By revealing information on the community in Spain; who was living where, and the details of their activities, including their connections in England, he had bargained for the promise of personal immunity to arrest and charges. The rumours grew because of added pressures; talk of the possibility that the lapsed extradition treaty would be reinstated within the next few years. Time was running out for all of them. Some were already looking for other havens much further away: to the countries in South America.

Even this was not the hardest part for Lisa. Madge confirmed what she now realised might be the consequence of that distrust and fear coming to a head in a deliberated outcome amongst the others. If Ray had 'ratted' on them, then the 'accident' could result from his perceived betrayal.

Whatever the supposed cause, suspicion of complicity fell on Lisa, too, apart from the desire for revenge. "You're educated, learning Spanish ... even the way you speak," Madge said.

Although wives and girlfriends had some idea of what their men got up to, they kept them in the dark, for their own benefit, as much as anything else. Lisa was different. She lived a life separated from them all. Madge was her only real friend. Many of the women described Lisa as thinking she was 'superior', and Ray was too 'upper class'.

This further scared and alarmed Lisa. She did not know what to say. Her head ached, and she felt so alone. There was no space for her to grieve, no time to make plans. She knew she had to depend on these two people who were the only ones she was sure meant her no harm.

Madge poured her a small brandy and insisted she nibble at the untouched savouries on the table, the fresh tapas she had made herself.

"You need to settle your stomach, my girl," she said.

Lisa looked up. A chiming clock, an anniversary present from Ray, she remembered, was marking the hour. Bed soon, and she would take a sleeping pill. The doctor had left her a few. *I don't want to think about it*, was the only idea running over and over in her head.

Madge changed places with Brian after whispering words between them, no doubt to pursue what they had achieved this far. "You *have* got a cache, Lisa? A stash of valuables?"

"Yes, when we were in Switzerland ...," Lisa said.

"Don't tell me any details!" Madge waved her arms. "You have a personal safe here? Everyone has them in the villas." Madge cupped her chin in her hands and leaned close towards Lisa. "Here's what you have to do."

Chapter Eighteen

'Keep on moving,' Madge had warned her. Barcelona bustled with a rising population; an easy place to hide, and Lisa had plenty of cash to do so. The city was still in a state of flux, following the revival of democracy and the end of the dictatorship after Franco's death several years before. It suited her purposes because nobody in the city took much notice of newcomers.

She had lost weight and her clothes no longer fitted, so she must buy a new wardrobe. It reminded her of Ray's insistence on fitting into their surroundings. It was as if all those precautions had trained her for now, and remembering them strengthened her because she felt Ray had not gone entirely. But she wept each night with the certainty that it was only a stage in her bereavement and the worst was yet to come. What was it Madge had said? 'For the first three years, you still believe that one day he will walk in the front door.'

Her priority was to find a suitable school for Sophie because the child was ready to learn and mix with others. Lisa took advice and selected a modern suburb in which to rent an apartment, where the burgeoning immigrant population spoke only Spanish. She signed a rental contract for a furnished place on the first floor, soon gained a reputation for reclusiveness, so that neighbours did not trouble her. English was the language she spoke with Sophie in their apartment – she could not call it a home – though in public spaces she tried to speak Spanish to attract less attention.

They settled into a comforting routine. If she often glanced over her shoulder during the first few weeks, the habit soon lost meaning, and though she continued to look, and note, who was behind her or across the street from her, or who lingered near her at a market stall, she did not know what she was looking for.

Summer in Barcelona was festive. Tourists flocked to the city, attracted by the Catalan *teatre Grec* (Greek theatre) and the festival of the Arts. Lisa acted as a tourist, and took Sophie to the circus at the amphitheatre, built in a quarry on Mount Montjuïc. It offered a variety of entertainments. She felt safe in crowds and the sights proved a distraction.

With a great effort of will, she displaced her overwhelming grief by present practicalities; the need to escape from the criminal element they had lived among and to secure a home for her child. As she concentrated on and formed plans for Sophie, she pushed away tears, forced them to be of the night, after her daughter, put to bed, lay in innocent and peaceful sleep, cuddling her bear, a soft toy they had bought when she was not much more than a baby. She compartmentalised the shock of Ray's death and, by that means, made her distress controllable. She experienced sudden, troubling, vivid remembrances of her mother and her siblings in childhood. What were they doing now? Where were they and should she return to England to find them?

Since those last days at the villa, Sophie had not once mentioned her father. Was that normal?

****

It was not long before someone found her. Lisa returned home one morning, having left Sophie happy and involved in colouring letters in a workbook, while chattering away to her neighbour at the nursery. Feeling on edge, even as she approached the front door, she put her key in the lock, noticing the scratch marks surrounding it. Expecting the lock to be broken, she took a step back, frightened of going inside. There was no sound from within. With a clammy grasp, she turned the key and tiptoed in, listening. Not a sound. Grabbing a bronze figure from the side table in the hallway, Lisa moved towards the open door of the kitchen. Barely breathing, she slid a knife out of the block on the work surface and grasped it in her right hand.

"Put them down and you won't get hurt." A hand clamped over her mouth. The hand was dry and tight; in some way familiar. Her first concern was for Sophie. At least her daughter was not there, but safe at school. He allowed her to turn around, and she stared at his face, then away again, confirming what she had sensed. He was the stranger they had met in the Rosengarten in Bern. The man with the red blemish like a scar or a birthmark.

She remembered, in a flash of images, holding Sophie in her arms on that day, waiting with Ray as the man approached them. Sophie had just walked with the help of reins. A happy time, but the thought that the man had been watching them had disturbed her. He had soon made it clear that he knew Ray and, with no introduction, shook her by the hand, lingering over it. After Ray had cut short the encounter and expressed his dislike for the man, he said she would feel the same way, too, if she knew more about him.

Now the same man pushed her by the shoulders into the sitting room. He had closed the shutters and, in a glance, she noticed he had ransacked the Spanish Secretary desk, breaking open and damaging the little drawers. Bits of marquetry lay scattered below the desk. What was he looking for?

He made her sit on the sofa and loomed over her, telling her what he wanted, knowing about the Swiss safe deposit boxes in the Bern bank. He knew; it was not a guess. She realised that someone who worked at the bank must have told him because Ray would never have revealed their existence to anyone. Had he known it all the time they were there and playing the part of tourists?

She must get ready to travel early the next morning, he instructed. They were going to Switzerland to Bern. He wanted to see both sets of keys to open the boxes at the bank. He insisted she had them somewhere in the apartment. "Get them, now!"

She was shaking as she got up, bemused, knowing her mouth was open wide in shock at his presence. She struggled to speak, but he pre-empted what was most pressing. "You can take the child with you tomorrow. Collect her as usual today, and put her early to bed." He looked at her, holding her gaze for a few seconds, and added," I don't touch kids."

Her bedroom showed evidence of a rough search; scattered clothes, drawers emptied, and the bed was in a shambles, with the mattress half on the floor. Lisa stood in the middle of the room and took several deep breaths. She realised it was not a thorough and methodical attempt to find the keys to the boxes at the bank, or anything else; instead, it was a way of frightening her.

When she returned with the keys, he reminded her to bring them the next day and keep them safe and on her person. She nodded her agreement. He opened the drinks cabinet and poured her a whisky. Did he even know her preferences in alcohol? She sipped it as she watched him cross to the window, standing to one side of the gap in the shutters, and peering down. Did he have an accomplice? Or an enemy waiting outside? What was his connection with Ray?

Drinking the whisky felt wrong, yet it steadied her. He took nothing for himself, but sat down opposite her and leaned forward. "Call me Ken," he said, "when we travel tomorrow." He clasped his hands together, raised them in a thoughtful pose against his face. "What's the name on the passport you're using? I need it for the tickets."

What else could it be? She wondered, frowning as she told him.

They remained in silence for a few more minutes. She could hear traffic outside the window, a lift ascending, voices from the street. All the normal sounds. Her hands shook again as she put down the tumbler and she held them together to still them.

"I don't want *your* money – cash or valuables. Nothing like that. You can keep it all. It's Ray's box I need to see."

She had never seen what was in Ray's box herself.

****

They arrived in Bern mid-morning. Lisa was wary because he distanced himself from them on the flight and sat towards the back of the plane. Afterwards, he was at her side, but not with her. A quiet word, a nod of the head to show the right direction to follow. That was his method of guidance. He had reserved a room for her at a hotel. Not as splendid as the one Ray had booked for their holiday visit to the city. The hotel was in a quiet area catering for short-stay business class visitors, but old and respectable, offering a wide range of facilities, which she had read on the information brochure in her room. They ate lunch in the restaurant on his recommendation. By that stage, she followed whatever he suggested, eager to get it over. If she did what he wanted, she believed he would not harm her, and Sophie was safe.

In the hotel room, she waited to hear from him. She perched on the edge of a chair and gazed down into the street below. A week day and there was only the traipse back and forth of those returning to work after their mid-day meal. Bern brought to mind so many memories. Dusty in the heat of summer, she could even recall and recognise the sweet smell of the azaleas wafting up from the front of the building.

"Get yourself ready now. I'm coming to collect you." His first words when she picked up the handset by the bed.

"What about Sophie? Where are we going?"

"You can guess where we are going. I've got an appointed time for us. There's a crèche service here for kids. Ring the number in the information you've got there and take her down. They are waiting for you. Do it now." He rang off.

Afterwards, she remained alone in the hotel reception, waiting for him as she had been told, feeling uneasy about her daughter, and wishing it would all be over. They picked up a taxi to the bank. He handed her an ordinary shopping bag and said she should use it to empty her safe deposit box.

They opened both boxes, and she showed little interest in confirming what she knew was inside hers. Not that she had examined the bound papers, merely fingered the jewellery and the cash when she went there with Ray. At first, the man – in her head she would not use his name – blocked her view of what he was doing in the other box. Then he pushed across two passports from Ray's box. They were for her; the same small photograph of her head and shoulders, everything else the same, except for a different name. They frightened her. Why did Ray have these made?

"Take them with you," he said. "You might need to use them."

She saw him unwrapping the small handgun he withdrew from Ray's box. There was no mistaking what it was, covered in a thin cloth, and she felt a rush of blood in her ears as her heart pounded in alarm. She looked away while he hid it somewhere inside his coat.

Next were more documents from Ray's box. Leases, he informed her of various properties as he passed them to her. She should take those, too. "You'll need money, an income. Ray set you up for that, by the look of it."

During the return journey, he gave her a business card. "This is a financier. He's clean, straight, and will sort out your finances before you leave Bern. He can deal with the jewellery, too. Phone him."

At the bar in the hotel, they had a silent drink together. Then he showed her the return travel tickets. "They're dated for a few days ahead. Get yourself sorted for the money and assets before you go," he added, jabbing at the envelope which held them.

"You can collect the kid, now. It's finished." He paid the bar tab and took the lift to his floor. She did not see him again. It had all dazed her.

She returned to Barcelona but did not stay long in the furnished apartment. Time to move on. How had that man found out where she was?

Lisa paid the rent well in advance, so she gathered up her personal possessions and a few clothes, plus Sophie's necessities. They left late in the evening, and she forwarded the keys to the agency by post from the railway station.

Next stop was Amsterdam. The financier in Bern had recommended it for the sale of the jewellery. Her contact with him was her most prized asset for the future, and she would rely on frequent trips to seek his help in maintaining her wealth.

Chapter Nineteen

Lisa studied the literature. Amsterdam's population was in decline, but the new 'growth areas'; suburbs promoted by the government were ideal for anonymity. This was what she needed and would look for.

On first impressions, she felt comfortable and relieved on arrival in the city; the tall buildings with their gabled roofs and the canal traffic appealed and offered interest. According to the brochure she had picked up, before she did a circular tour on a tram, the restored historic centre was rising in popularity with the wealthy. No doubt already unaffordable for most of the locals. More significantly for Lisa, the changes drew attention to those who could live there, so it was the latest constructed suburbs she turned to in preference. Reputed to be very mixed communities, providing temporary accommodation for those of all nationalities in transit.

Although English was only the second or third language used in these areas, she saw that as a minor drawback. It was a good place to hide. The language barrier, on any level of social contact, kept her at the distance she chose. She need not worry about another sudden forced entry into her home by the likes of Ken. Even if he tried to follow her escape from Barcelona, she doubted she had left much of a trail.

She had seen in the history section of the information she read through that Amsterdam had always relied on trade and tourism. This strengthened her conviction she had made a good choice. It would be both safe in protecting her solitariness, and convenient in the contacts of everyday life. Almost as soon as her search began, Lisa decided on a new suburb and paid an advance on a short-term rental basis property.

During those first few weeks, she took to cycling, with Sophie secured in a child's seat on the back. It gave her exercise, a sense of freedom, and was a common and safe method of transport. She explored with enthusiasm: crossing the bridges over the seventeenth century canals, finding her way around, gaining a welcome distraction in distancing herself from the recent events in Barcelona and Bern.

She had taken Ken's advice and sought the help of the financier in Switzerland. Now she wanted to forget that time. Though she disliked Ken, he had been helpful and, she sensed, instructed in what to do when they were in Bern for her benefit. Yet gaps in her knowledge tormented her. She still did not know if her husband had been a former criminal. Had he secured money, all of his wealth, through investments? How often he had brushed aside her tentative queries during those few years they had spent together! Not that she had persisted because they lived well and she enjoyed it. Perhaps an inheritance had been the basis of his income? During that first stay in Bern, why had he warned her she would not like Ken if she knew him better? Because he was involved in crime? Vicious , too, she imagined, remembering the scar on his face. The questions returned again and again, but were impossible to answer.

There were moments, hours, even days when images struck her in Amsterdam, surprised and delighted her, making her happier. They were of youth and different from anything seen in rural Spain. She gazed, fascinated at the newest punk dress and behaviour of the many young people whom she passed. Others wore the long hair of a preceding fashion and appeared similar to what she left behind in the streets of Spain. The contrast amazed and absorbed her attention as she pedalled along. The sights, combined with the street-protest graffiti, also intrigued her. Amsterdam seemed another world from Barcelona.

She noticed a stirring of exhilaration and realised, although she had a child and responsibilities, these young people were at least near to her own age. She must have something in common with them, even though she married Ray when still a teenager and was now widowed. For many older women, widowhood would mark another stage, a restricted one. For her, there must be some chance of a social life, of purpose, and companionship in this city. Having escaped pursuit and secured her finances for the future, she was free to respond to that stimulation; all the sheer excitement that the new environment and culture offered.

The weight of her grief lifted, as loneliness itself – something different from sorrow and depression, even if still a part of it – spurred her towards risk and adventure. She knew she could travel and secure her place anywhere now as an experienced adult, with additional financial security for Sophie. She could do anything. The young people she saw had a distinctive air of self-confidence, which she also wanted for herself.

She found a playschool for Sophie, which specialised in English as the common language encouraged between the pre-school children. Her daughter was one of the oldest, sturdy and taller than others, which enabled an easy dominance in any squabbles. She was also used to change. Perhaps that was why she could smile often enough, as Lisa lingered to watch how they received her daughter, and saw her enjoying activities, making new friends.

The person who interviewed them praised Sophie's abilities, both linguistically and socially. "She is very young to be so adaptable," she said. "Your child will settle in. The other children want to be her friend." That was comforting. Meanwhile, the young woman offered help in recommending an excellent, reliable student who looked after children from the school, on short notice in the evenings, to help maintain herself in her studies. Lisa appreciated the suggestion because it seemed to be given in recognition of her youth and the need for a social life.

This led to the club Paradiso in Leidsplein: Amsterdam's most famous 'pop-temple'. A group of women celebrating a birthday drew her into it, encouraging her to join them on a night out. Though a little older, they kept a slight hippie air about them. They joined in with the vigorous jumping to the music of a punk band, and everyone ignored the areas inside the building, which were covered in drink stains and cigarette stubs. It was all very different from the England she left years ago, or the area of rural Spain where she lived with Ray and their daughter. How distant that felt. It seemed as if she was catching up with the present.

Accompanied home earlier one night, she dismissed the babysitter, with her usual taxi-fare, and asked the man she had danced with to stay. The next night, he introduced her to the coffee shop culture, which he told her was flourishing under the recent government tolerance policy, and encouraged her to try cannabis. To her surprise, with its use, her confidence soared. The weed soon replaced her dependence on alcohol during her grief after Roy's death. It lightened her mood and convinced her that this life was what she wanted.

It did not last. A series of brief love affairs ensued until she wearied of the sudden surge in her own sexuality. She seemed unable to trust anyone enough for a proper, long-term relationship instead of a physical one, and she worried about Sophie's reactions. She took greater care to ensure Sophie was unaware of the people she met by pushing her lovers out of the door with the dawn. After Ray, she soon found the men callow and uninteresting, even if they reminded her she was still young.

One morning after a series of late nights, she sat in front of the dressing-table mirror, and pulled at the bags under her eyes, grimacing at the blotchy redness of her cheeks and her lacklustre stare. Was this the lifestyle she wanted? It was all loneliness at heart, wasn't it?

****

She wrote to her mother. A brief letter saying she was thinking of returning to England, but giving no details. How could she mention Ray and her child? In her mother's eyes, she was still married to Ted. Therefore the child must be illegitimate and despite all the changes Lisa had noticed in attitudes over the last few years – the decline in marriage itself – she knew that her mother would consider her relationship with Ray and the birth of Sophie as wrong; sinful and a cause of gossip and ostracism if known. How much worse if she dared to reveal that Ray had married her, made an 'honest woman' of her, while innocent of the fact that it was bigamous?

Afterwards, she regretted the letter; she thought it would be a relief if there was no reply and she would have to reveal those details in meeting her family again. Yet, the lack of a response to her letter also upset her. This lack of contact festered in her mind, and she found no outlet for it. After a year in Amsterdam, she contemplated making a brief trip to England to visit her home town unannounced. It came to nothing because Sophie was unwell.

Lisa's chief concern had always been at how little Sophie referred to her father, or his absence. She showed Sophie the photographs she had kept in an album at regular intervals. These were for Sophie's development; a record and a pleasure. It remained a melancholy activity for her, but she wanted their daughter to remember her father.

The child threw tantrums, rages more commonly associated with that of a two-year old. Was this connected to the loss of her father? The school, which had praised her adaptability and temperament on entry, now brought to Lisa's attention the fact that dominant by her stature, she had become aggressive.

"Other mothers are complaining about your child. The situation is difficult for us," the same member of staff at the school now informed her, "we have to consider all the other children. That is why we are so careful when mothers apply for a place." In the end, the occasional babysitter lost patience, too.

A lengthy period of withdrawal from the social scene was already inevitable, and it was time to try something else for the sake of Sophie, too. Was the child bored? Lisa withdrew her from the pre-school and they moved further west along the coast and into Belgium.

Additional stimulation seemed to be the answer; it was what the guidance in the books of the day for mothers of young children recommended. She continued to practise numbers and counting with Sophie, taught her letters and the names of animals. The child liked train journeys and talked at length about scenes flashing past while, in contrast, she slept through journeys in the car. Belgium was as flat as the city of Amsterdam, and Lisa took up cycling again, both for the exercise and Sophie's delight. They both enjoyed being in the fresh air.

One bleak morning, when she realised she had not spoken to anyone, her misery made her maudlin, as though she was a drinker, whereas she had given up alcohol. Desperate for a contact; she had already sent Madge many postcards of the tourist sights as they viewed them; she sent her mother yet another letter. This time she included a photograph of herself with Sophie, courtesy of a pleasant young woman seated at the next table in a street cafe in the centre of Bruges. They had exchanged a few pleasantries, and Lisa found the words tripping out so fast from her mouth, in her enjoyment of their conversation, that the young woman had laughed and cautioned her to slow down, as her own English was not that good.

She wrote in the letter to her mother, with such pride: 'You are a grandmother. I hope you like it!' A grandmother for the first time, she thought, as her sister Brenda was too young yet, and her brother even younger. Intending to stay in Belgium for at least six months, her usual tenancy agreement, she gave a poste restante address, in hope of a reply this time.

Afterwards, she had no immediate regrets. Whether or not her mother responded, she would keep sending letters and hope that in the end, her mother would give in. Did she show the correspondence to Lisa's siblings? They might have something to say on the matter since they were older now. If her mother had not kept them in the dark, made up some story or another. If she *had* done so, she would be appalled if Lisa ever had the courage to turn up on the family doorstep.

Once she had made that resolution, her life seemed simpler. She planned for Sophie's education in England. After all, Ray had taken care to ensure she was born there. Boarding school would be the answer and it would leave Lisa free to travel the world in term time. Her trips to Switzerland to contact her advisor enabled all her assets to extend and accrue.

She had no intention of making England her home, where there were too many terrible memories. Yet, even that resolve weakened as the years passed.

Chapter Twenty

Years Later in England

Madge had agreed to a date and Lisa left early that morning to collect her from Bristol airport.

She looks different now, more her age, Lisa thought, as she caught sight of her at the baggage handling. Although, allowing the grey to come through, abandoning all the bleaching and opting for a short cropped style, gave her friend a more sophisticated appearance. The wrinkled, dry skin from too much sun was now covered up, especially her neck and arms, enhancing the improvement. I expect the latter is because of the expected drop in temperature rather than anything else; Lisa thought, as they hugged each other with affection.

The contact with Madge had been sporadic as the years slipped past. This reunion struck Lisa as poignant. I expect she thinks I have aged, too; not a young mother any more, but a mature woman – in years, anyway.

It was not Madge's first trip to join her in the cottage in Cornwall, but Lisa sensed it could be her last. 'I'm not like you gallivanting all over the place,' she had said in their last phone call. For Madge, living in Spain for so many years, through widowhood, later losing her brother, Brian – the last of her family – had hardened her appreciation for being settled, secure in one place, and that was Spain. Besides, travelling was so much more arduous now, she insisted; fraught, crowded and exhausting, and she did not enjoy it.

As they sat over an evening meal in Lisa's cottage, she put forward a few plans for the visit, gauging Madge's reaction and amending them as they went along.

Madge kicked off her shoes and sat on the sofa with a glass of red wine. The meal was over, and she patted her stomach and said how glad she was to be there. "Have you put down any real roots yet, Lisa? Where's Sophie and what is she doing now? I haven't seen her for a long time."

"Well, I am living here permanently now, and it's been ages since I went anywhere else on a trip. And before you ask, I am not in a relationship either. Sophie is still at Uni. It's her last year. She will get a good degree and she's made a life of her own. Boyfriends, all the usual things."

"You're not frightened any more of someone knocking on your door?" Madge smiled and drained her glass.

"You always ask me that, and I always tell you the same thing. I had a constant reason to worry about that man and the trip to Bern. You and Brian, bless him, had hurried me away from Spain soon enough after Ray's death and put the fear of God into me. Remember?"

Lisa got up and refilled her friend's glass. Madge had nothing more to add about Ray's death, and Lisa had given up asking her. Her experience years earlier had precluded investigation, Madge said. She had explained that, after her own widowhood, the English expats excluded her from any talk about suspect activities, and she had thereafter gathered most of it from her brother Brian on his visits. When it was all long over, the men and their families scattered far and wide to new havens elsewhere. South America being the favourite option.

Lisa wondered if Madge had been lonely even before her brother Brian's death. There were so few English left living in the isolated hills at the back of that stretch of tourist coastline. Madge could have moved elsewhere, but she guessed that the attachment, the memories of her earlier happy life in the Spanish villa, had been too strong.

Lisa knew how feelings lingered from that period in her life, although you thought they were over. A few years ago, she had returned to the cottage in Cornwall from a long trip in Asia and encountered the same old fears at what she supposed to be a break in. All the old insecurities had flooded back. She had been away for months and apart from the general overgrown, neglected look of the garden, the temporary wooden panel over a ground-floor window was the first thing that caught her eye. Turning the key with caution in the front door, she had breathed seeing the absence of debris in the short hallway, and held a hand to her chest as if to still her heartbeats, as she looked through the open door to the sitting room further along. No sign of turned-over furniture, wrecked ornaments or pictures, or strewn papers. Everything looked normal.

The sign of forced entry, if that was what had occurred during her absence, turned out to be nothing to cause concern. In that period, she made sure she left little evidence of her existence in the cottage, and certainly no valuables. In her absence, her nearby neighbour had undertaken to get the window boarded up. Local youths had been stone-throwing because holiday cottages had become an important issue, depriving locals of the opportunity to live in the area in which they had grown up. Lisa's home was one easy target.

Madge was saying something else and Lisa, distracted by these memories, asked her to repeat it. "Do you still feel the same way about contacting your family?"

There was no change in that, Lisa hastened to assure her. For a moment, it tempted her to explain why. It would be a relief to tell Madge about Ted and why she had left home. She had always avoided disclosure because of the entanglement with the bigamous marriage to Ray. She held back, as she always would. The marriage was a wicked and immoral act for which she had no excuse except youth. As the years went by, the folly of it did not fade. She doubted Madge would turn against her, but it could further complicate the delicate balance of their friendship. Lisa did not want the relationship to fail; she valued it too much.

Though Lisa no longer feared the long arm of the law, her upbringing within the church never quite let go. Recently, she had returned to a Catholic church in the nearest local town. Not with any regularity, rarely enough to engage attention, and of course she could not take communion, but confession … would it help? That was still available to her.

PART THREE

Chapter Twenty-One

2018

Sophie tripped on the overlapping slate pathway. By instinct, she thrust forward, her hands flat, palms down. The impact shot a burning pain right up to her knees, and it nauseated her when it reached the bridge of her nose. Had this venture to see her mother rekindled her clumsy behaviour? Previously, they had only met on neutral ground.

There was no time to recover from her humiliating fall. The primitive wooden peg of the latch lifted, and the front door of the tiny almshouse opened. Sophie struggled up onto one elbow and, unable to raise her head, dazed, she studied the tips of her long hair brushing against the doorstep. She lifted a grazed hand to her face to see if the fall had broken her nose.

Sophie struggled to look upwards. She was in time to see a smile disappearing from her mother's mouth, although her eyes remained wide in surprise. "Good lord, Sophie! Talk about making an entrance," Lisa said.

She stooped, dragged her daughter upright, and eased her inside the room onto a hard, slatted wooden chair. Sophie breathed hard and decided her nose was intact. She held out her injured hands, which felt as though a fiery flame scorched them. Nothing had gone according to plan, and she felt foolish, almost tearful.

Her mother crossed to the sink in three strides across the floor of the small space, moistened a cloth, and returned to wipe the grazed hands.

She knelt down, muttering. Sophie leaned back and watched with unease while the top of her mother's bowed head bobbed about during her ministrations.

My mother's hair is shorter, greyer, but she still wears it with the same parting in the centre. Though that gap is broadening out; Sophie thought. At least she hasn't covered her head with anything in order to conform to the rules of this ridiculous environment.

Lisa stood up, looming but somehow reduced; lacking in any excess flesh compared to her sturdy daughter. "Cup of tea?" She repeated it with a flicker of irritation, a momentary pursing of her lips.

Sophie nodded, massaging her knees with only her fingertips, wondering what to say, or even how to begin.

Lisa, as usual, took the lead away from her. "Well, what do you think of it?" her mother said, as she turned from the tiny kitchenette, holding a small tin kettle in one hand, and waving around the room with the other hand as if she was an estate agent drawing attention to its good points.

The question distracted Sophie's light-headedness after her stupid fall. She inched back on the chair and raised her head to study her mother's new lodging. It was her first time here in this strange enclosure in England. The dark, low-ceilinged room felt warm. She spotted a modern radiator plugged in under the window overlooking the grassed square, around which there were several more single-storied houses. A terrace of bijou dwellings; Sophie thought, still on the estate agent's theme somehow, and it made her smile.

It was one sparse room, with a narrow bed standing against the wall. The low bed comprised a primitive wooden structure with only a thin mattress, but Sophie noted the thick duvet folded back on top of it, which seemed a more promising sign of comfort. The bed looked strange, old world, with its blue-checked canopy to the back and sides, and the short pelmet of matching cloth hanging down. It reminded Sophie of a 17th century Shaker or Quaker dwelling in America.

However, the second chair, aligned next to the bed, was a *prie-dieu* with its knee-rest at floor level. Yet, there was no sign of a prayer book, nor any other religious symbol. In increasing confusion, Sophie glanced at the old print hanging on one wall, and guessed it to be that of the historic Belgian *béguinage*, on which this entire complex in England was modelled.

What to say in answer to her mother's question? Sophie felt tempted to be honest and admit she did not like the accommodation, but refrained at the last moment. Instead, she watched and waited while Lisa made the tea. She took the time to continue her observations of the room – for that was all it was; a partitioned, small space.

A kitchenette in the corner gave some concessions to modernity. The tiled rectangle of the floor held a sink, a gas hob, and cupboards above and below that level. A sliding door in the side wall, with a thick glass panel, suggested there was a toilet or bathroom. The tiny size and sparsity of the multi-functional room appalled Sophie, but it seemed to have some basic comforts, and it would not kill her mother to stay here. She sniffed at a musty smell and it turned into a sneeze.

"What on earth are you doing here, Lisa? I mean, *really?* You're not religious! " Sophie said.

"I'll give you a guided tour later, and then we can have something to eat." Lisa placed the cup and saucer in Sophie's hands, and picked up a piece of lace from a narrow shelf beneath the *beguine* print. As Sophie sipped at her tea, her mother sat down on the edge of the bed. She looked at her handiwork, and straight-away had to get up again to hunt for her glasses. Sophie sighed.

****

When her daughter had gone, Lisa laughed as she thought about the visit. The sound surprised her because it echoed loudly in the under-furnished room. She realised how much Sophie had looked like a supplicant earlier in the day, when she entered and stretched out her hands for cleaning. Like a child wanting sympathy for wounds sustained in some playground scrap; Lisa thought. She wasn't hurt much. And she always held her own wherever I sent her to school. It is her ungainly frame; I suppose. Yet, she had bathed the hand with tenderness, and the memory of other occasions, tending to Sophie's cuts and grazes, had surprised her with the pull at her gut. 'The more you fuss: the more children cry.' Ray had always said, but he was a kind man, too, and he had loved their daughter.

As Sophie and her mother had been sitting eating tea together that afternoon, at the big refectory table in the communal room of the béguinage, Sophie's expression, or lack of it, which Lisa was sure masked rising irritation, made her determined her daughter should leave the enclosure in good time before the second office of the day.

Sophie's visit had awakened a sense of intrusion and she parted from her feeling irritable and relieved at her going. Lisa licked her lips, passed her tongue around her teeth. That metallic taste again. She shook her head. What was it?

No, that was the wrong word! Not the 'second office' of the day, but the 'Contemplation'. That's what they called it here. She smiled because she remembered it.

Now that Sophie was gone, she tried to slip into the familiar self-disciplined mood of calm neutrality. A sustained nothingness which she believed was what she should aim for. She tied a scarf over her hair, unlatched the door, bent her head to avoid the low lintel, and stepped out onto the slate pathway. Lisa walked with a brisk step towards the Dame's house at the far end of the enclosure. In her peripheral vision, she glimpsed other doors opening; all its female inhabitants were leaving the parallel row of terraced almshouses.

She heard the incisive tap of thin, pointed high-heels behind her; a warning that Jeanette, the woman who had seen fit to take Lisa under her wing, was approaching.

"Good evening, sister. A fine one after all that rain." The precarious heels gathered pace. "Visitors today?"

Lisa glanced sideways at Jeanette. She looks preposterous in that hood and scapular, especially with those heels. Who or what does she think she is?

"Some late evening sunshine. Very agreeable," Lisa acknowledged, and ran up the steps, slowing to a walking pace once she had crossed the threshold of the main house. Inside, she turned left, ignoring the holy stoup, and hurried to a short bench near the back of the room. She inched her bony hips onto the edge of the polished wood. The other women's heads were already bent in serious prayer.

The silence made her sleepy. Lisa tried to focus on the only religious artefact the room contained: a tall, flickering candle surrounded by a wreath of interwoven flowers. The problem was that she could not get into the right frame of mind. Memories flooded back all the time. The recent retreat in France in that setting of the forest. During the months spent there, Sophie's visit to the holiday home had seemed to draw them closer together. Not that the period was without drama, she mused, thinking of the injured hermit; his harsh advice to her, and that terrible muddle over his sister Barbara and her death. Marianne still had hopes for Liam. She was the one person Lisa had kept in touch with in France. In the end, he must realise that none of it had been the fault of either sibling, and also that Marianne loved him.

Someone coughed and slid off the front bench, falling to her knees. A muffled cry and a shuffling resulted from the other benches, mingled with a suppressed laugh.

Mere ostentation, Lisa thought, and shrugged. Complaining about Jeanette and her ridiculous outfit had not been effective, either. The Dame had said that Jeanette would not stay long in the béguinage. Twisting her blue-tinged, veined, dry hands together, the Dame had sniffed and summarised her opinion: 'Jeanette retired recently and is trying a retreat until she decides what she wants to do next. No spirituality there. None!'

Lisa reasoned that Jeanette must be a reluctant celibate who was filling in time; only widows and women of single status could apply to enter the community. If you can call it a community; Lisa thought. We don't even have to take meals together.

She remembered how she had steeped herself in all the lore surrounding the semi-religious institution and regretted the effort. Much of what she had learned no longer applied. But then, why should it? She knew that even in Belgium, the original medieval movement had expanded and retreated in a pattern over the centuries. Threatened, persecuted, and revived, it had died out, with the last of its practitioners, during the 20th century.

How significant that return visit to Bruges had been after the months spent in retreat in the forest in southern France. Although she had not known it then, the tranquillity of the béguinage in Bruges, which she had visited so many years before as a young widow, and the possibilities it offered to women of single status, had lodged in her mind. Perhaps it had been part of that long period of acceptance following Ray's death, during which she allowed the idea of seeking refuge with others from her loneliness and loss, before all her subsequent travels thereafter had further blotted it out, and she had decided she was much better on her own. There had still been Sophie to care for, of course, throughout those independent years, and that had occupied her time.

When she and Sophie were still living in Amsterdam, she heard and read about the béguinage complex in Bruges. She had admired it from the outside and the beauty of the architecture of the site had struck her first. She had read about its purpose and meaning, but seen it only as another institution of its time. A way for women long ago in history to have an independent life and not to be forced, as widows, into another marriage for the money they brought to it. All the tourist information she saw at the Bruges complex emphasised that overwhelming conflict. Wealth in lands in those days, she supposed, which the widows owned, or other rich prospects when inheriting some medieval business their late husband had followed.

What did she expect from this present institution set up in England, based on the original medieval one, which she had come to? After Sophie's visit and obvious disapproval, she questioned its purpose. Was it a mere mockery of the need for a woman's protection? In England in the 21st century?

Chapter Twenty-Two

Sophie hauled her two bags of shopping up the twelve steps to the ground-floor flat, while listening to her own breathing. I must get fitter. Healthy body in a healthy mind. I have let myself go a bit; she thought.

David surprised her by opening the door. "Heard you coming." He took one bag, then the other, and deposited them in the hallway behind him.

"In the kitchen, please. No … wait, I'll take one of them. Not that heavy. It will do me good."

"I take it that Lisa is now in rude physical health?" He ignored her attempt to take a bag, and grasping one in each hand, walked the length of the corridor before she could protest.

"David, she was ill. I wish you could realise how frightened we both were of the outcome. That so-called retreat in France, after the awful treatments for the condition, didn't do her much good either."

David ignored the criticism and asked, "What have you done to your hands?"

"Nothing. Fell over in the cobbled courtyard. Is that another letter from the bank?" She picked it up from the kitchen table, brushing aside the torn and crushed envelope which lay discarded beside it. "Not looking good, is it?" She glanced down the page to the final balance – they were into the overdraft already. So much for her idea of being self-employed.

David took the bank statement from her hand and held it behind his back. "What is she up to, and how long does she intend to stay there? Did you find out anything?"

"No. We just had tea together. It's such a weird place. I hate to see her there! What on earth is it for?" He drew her close, and she tucked her head into the niche of his collar bone as he stroked her hair.

"Plan B, then. We'll have to make an appointment to see the head – the Dame. That's what she calls herself?"

Sophie made a noise in her throat and he lifted her chin and wiped her tears with the back of his hand. "She was alright when you went out to France, you said. In fact, you were pleased to have seen her again, and I noticed the change. We talked enough about her when you came back from France."

Sophie nodded and broke away from him. She thought, but did not utter the words; why is she living like that, and what is she doing with all the money? It was like a negative mantra, which they had both repeated.

"I don't want to mention money. She has always supported me. Generous, too. We've been through all of this before. I'm almost forty and I need to stand on my own two feet."

" I agree. It isn't about us, and we will manage. But what if that place has gained a hold over her?"

"My mother is tougher than that. No-one gets even close."

"Yes, but she may be ill again, and not just physically this time. It is very odd behaviour, and we should do something."

****

Dame Alice shifted papers from one side toward the front edge of the gleaming, polished mahogany desk. Like a barrier between us; Sophie thought. She edged her chair forward and sat erect, planting her feet hard on the floor to look more imposing.

164

"Of course, my mother can live where she likes." Even as the words left her mouth, Sophie could not stop herself from redirecting her gaze to over the Dame's shoulder. The woman's hard, fixed stare deflected all her resolution, and Sophie felt her confidence ebbing away. Besides, it always appeared that she was only after her mother's money and could not wait for an inheritance. This was not the first time she had insisted on speaking to the woman who had given herself that ridiculous title of Dame. She had not been ennobled. It was an affectation; a title from centuries ago, as far as it had any religious context.

"I think I understand your concerns," the Dame said. "As I have told you

before, your mother had her health checked. I am aware of some problems with memory. This is common with age. I suffer from it myself to a degree. But it is not even the *early* signs of anything … of course it is not dementia, which you suggested. " The Dame's eyes flashed and her mouth tautened. "She is happy here."

Dame Alice sat back, fixing a taut smile which did not reach her eyes. It involved the barest movement of facial muscle.

Sophie noted that the woman had not responded to her comment about her mother's slender frame; her lack of any excess flesh. She tried another tack. "As her daughter – the only family she has left, by the way – I have to think of the future. A priority must be how she will be situated when she leaves this place." Her fingers twisted together in her lap. She glanced down to see what was hurting so much and unfolded them; leaving them arched and palms upward. Of course, her hands were still tender from the fall on the doorstep of her mother's cottage. Aware that their position could now suggest entreaty, she turned them over and placed them flat down on her knees.

"If, as I suspect, you are talking about finances, let me make it clear once again. Your mother contributes a modest amount toward her … sojourn with us. The land and the buildings of this beguinage are all endowed, and as you are also aware, the beguines – members of my community – are free to conduct a business, or dispose of their capital and investments in any way they choose. Providing they live within our enclosure, do not marry, and can always meet the spiritual needs of their commitments here, of course."

Sophie felt the blood rushing to her cheeks and a mingling sensation of embarrassment and anger. When she opened her mouth, the words came out in a rush. "My mother has led an independent life for decades and various arrangements dating from her widowhood ensured that she could do so." At that point, she tailed off because she did not know what the funds or income were, nor if the statement was correct. Had her mother received money, an income, from any work she had undertaken? Neither did she want to reveal the long estrangement from her mother, before she had been called to visit her in France, or that they had recovered their relationship so recently and only in part.

"My mother has acted out of character in coming here, and I am certain she has no religious leanings."

"I find your obvious hostility difficult to deal with, Sophie. Your mother is looking for a little peace, that's all. I don't think she relishes your visits here, either. What is it you want from me?"

Sophie cleared her throat and swallowed hard. I bet my mother's already tied up all her assets in this place; she thought, but did not dare say.

"When the time comes. Will she be able to support herself in a home, or with nursing care? Those are my concerns." The sound of her humility made her cringe.

"There is nothing wrong with your mother, or how she chooses to live her life. She is not an elderly woman who needs looking after. I think you should stop interfering. Please make no more requests to see me. I am a busy woman." Dame Alice rose to her feet, marched across the room, and opened wide the door.

Sophie had no choice but to leave.

****

Lisa could not find her cheque book, and when she did, she could not remember which day it was. She peered at the calendar where she had been marking off the days. The fifth of April, it seemed. The rain dripping down the window suggested this might be so, as April was often a wet month, but she took down the calendar from the wall and flicked back a page to make sure she had crossed though the previous month.

As she sat with the poised pen, having written the date, the blank cheque appeared unfamiliar. For a few moments, she struggled with the choice of where to write the name of the recipient, and on which line to write the amount in words.

A tentative knock on her door, followed by heavier blows from the sister, summoned her to the Dame's office. Lisa paced with caution over the slippery slates to the main building.

"Goodness, sister! Where is your coat?" Dame Alice pushed the bell button on the ledge at the front of her desk, and another sister came, went, and reappeared with a towel before Lisa had even made herself comfortable. Lisa took the towel and scrubbed at her hair, dabbed at her clothes, and gave a cursory wipe to the tops of her boots while Dame

Alice watched.

Sometimes Lisa wondered if her memory lapses were artificial. Perhaps they were signs of a cultivated eccentricity, rather than anything more sinister. Today was – well, just a bad day. Lisa proffered the towel, and the Dame took it with a sigh.

"Is something wrong?"

"Your daughter, Sophie, has been to see me again."

"I can't imagine why. I have been here … long enough for her to accept my decision."

"She is still your daughter and, as she reminded me, your sole relative. When are you due to see your doctor? It is a while since your last check-up and my duty is to see we meet these consultancies." Dame Alice flicked through the index cards in the box on her desk and pulled one out.

Although Lisa knew the Dame was computer-literate and had a well-used laptop in her study, there were these outward appearances, or gestures, to the past, as many of the others referred to them. Lisa smiled at the hypocrisy and winced at a twinge from her bunion. There's more wrong with my feet than my head; she thought. Those pointed shoes I wore when I was a teenager.

Ignoring the lack of response, Dame Alice continued, "I think someone should accompany you next time. Why not let your daughter go with you?"

"Oh, she will only fuss. I can find my way there and back home, you know."

"Nevertheless, it would be remiss of me if I did not insist on it this time, Lisa. You will choose one sister, then? I *will* follow this up. So make sure you keep me informed."

"That's all? I can now go about my independent business?"

"Independence to a degree. This is a community, as you are aware. We all care for each other." Dame Alice stood up and Lisa took her cue.

As it was still raining and she felt rather damp, Lisa tried the prayer room once more. The high heating level which was maintained to encourage its use could be overwhelming and make her sleepy. The women called it a chapel sometimes, but it was hardly that. Lisa took a seat, having first noted that only three others were present, who paid her no attention.

The tall, elaborate. central candle was lit and flickered in a draught from the door, which was wedged ajar. I am not the only one who finds it over-heated; she thought. She closed her eyes and bent forward in an attitude of prayer, but could not empty her mind. Her daughter's visit had triggered all these memories. That and her recent involvement with the church.

Images of Sophie running along a beach, her feet leaving a trail of tiny-toed, splayed imprints, zoomed and faded like a photographic display on a screen. She could smell the seaweed and hear the lapping of the sea. Ray bent double with arms outstretched, calling 'Come to Daddy', and scooping her up into his arms, pulling her fists away from her eyes and making her laugh. Lisa was not visible in this scene, but she felt her own presence in the background, amused and disapproving in the same scant breath. Perhaps it was so long ago that she could not picture herself as a young mother, or did not want to.

Her chest hurt at the memory of Sophie's vulnerability and her own after Ray's death. Though she had done everything she could to keep her safe. In the end, boarding her at school in England had been the best answer. I would have kept her by my side if Sophie had ever shown any sign of distress; she thought. Why all this guilt now?

What of this man she's living with? David. Is he any good? I hope she is a better judge of character than I was. First there was Ted, and he left me on my own almost as soon as we were married. Well, I abandoned him. Ray was altogether different, but Sophie was too young to know her father.

She opened her eyes and gazed ahead at the dipped heads of two of the women sitting at either end of one bench in the gloom of the prayer room. Why was this space so plain and the light so low? At least in the faith of her childhood, there had been some grandeur and colour. She remembered sunlight casting coloured patterns onto the modern tiles, or the older stone slabs of the walls and the church floor in the nave. How often as a child she had focused on that in her boredom.

There had been three other people in here with her, she recollected. Now there were only two. She wondered where the third woman was, and turned her head to make a discreet survey of the other benches in the room, although she failed to find her. Lisa tilted her head to one side and listened. Perhaps the rain had stopped. The room did not echo like a church either. It had no atmosphere to it.

As she left the main building, pausing on the step with one hand raised to test the weather, she saw Jeanette. Lisa tried to outpace her, but the path still needed caution, and Jeanette caught up.

"Sister! How are you?" A breathy rasp. "Could you slow down a bit?"

Lisa grimaced, but felt obliged to stop. "What is it?" She gazed upwards in a theatrical gesture, sure to distract Jeanette . "We are bound to have another shower at any moment."

"Just seeing how you were." Jeanette patted her on the arm as if to gain her attention. "I understand you might be glad of a companion on your next medical visit. It would thrill me to be that person. Indeed, a great honour."

"Been talking to the Dame, have you?" Lisa muttered and kicked the toe of her shoe against a raised edge of stone. She looked up again at the darkening clouds. "I notice you are no longer wearing a nun's habit, Jeanette. Have you decided it is not for you, then?"

Jeanette launched into describing the traditional head-wear of nuns in the past. Lisa ignored most of what she already knew; the variety of clothing worn by beguines over many centuries. One aspect of Jeanette's explanation, though, caught her attention.

"The sides of the wimple, the head-dress, came so far forward over the face, it created a sort of tunnel vision," Jeanette said. "Modesty of the eyes and all that, yes. But imagine after years of it. Must have limited your vision all the time, wouldn't it make you turn inwards, too? I mean, it could help in spiritual progress?"

"The beguines were not nuns! Semi-religious at most, Jeanette. They came together for safety and independence; to avoid being married off again, or even for the first time. What we have here," Lisa waved her hand around the buildings in the courtyard, "isn't an instruction ... instant ... institution." Her problem of grasping for the word made Lisa stop; she had forgotten what they were talking about. Jeanette's expression in reaction to this difficulty worried her, too.

"I'll come with you then? To the next medical?" Lisa nodded.

Chapter Twenty-Three

Lisa had so many prompts for her medical appointment that she thought it was impossible to forget it. Yet, she had written out a note in large, block capitals and pinned it to the cupboard above the sink, where it was in her eye-line, and the number of times she had read it over the last few days irritated her.

Having set the alarm for the morning of the much prompted day, she awoke with the instant recollection of what it was for. She had washed, dressed and breakfasted when she heard Jeanette's summons and opened the door.

"You look smart!" Jeanette said. "Have you got everything?"

Lisa looked downwards at her own neat, dark suit and crisp, white blouse and smiled in self-mockery. I could almost go for an interview for a job in this; she thought. Medical appointments now seemed to draw out in her an overwhelming desire to look competent and assured. She had defeated a terrible disease, and survived radical treatments. She had recuperated by retreating to the forest holiday home in France. So, at least her confidence had grown in her physical health. She grabbed a short coat draped over the back of the wooden chair, and they set off.

They crossed the quiet courtyard in an early morning half-light, and the prospect of the train journey reminded Lisa of others taken to meet Ray for a weekend in a city somewhere in Spain. His business absences were always a mystery and one she had learned not to question. When he asked her to join him, on those occasions, Lisa had looked forward to the Spanish city crowds, the thrill of watching so many people bustling towards an array of long-awaited activities at the end of the working week. Shopping whilst based in a luxurious hotel for the weekend had also excited her.

Later it was travel itself that stimulated, but that was long afterwards, when Sophie settled in boarding school in England. Every half-term, she took her daughter somewhere new in Europe. Part of it, of course, was her desire to complicate her exact whereabouts if anyone was looking for her. Yet, it became a habit, long after the fear of discovery was past.

Leaving for her medical appointment on this morning, she and Jeanette passed in silence through the main gate of the beguinage complex. Lisa looked back, aware of a slight discomfort in the pounding of her heart. She smoothed moist palms against her skirt and recognised what it was; the fear of leaving a place of safety. Was she becoming agoraphobic? That was too ridiculous to contemplate.

They walked at a brisk pace to the railway station; mindful of the recommended exercise they should take, and the need to observe some frugality at mealtimes. They lived such sedentary, enclosed lives. Jeanette breathed hard like an athlete and swung her arms.

Although no restrictions applied to them, the women of the beguinage shunned the town. We are in retreat, Lisa reminded herself, that morning. She knew that isolation was the principal attraction, and many joined the community to get away from people or situations. Yet, today, as they boarded the train, she wondered how she would react when they arrived in the bustle and noise of the city. It was a year since her last appointment. Even Jeanette was quiet for once.

They took a taxi to the clinic. On arrival, passing through reception, someone whisked away Jeanette to a communal waiting area. They identified her as neither a relative nor a carer.

Lisa braced herself for the various tests. She doubted she would see the same psychologist as last time. The questionnaires did not worry her. The memory tests and other 'games' seemed to pass without calamity, but she disliked the one-to-one interviews and the interminable, intimate questions. They seemed more probing today. Perhaps she felt the lack of anyone to corroborate what she said about her own reactions, feelings, and behaviour. Like a court of judgement, but without a witness to confirm it. Would it have been better if her daughter had accompanied her?

She disliked the fact that they already had notes about her, with a full record of her move to the beguinage. No doubt her GP had advised them of this. He had made the referral, Sophie had prompted it, and Lisa's ability to pay for a private consultation had enabled it.

The psychologist, a woman of middle years, leaned forward, smiled, touched Lisa's hand, while she reassured her it was normal and necessary to work out new goals from time to time. It was important, she stressed, to avoid apathy. Did she have sufficient stimulation – interests and things to do in this remote community? How long did she intend to stay there? Was she depressed? On a scale of one to ten, how happy did she feel most of the time?

The last question reminded Lisa of an absurd personality quiz in a women's magazine. The assessment ignored her situation. It wasn't in a remote place. How often did she have to explain that the community was on the margins of a sizeable town?

"This afternoon, you could join in with an occupational therapy group and enjoy rug making, expressive artwork, even pottery. We have a separate unit for that," the psychologist said. Would she like to stay for lunch?

"You might benefit from a new activity, for example," she said.

174

Lisa declined all of it and went to find Jeanette. She paid for her session and they left.

******* found?

Lisa picked up the letter, turned it over and looked for its origin from the foreign postmark. Of course, it was from France, and it could only be from Marianne. They had been in contact at New Year, and she had given her the address of the beguinage.

After the usual greetings, she read of the real reason for the brief letter; Marianne had persuaded Liam they should get married. They had been living together for a year and the relationship was flourishing. She wondered if Lisa wanted to come to the wedding. This was all very pleasant, but the last paragraph, added as an afterthought, disturbed her. Someone had been making enquiries about Lisa and her stay in the forest holiday house. This person was interested in finding her and had consulted the village Mayor. It was a woman of a similar age to Lisa herself.

Lisa made black coffee and took a bottle of brandy from the back of the cupboard under the sink in the tiny kitchenette. It was unopened. The impulse was an instinctive reaction to a deep-seated fear, and she recognised it. For decades after Ray's death, she had struggled to avoid discovery. Long after she knew that as an accessory, if Ray's activities had been criminal, the chance of her being brought to justice was unlikely. Her other concern was that if he had become an informer, turning on his own associates, further danger after Ken's arrival on the scene could have followed. Someone might want a share of her considerable assets. Ken had only wanted Ray's gun. Nothing had occurred to support either anxiety, but she remained wary and did not lead an ostentatious lifestyle.

She added a generous amount of brandy to the coffee and sat on her bed, sipping the warming liquid. It will do me no harm, she thought, I got over that years ago.

It consoled her that it was a woman seeking her. A woman near to her own age. English? Marianne had not said in the letter.

Later that afternoon, when she knew Marianne would have finished work, she sent a text and asked her to call.

Marianne was sympathetic to Lisa's wish to remain in seclusion. She understood because she had spent over three years herself in the Buddhist sanctuary in France. Though she was now busy and excited with her wedding plans, she promised to try to obtain more details about the woman looking for Lisa, and that she would be discreet.

A few weeks later, Marianne contacted her again. The stranger was related to Lisa.

Shocked and confused, Lisa turned to Sophie for advice. It was possible the woman had left an address with the Mayor. Should Lisa contact him and delve further into the contact and its purpose?

She asked Sophie to meet her in a coffee shop. She did not want David to be involved. I will have to tell Sophie about the past; she thought. Had Marianne's wedding invitation and Liam's advice to her in the forest stirred this need to tell the truth and not to hold back secrets? Or was it just age and reflection on the past? Did everyone feel like this when they reached a certain time in their life?

Perhaps I have started on a long road towards making amends; she thought. Am I looking for something redemptive which will give me peace?

On arrival at the coffee shop, Sophie looked flurried. What was it she did for a livelihood now? Lisa wondered. I must ask her, without pressing too hard. Sometimes she seems secretive, too.

"Let's have coffee and cake, Sophie. Are you hungry? Call it an early lunch if you are weight watching. Not that you need to be, of course."

Was that the wrong thing to say? She had averted her gaze when Sophie dropped her handbag and half of the contents came tumbling out. Sophie scooped up everything and thrust it back inside. Lisa caught the waitress's eye and placed an order.

You have a certain effect on me, mother, " Sophie said. She edged around the table to the window seat, unbuttoned her jacket, and smoothed the hair away from her face. She leaned forward to kiss Lisa's cheek.

"My word, that's a cold, red face, Sophie. Why don't you wear a hat or a hood or something, like everyone else? Sorry, I didn't mean to be critical. How are you?"

When the waitress returned, they sipped at the coffee, and Lisa forked two mouthfuls of cake. She wiped her mouth with the paper napkin and abandoned it. When she spoke of Marianne's letter, the wedding interested Sophie, but she made no comment about the mysterious woman.

"Go ahead. Ask the Mayor. Your French is fluent enough." Sophie swallowed the last of her piece of cake.

"You said we had *no* relatives, no family members. You lost contact with everyone. No-one approved of your marriage to my father. That's correct, isn't it?"

"Not exactly. I isolated myself from them. I wrote to my mother, your grandmother, when we lived abroad. Several times. She never replied, and I gave up trying to contact her."

"Well, she could have moved away, or died. My grandmother. Strange to think I had any relations. People get illnesses and pass away. And they were not well off, so perhaps she was not in good health either. Anyone else? You never mentioned if I had any aunts or uncles. I always supposed you were an only child, like me."

"No, I had a brother and a sister."

"There could be lots of us!" Sophie laughed.

Lisa felt her stomach lurch, but with what emotion she was not sure.

"Would it make you happy if there were?"

why hadn't Sophie tried to find family?

Chapter Twenty-Four

It was Sophie's idea that Lisa should try some voluntary work to keep in contact with 'normal' people. Lisa accepted the suggestion.

One morning, several weeks later, she set out to walk at a brisk pace in the frosty air to the charity shop. As she passed along the side of the enclosure, looking back at its high wall, she sensed release. Perhaps Sophie was right, and she should abandon the experiment of life in the community. Was it helping? Her memory might improve now she was talking to people and doing something useful. She admitted that stimulation was important; all her reading confirmed it. The beguinage environment offered nothing other than the internalisation of limited ideas, which were not shared, discussed or communicated, just dwelt on. It could lead to depression.

Her colleague at the till that day was Cheryl, who mid-morning went into the back store room to make coffee. The frequent opening and closing of the shop's door dispelled much of the heat, and it was not a comfortable environment. They were not busy that day, and Lisa was rearranging more valuable items on the shelves nearest to the till for something to do, when a couple entering the shop caught her eye. The woman looked her way and smiled. The man did not, but Lisa blanched at his appearance. Her heart thumped erratically as she watched him guide his companion towards a section of menswear. It was a powerful recognition, and she stood immobile with her gaze fixed upon them both.

"Can I take this, then?"

Lisa turned to the woman waiting in front of her, who pointed to an item of child's clothing she placed on the desk before her.

"Sorry, yes, of course. I was miles away." Her throat was dry, and the words were only just intelligible, but the young mother was already busy finding her purse while Lisa searched for the price tag.

"Could I have a bag?" The shop kept old plastic carrier bags on a hook, and Lisa pulled out one of those from the shelf below the desk.

Afterwards, the purchase over, she glanced around the shop floor, which had almost emptied for the couple. He continued to look at the menswear, and she had wandered off to the books. Lisa dared another darting glance to confirm what had alarmed her. The man's face looked like Ted's. The eyes and jaw as she imagined he might have looked after the passing of so many decades. She saw at once the similarity in the profile. His height, the way he moved and bent forward, circling the trousers hanging on a stand, strengthened the impression. She knew it was ridiculous, but just before Cheryl returned with the coffee, she grabbed the phone from her handbag and took a surreptitious photograph of his face. Her own burned with embarrassment and shame. A stupid act, but one she felt compelled to do.

When Cheryl put returned with a coffee mug, fearful that the couple might soon approach the desk with a purchase, Lisa asked, "Do you mind if I drink it in the storeroom? I want to make a call."

"No, of course not. Something important? Is everything OK?"

"I'll be about ten minutes. We're not really that busy, are we?" She took the mug in one hand, her phone in the other, and weaved her way around the side of the shop, with her head down, until she reached the storeroom.

She had to put down the mug; her hand was shaking. Yet, the more she looked at the image, the less certain she was. She archived the photo, reluctant to delete it completely. Part of her had wanted for a long time to see Ted, find out what happened to him, and make amends. My memory loss and now this nonsense, she thought.

The coffee restored her, and after a peep outside to make sure they had gone, she rejoined Cheryl.

The morning session dragged on. By the time she left, she felt weary and had a desperate need just to lie down and sleep. Was it talking to her daughter and opening up a little, which had caused her reaction? She had built up so much anxiety, wondering when she should tell Sophie about Ted.

They were on closer terms, so how far should she limit the disclosure? Did she need to say she married Ted? Perhaps she could describe the relationship with Ted as his being her first lover and not for long. Which was true. Otherwise, it would lead inevitably to further admissions because Sophie knew the time scale; her own birth and how young her mother was.

Lisa could not contemplate how Sophie would react to the knowledge that her mother's marriage to Ray, Sophie's father, was bigamous. It made her daughter illegitimate under the law and, more pertinent from her own religious perspective, born of mortal sin. It shocked Lisa how much of her faith remained.

****

The town centre provided an internet cafe which Lisa used. The community of the beguinage did not approve of social media, nor the up-to-date technology of instant messaging and communication. Yet, as far as she was aware, everyone possessed a phone, and they were all entitled to run a business. How could you do that without easy, modern communication?

Inside the cafe, the warmth hit her. She took up a free position at a monitor, unbuttoned her jacket, and logged on. She was used to technology and not frightened by it, but today was personal, and her searches felt disturbing.

There was a low buzz of chat from one corner of the room, where some sort of guidance or training was taking place. Otherwise, all eyes were intent on their respective screens. It was not her first effort to find information, as anonymously as possible, on bigamous marriages.

After a desultory forty minutes – she had promised herself that she would not waste too much time, and kept checking her watch – Lisa realised she was uncovering the same websites and generalised legal statements as before.

They all stated that bigamy was a crime and carried a prison sentence. According to a clip from a tabloid newspaper, referenced to the Matrimonial Causes Act of 1973, which used legalese and was almost incomprehensible, it was punishable by up to seven years' imprisonment. A recent case exposed in the news of a celebrity brought to court found him guilty, but he only endured a six months' prison sentence. Another quoted ten years or a fine, while it also inferred that mitigating circumstances could reduce both. It was so confusing. The latter highlighted a get-out clause. It all centred on whether the first marriage was annulled or void. This circumstance could mean a lightening or lessening of the severity of the case. Lisa worked out it was about desertion, or one person believing the other to be dead. Could desertion apply to her? What about Ted? Did he remarry?

She had read it all before and even made notes on it. She pushed back her chair and rubbed her eyes. In the end, the closeness in the room's atmosphere, filling up with other internet users, had brought on a headache, and she had achieved nothing.

Lisa could hear Sophie's voice advising her to seek professional advice. Logical and straightforward as her daughter was. But she knew nothing of this, and Lisa did not want to reveal it to her daughter.

In the dusk of late afternoon, she returned to the beguinage. It was still and silent. The smell of acrid wood smoke from the hearths calmed her; a reminder of the retreat in France. There had been moments of peace there. The cobbles were slippery, so she slowed and stepped with greater care, watching the wispy spirals of her breath in the cold. Lisa realised all the women who wished to take part must be inside the prayer room for the brief service of benediction.

The service had no similarity to either the modern or the Latin rite, but the Dame always enthused about it. She saw it as a gathering in which prayer, listening to a choral recording of a hymn – she encouraged them to join in the singing, and the wafting of a floral perfume – a substitute for incense – enabled the community to finish the working day spiritually.

Lisa did not join them in the service. As she opened her cottage door, she stepped on a long envelope and left a dirty, obliterating footprint on it before she picked it up. An immediate sense of dread accompanied the sight of it because she received so little post.

It was only a letter from Madge, but she checked the seal before she opened it, always suspicious of the Dame in the delivery of personal correspondence.

At first, the letter made her smile. Madge had a very peculiar idea of the beguine community and the life Lisa was following. For years, the two women had kept sporadic contact. At first, with postcards. When

Lisa settled in one place for longer, they used a poste restante address for various cities or towns in different countries. With the ease of mobiles and emails as they developed over the years, the communication grew regular.

Madge had followed her movements at a distance, in both time and space. She lived in Spain herself, but on rare occasions they had met for a few days in various European capitals. These were during the periods when Sophie, still in education, visited her mother all over the world. 'Part of your education,' Madge told Sophie. It was how Lisa viewed the travelling, and Sophie seemed happy enough.

By the time Madge visited Lisa in Cornwall, they both knew she would pass her remaining years in Spain.

Lisa read with amusement that Madge was concerned she had 'walled herself up, like in a convent,' and she threatened to phone the person in charge, if she did not hear from Lisa soon, because they denied her contact with the outside world!

Madge raised one serious issue at the end of the letter, which Lisa guessed was its real purpose. There had been a woman asking for information about Lisa. She had arrived on a visit, not a holiday, in the English community in Spain where Lisa and Ray had lived.

The woman had detailed knowledge; she referred to both Lisa's maiden and married names, her date of birth, her marriage to Ray and that she had a child called Sophie. Surprised but curious, Madge had been evasive with the stranger, but had not denied her friendship with Lisa. The woman seemed inoffensive enough. Afterwards, the visit and enquiries puzzled her, and she wondered what it was all about.

Lisa could not still be worrying about the old days and maintaining all that secrecy? She had returned to England and lived there for many years. All of that life in Spain was over for her. Madge hoped, therefore, that she had done nothing wrong in giving what amounted to very little information.

She read between the lines; Madge wanted reassurance. She emailed asking for any further details and slept badly that night. It was all too much of a coincidence. Could this be the woman who Marianne had also talked to? The same woman about whom Lisa had contacted the French Mayor? He had remembered Lisa's stay in the forest because of the problem between Liam and the hunters. Of course, he had some involvement in that episode.

Lisa hesitated to admit her concern. A few days later, she checked her phone for notifications, a timely event, and read a quick message from Madge. A pity she had not heard from Lisa, especially as the woman had returned and claimed she was Lisa's sister! She had shown Madge her birth certificate, which included the same surname as Lisa's and the same town as her parents' address. Madge remembered them both from early conversations when she first met Lisa in Spain.

Worse followed. An urgent email from Marianne, who also had heard nothing from Lisa. She had relented to a request when the 'women' had contacted her again.

'Be sure to check your junk mail,' she had written. 'If I have done something against your wishes, then you can delete and block the woman,' Marianne emailed. 'She said she would approach you that way. Sorry. I still do not know who she is.'

Chapter Twenty-Five

"You two need a break and I could get to know David if we spend time all together," said Lisa, sitting on the edge of her neat bed with the phone held out near the window.

Sophie did not reply, and there appeared to be a disconnect. Perhaps it was too early in the morning, Lisa thought, blinking in discomfort at the sun's rays filtering into her cottage in the beguinage. She had not slept well. Perhaps she could call back later in the day and attempt to go outside for a better reception.

I am losing more weight, too. Glancing through her wardrobe the day before, she acknowledged her clothes were falling off her. I will get some new outfits in London, she consoled herself and waited. There was a rustling noise and Sophie's voice came through again.

"Yes, of course, that's a good idea, and a weekend away appeals. But wait a minute, mum, I want to find out first what this is all about. I am guessing you need to talk and want to be on neutral ground, right?"

My daughter is becoming more intuitive; Lisa thought. Or curious now that I am more open with her. They agreed to meet in London the following weekend.

David remained at home because it would be intimate women's talk, Sophie suggested. Her mother had accepted the excuse she offered on David's behalf without demur. Perhaps that was because her mother had second thoughts about David's involvement, if the matter for discussion was delicate.

Though she had wondered what it was all about, Sophie had come to no conclusion, except that she was going to be asked to do something. At one point, mulling over possibilities, she had even wondered if Lisa wanted to be a grandmother and hoped for news of it. As the plan was to have included David, perhaps her mother had been assessing him as a prospective parent. The idea of a pregnancy made Sophie smile at the improbability. Although women have babies later and later; she thought.

The two women shared a twin-bedded room in an expensive hotel in the centre. Lisa had bought tickets to a musical for the first evening of their stay. They intended to do some shopping, a visit to a museum, and a gallery. This was her mother's agenda, and Sophie had no preferences. The main purpose of the visit to London was a medical appointment.

Lisa seemed distracted, but had been compliant regarding her organised appointment with the specialist. Although Sophie was to accompany her, she did not want to talk about it, as there was no point until she received the results, she said. Sophie thought this was fair enough.

The following day, they sat drinking coffee in the museum's restaurant. A quiet time of year, but soft background music covered their conversations. When Lisa, looking agitated, plunged straight in, she took Sophie, who was shuffling a few souvenir postcards and wondering who to send them to, by surprise.

"Marianne has been in contact again about the woman who was looking for me," her mother said. She stretched out her hand and covered over Sophie's postcards, demanding her full attention.

Sophie realised this must be an important moment. Her mother's serious expression suggested openness or even some sort of revelation. What was the last piece of advice she gave to her? "Did you talk to the Mayor?"

"Thankfully, it was unnecessary, after all. The woman now has my email address via Marianne, so we can use that."

Sophie raised her eyebrows and put down her empty cup. What to make of that? They had a coffee pot between them, and she refilled her own and her mother's cup, giving her time to reflect.

"Do you *mind* that, mum? Giving away your email address?" Sophie wondered if there was any intention to make contact. "Aren't you intrigued at least?"

"The whole thing is … escalating. That's the only word for it. I don't know how to tell you this, but Madge met this woman in Spain, too, and saw some documents she offered her as proof!" Her mother withdrew a trembling hand.

Sophie gaped, her mind racing. Proof of what? She knew who Madge was and, although she did not remember her from when she was a young child, she knew her mother had maintained their friendship, and she had met Madge once or twice on visits. Why was her mother so fearful?

"This woman, she's my sister, Brenda." Lisa bent her head. Tears ran down her cheek. She caught them with the napkin by her saucer, and wiped the streaks away, while looking all around at nearby tables to see if anyone had noticed. As the tears dried, a flush rose from her neck. Sophie got up to offer comfort, but Lisa motioned her back into her seat.

"She's not here – here in London, *now*?" Sophie asked, leaning forward across the table in alarm. "That's not why you got me to come? Are you scared by all this?"

"No, no. Please, Sophie, don't get the wrong idea. I am overwhelmed by it all. It has been building up," she paused, sniffed, and searched for a tissue in her handbag. "There's guilt, too." She lowered her voice. "I abandoned Brenda and our brother when they were young – not much more than children. Just upped and left to go away and be a barmaid of sorts. They relied on me to look after them, but I had to leave home. Well, you know about what followed. I've told you the story before." She paused and sipped at the cold coffee.

"Yes, the sailing club where you met my father. That was decades ago, mum, and your sister isn't a child any more; she will have made a life of her own. Don't you want to see her? She obviously wants to see you."

"But what will it be like? She could be angry and ...."

Sophie clasped her mother's hand, now resting on the table. For once, Lisa did not resist.

Sophie smiled. "I doubt that. It's all in the past. She may have information about your mother and your brother, too. That's exciting, isn't it?"

Then another consideration occurred to her. "I hope it's not just that people have died." She squeezed her mother's hand. "It could be a reconciliation, mum. Wouldn't you like that?"

By the time they parted at the end of the weekend, Sophie had persuaded Lisa to meet her sister. Full of an equal measure of hope and doubt, Lisa replied to the brief email that Brenda sent. She had sensed a warmth in her sister's messages, and it pleased her that Brenda seemed happy to follow whatever arrangements she suggested. Though Brenda stressed that her time was limited and pressing, and they should 'break the ice' soon.

****

Their nearest point of contact between where they both lived was further along the coast. "You probably appreciate the area and its resorts much more than I do. I am not a traveller like you," Brenda texted. "Could you book us rooms somewhere nice?"

Lisa was happy to do so and, because Brenda was coming by train, they met at the railway station. Lisa held an enlarged photo of Brenda, printed off from an email attachment. She studied it as the train arrived, excited at the idea that it was bringing a sister she had never seen since they were children. Brenda held aloft her photo of Lisa when she stepped off the train. The planned sign made them both laugh as they hurried towards each other.

Lisa shook and withdrew quickly from Brenda's hug. She now felt sick from all the anticipation. "There's a decent cafe here. Shall we have some tea before we set off for the hotel?

Brenda agreed and waved away Lisa's offer to take her handbag for her – a large, floppy, tote bag, which bulged with odd-shaped objects – while Brenda lifted her modest suitcase with ease. "Where's yours?"

"Mine is already in the hotel. I have booked in for us both. Are you sure you can manage?" There would be time to take stock of each other in the cafe; Lisa thought.

Later, Lisa could not remember what they said during that first encounter. She looked in vain for some facial similarity, listened for the local accent of their childhood from long ago, and recognised only a vague twang in her sister's speech, which could have been from anywhere. She made some sort of comparison with Sophie; in that they were both taller and appeared more robust than her own petite frame.

Brenda talked a lot, smiled all the time, and ordered cake. "I'll get it, shall I?" she said as they got up to leave, fumbling in her bag for her purse.

"No, no. Let me, I must," Lisa insisted and passed her bank card over the machine. "All done," she said, and wondered when she would say her sister's name. What was holding her back? There did not appear to be any terrible conflict between them about the past.

At dinner that evening, Lisa resorted to alcohol to get her tongue working. Brenda filled in all the gaps in the conversation, sometimes with questions, and seemed eager to know what Lisa was doing now. Lisa's curiosity was about what had started the contact.

They had moved to the bar area and Lisa insisted on paying at every point. At least she could do this for the sister she had turned her back on all those years ago. Brenda warmed the brandy glass in her hands, swirling the oiliness against the sides. Neither woman had changed into anything special for the evening, only adding a few items of jewellery, and re-arranging their make-up and hair.

"Well, you sent *our* mum several postcards to begin with, and then there were the letters. Mum wasn't interested, of course. I'm sorry ...," she leaned forward as Lisa's face crumpled.

The constraint and effort of the day, Lisa thought, I have had so much bottled up. She used her handkerchief and straightened up in the chair, recrossed her legs, and told herself to stop being embarrassing.

"Mum kept your letters with the addresses, and I saw where she hid them," Brenda said.

Lisa nodded and picked up her own glass, but determined not to overdo the alcohol even though tempted. There were more blanks she wanted filled in. A lifetime of missed moments and important events.

"Your letters often gave poste restante addresses abroad, but I read them, and as time passed, you always included more and more details of where you were. Especially after you were so ill, and in those more recent ones in France, too."

191

Lisa saw that Brenda's glass was empty. "Like another?" She gestured to the waitress, to whom Lisa had already slipped a tip. She was keeping her eye on them.

"I never got an answer to any of my letters. Not one," she mumbled, with her head down to avoid Brenda's reaction, or her own response in voicing what had hurt her the most.

"What did you expect?" Brenda said. "I'm surprised she even *read* them, let alone kept them." She broke the harsh tones of the comment with another smile and slapped her own hand as though she were a naughty child.

"You wrote a lot of things about your daughter ... *my niece* ... Sophie, in your letters towards the end. You thought our mother would be pleased that she was a grandmother. I remember reading that.

"Also, I got someone professional to help me. He tracked you down and it was easy after he found the place you bought in Cornwall. A neighbour there held your daughter's address for another contact. He even spotted you with Sophie in the town nearby, where you moved to next. What on earth are you doing in that peculiar religious place? You're not still living there, are you?"

Lisa put down her glass to prevent stilling the contents. This story of searching, tracking, and spying by Brenda and someone else, in order to find the whereabouts of her various homes, alarmed her. The same deep sense of threat, emotions from years ago, flooded her. They were from the time when she had believed it necessary to move home constantly for her own safety and Sophie's. These revelations were not what she had wished for. It took a great effort to stop everything from overwhelming her.

"I need to visit ...," she waved her hand toward the toilets.

Chapter Twenty-Six

"Well, how did it go?" Sophie was full of questions. Lisa had retreated to the beguinage in relief after the weekend away, and stood in the drizzle outside her cottage where she could get reception. She ignored the disapproving frown of Jeanette, her pointed glance at the phone, as the woman tripped along in her high heels towards the Prayer Room.

We've all got phones, even you, Jeanette, so you can ignore mine; she thought.

That morning the light levels seemed higher as the Spring advanced and that helped her mood, but Sophie's insistence on hearing everything she and Brenda had talked about did not. It also annoyed her that the Dame queried her frequent absences, though now she seemed satisfied that they were temporary and because of family matters. This time, she listened harder to Sophie's response and explained.

"Brenda blames me for leaving them," Lisa said. "They were only children when I went away."

"They had a mother, too. It was not your responsibility. It sounds like you did far more than anyone could expect before you left home, and you wouldn't have gone without that pressure. Anyway, do you like her? How did you get on? Tell me something about her!"

"You're too kind, Sophie, but I can't shrug off the natural reproach and criticism which Brenda soon made. Although I appreciate you defending me, I was only thinking about myself when I abandoned them. I admit there were other circumstances, too, and I was also very young. Some excuse, I suppose." Lisa looked up at dark, looming clouds. Not a day with much promise, despite what I thought.

"As for Brenda, she's my sister, and I care about her, of course. But it was difficult. Not talking about our childhood; she does not want to go over all that ground. Which leaves me with not much point of contact so far. Also, there are things she hasn't mentioned, and I don't know why. And no, I am not going into it all now. In fact, Sophie, I am going back inside as I am getting soaked."

Lisa finished the call. She turned around and stepped back under the ornate lintel into the cottage. The information Brenda gave was disheartening and confused her further. She kept mulling it over, but reached no conclusions. Their younger brother, Ryan, had come to nothing. He had spent some time in prison, following several offences. Afterwards, she did not know where he went and had not heard from him for years. 'He'd only be after your money,' Brenda said.

Their mother was in a care home, and they should visit her together, but not yet. There were complications at present, and it was a long way up north. So what was Brenda now doing living down South? Lisa wondered. With these bare, unpromising facts presented to her, it seemed the whole family was doomed.

Meanwhile, there was some post to attend to, she saw, as she stepped over the threshold. A brief letter on thick, quality paper with an impressive letterhead, with several pages of incomprehensible statistics, tabulated on separate sheets, and all stapled together from the consultant in London. Her medical assessment.

She glanced over the first paragraph and finding it encouraging, or at least not doom-laden, made as much sense as she could from the enclosed tables and statistics. These seemed to relate to blood tests and a brain scan; the former suggesting a remedial problem, and the latter that there was no evidence of disease, dying cells, or the dreaded conditions of old age, such as dementia and Alzheimer's. It was a relief.

After supper, which she had to attend in order to soothe the Dame and deflect the disparaging comments of Jeanette, or any of the other sisters. At meals, they had little else to do. She realised Sophie must hear her news. She wanted to assure her of what a good idea it was to initiate the appointment, and that the outcome was encouraging, with nothing to worry about. Her daughter would appreciate that.

In the dusk, pleasingly later in the lengthening days, Lisa hurried to the tiny library. More of an alcove than a room, it fronted the edge of the beguinage complex where the signal was stronger. It was also warmer than standing on the step outside her cottage to make a call.

It was David who answered. "How are you? I hear that the family reunion was OK? I'll get her, she's washing up," David said. "It's her turn."

Why don't they get a dishwasher? Lisa thought. Sophie works such long hours now that she's self-employed. She could hear David calling Sophie, before she arrived breathless at the other end.

"Before you ask me, I am fine. I have some good news." Lisa smiled. Now Sophie could relax and stop worrying, too. The solution was straightforward.

She explained from the blood tests that the problem was a deficiency in vitamins, particularly B12, which over a long period could lead to more than the absent-mindedness Lisa had attributed to her memory lapses.

"I need some injections, Sophie. And they will be in my backside!"

"Ouch," said Sophie. "So when are you going for those … and where? Not London again?"

"No. They can do them at the local surgery. I have the letter and must make the appointments. Once a day for the first week. It has to be built up without delay, they said. So, I expect I will feel bruised and sore."

"You'll survive mum. I'm guessing that the cause is diet? Not eating enough, anyway. You *are* thin, mum."

****

Brenda's visits became routine. If Lisa did not arrange a meeting for lunch, or an outing to the theatre, then she would arrive at the beguinage and seek her. During the week's initial course of Lisa's vitamin injections, she came early in the morning and insisted on accompanying her to the medical practice. As if she were a carer. Afterwards, when Lisa preferred to rest, Brenda dragged her off shopping and then, of course, it was time to find something to eat.

"I do voluntary activities, as well as working full time," Brenda said. "Charity shops, that sort of thing. I am having a break from them in order to for us to get to know each other. We must make the most of our time together. I am sorely missed and I'm using up all my holiday time!" She wagged a finger in admonition at Lisa. It was Brenda who prompted everything.

"Do you work locally?" Lisa asked. "There isn't anything near your home around here, I wouldn't think."

"On-line and I have to move around, fill in gaps. No travelling allowances, of course. Let's talk of more interesting things."

Brenda described their conversations, as well as the 'togetherness', as making up for lost time. Although, that was gone forever, of course. These repetitions made Lisa uncomfortable, and the platitudes which often flowed were no salve to her conscience. It was impossible not to feel affection for her sister, but they had not bonded as in a sugary Hollywood film. Lisa hardened her sense of duty. She could deny her sister nothing.

They only travelled once to where Brenda lived. She drove Lisa to a quiet hamlet further along the coast. The facade of the bungalow, in an isolated, peaceful environment, appeared well-cared for and in good order. It was tidy, if almost austere inside. Brenda made coffee and brought biscuits on a plate.

"My boys are grown up now, and I see little of them. In wonderful careers though, but you know how mobile all families are these days, scattered over the country for their work." She took a photograph album out of a drawer. There were several pictures of young children on a beach to show Lisa. "They're your nephews, Henry and Toby."

Brenda found her spectacles in her handbag and peered at the prints before offering them to Lisa. "See any family likeness?"

"I'm hopeless with likenesses," Lisa said. The photos were too small to make out anything.

Lisa had shown her pictures of Sophie at different ages, but Brenda just glanced at them without comment and gave them back, showing no interest.

"Are you really going to remain in that dreadful place?" Brenda asked.

"If they don't throw me out! I miss an awful lot of the community times, and I am not often present at meals." Though her remark was pointed, as Brenda occupied so much of her time, she knew the Dame was not pressing her and seemed well disposed to her sister. The idea of the two siblings, long lost to each other, coming together in later life – Brenda had given *her* version of events, when invited to join the Dame for tea on an introductory occasion – had sentimental appeal. Lisa assured the Dame that she had no intention of leaving the beguinage, nor any desire to live with her sister.

Brenda was divorced and had brought up her two boys on her own. She returned to her theme. It had been very difficult; she told Lisa, alluding to the sort of poverty Lisa had known in that part of the country as a child. She had to work long hours as a secretary and then as a personal assistant.

"You did well," Lisa said. "There was nothing like that available to me. How did you get the training?"

Brenda brushed that aside. "Things changed. Of course, you were out of the country by then." A revealing rebuff.

Lisa's coffee cup tilted and slipped on the saucer. She caught it just in time, grateful that it had only a few drops in it.

Brenda moved the cup away. "You didn't just leave us, did you? Left your husband, too. Deserted poor old Ted."

There was a glint in her eye, and Lisa recoiled. What had she glimpsed? A touch of malice?

She patted Lisa's hand and stood up. "I don't own this," Brenda said, waving her hand around the sitting room. "Just a rented property, and that's tough enough moneywise." She picked up the coffee cups and Lisa followed her out into the kitchen.

"I'm sorry, Brenda, if I have stirred up some … unhappy memories. Life must have been hard. I know how difficult it was sometimes with Sophie, and I had only the one."

"Let me do that." Lisa picked up a tea towel and rubbed away at the cups and saucers on the draining board, noting the lack of a dishwasher. Perhaps I could buy her one; she thought. I seem obsessed by dishwashers.

They returned to the sitting room, and Lisa took her purse out of her handbag. "Are you a bit short, Brenda?" She hoped it was not the wrong thing to do, since she paid for everything they did together, anyway.

Brenda smiled and moved closer to her. "Cash is useful, dear, but a cheque to help with the rent and bills would not go amiss."

There was that look in her eyes again. An intelligence, too, which Lisa thought her sister had hidden up to now. Brenda frightened her today.

Lisa always carried her cheque book, although she rarely used it. It held the same importance for her as her passport. Proof of identity came naturally to her, after all the travelling she had done, and the necessity for quick access to her finances gave her security.

She wrote out a cheque for several hundred pounds. Brenda told her to leave the payee blank and did not look at the amount, folded it in two and tucked it into the pocket of her jacket.

"You mentioned Ted. Did he come back then? I mean, after I left that place ... you could hardly call it a home ... where we lived together."

"Oh, yes. He often used to visit me and mum."

"Why do you call him 'poor' Ted, then?" Lisa surprised herself by the harshness of her tone. Was Ted still around? Her heart pounded in the early throes of a panic attack. She flapped her hand in front of her face. "I need some air. Does this window open?"

Chapter Twenty-Seven

"Mum's got a big birthday coming up; one of those decade celebrations. Could we do something special for her, David?"

"What did you have in mind? Not a party, of course? Not while she's still living in that place. It's all prayer and good works, isn't it?"

"No, and you've never been there, so you can't judge. I seem to get on much better with the Dame now. Reviewing my opinion of her, anyway. I don't think that she's after mum's assets. She might hope for an endowment, perhaps, in mum's will."

It was a Saturday morning, and they were both changing into sports clothes, ready to go on a run together. This was a new activity, and Sophie was not sure how it would work out. She hoped it would not be too competitive. In its favour, the clothing was tight but comfortable, and it pulled her stomach in. No bulges were showing.

"Will you invite Brenda to the 'do', whatever it may be? I've never seen her and you've not spoken about her."

"I only met her once. Just for cake and coffee; not time enough to have more than a slight first impression. I haven't made my mind up about her yet. I don't even think of her as my aunt, which she is, remember?"

They stood together in front of the mirror, admiring their running outfits and laughing at themselves. "We *look* the part," David said. "Come on." He took her hand as they walked down the hallway. "Keys?" She nodded. "You've changed over these last few months of seeing your mother."

"What do you mean?" Sophie pulled the door to, and slipped the keys into a pocket. "Wait a minute before we start, David." She caught hold of his arm. "In what way?"

"Both of you, really. *You* seem less ... wound up, less nervous, almost. I always thought you feared her. Well, her opinion of you. That she thought you were rather witless. That's an exaggeration, perhaps. Now you appear confident, and even over-ride what she says, contradict her sometimes. From what you tell me."

"Go on."

"Whereas ... your mother is hesitant, unsure about many aspects of her life. So it all seems to me. She was pleased, grateful, about the medical appointment you made for her; that's one example. Before, she would not tolerate your interference. And now ... all that clumsiness you only ever showed in her presence seems to have gone!"

"Thank you for that, darling," she kissed him. "Now let's go!"

******

Brenda needed a new outfit. If she was to accompany her sister as their only guest for the restaurant dinner, she wanted to be presentable.

Worn down by this insistence that her sister's wardrobe contained not one decent dress for the evening – Lisa went through the hangers and agreed there was not much there – they went to London early by train for a longer weekend to buy clothes.

Sophie had made the booking at the restaurant in London for the celebratory meal. She advised the hotel, where they were all staying for the special occasion, of her mother's wish to go to a favourite place to eat. Though the hotel would have catered well, she knew her mother's reserved temperament. She would hate a fuss. A restaurant in a quiet area, which had excellent recent reviews, and which a work contact had also recommended. In their discussions. The restaurateur compromised on some tasteful, simple decorations, and a restrained procession with the cake – after the cheese course, and before the desserts. They would have soft music and anonymity.

Lisa had warned Sophie not to contact the beguinage, nor notify them about her birthday celebration. She would tell the Dame herself before the weekend away. The Dame would understand her absence.

Sophie and David intended that on the second day of the booking, they would depart and leave the two sisters on their own to enjoy a show in the West End.

It did not disappoint Sophie in anticipating a happy, heart-warming birthday meal. The dinner was perfect, and her mother expressed her gratitude for all the planning and preparation.

When she saw Brenda come down the stairs to the waiting taxi, with her mother trailing behind, Sophie checked her astonishment at Brenda's appearance. Her stylish, tailored, rustling dress, and the matching scintillating jewellery which adorned her neck, ears, and wrist, were clearly expensive. As was the fine embroidered pashmina shawl draped over her shoulders. Only later did Sophie learn who paid for it.

Brenda smiled her way through the evening, but said little. It surprised Sophie. She had gathered from her mother that Brenda was loquacious in a social environment and strong in her views on issues – though she preferred to chat about trivialities whenever the two women were alone. She avoided questions relating to the shared childhood with Lisa, but made clear to everyone that she was, of course, the younger of the two. Brenda told Lisa that she remembered little of those early years.

To Lisa's relief, her sister did not mention Ted. Although Sophie had known for some time of her mother's first marriage – which did not last long before she married Ray, Sophie's father – it seemed Sophie did not want to quiz her mother any further. The revelation about Ted had come when mother and daughter were not on such close terms, and perhaps explained why Sophie had not pressed for more information. Lisa dreaded the moment, if it arrived, when either Brenda or Sophie raised the subject of Ted in relation to the second marriage. Dates concerned her because of the bigamy aspect. It was on her mind during the meal, and she was relieved that Brenda appeared happy to drink and eat, but raised no embarrassing subjects.

"My mother ate well. She looks as though she has put on a little weight, don't you think?" Sophie asked David the following morning. "She has some colour in her cheeks, and it isn't all down to make-up."

****

The excursion to London for her sixtieth birthday marked the start of further unsettling developments for Lisa. Soon afterwards, the Dame asked to see her. Was she going to query yet another absence, despite Lisa's forewarning of the birthday weekend?

"Come in, sister. I have asked for some coffee." She greeted Lisa with a flourish of her hand and guided her into the centre of the room. They sat on either side of her desk and not, as was customary with less official social meetings, on the informal chaise longue and the two leather armchairs at the other end of the office. Lisa braced herself.

"Congratulations again on your special birthday. They become something of an achievement as we age, don't they? We have seen so little of you. How is it progressing, this reunion with your long-lost relation?" She peered at her across the coffee cups and percolator.

Lisa smiled at the reference to age. She was not ancient and was continuing to be in complete remission. Settled and in good health now, she hoped, after the frightening course of treatment she had followed at what seemed a lifetime ago. She thought about how much had changed since that time when she retreated into the French forest. Neither was the Dame herself much more than in her early fifties, she guessed. Why all this emphasis on age?

"Brenda takes up a lot of my time. It is quite intense at the moment, I have to admit." She had offered an apology. "But then, so many years have passed …."

"Yes, of course. Your sister asked for a private conversation with me because she is anxious about you and not convinced that this is the best place for you to be. I had mentioned – that is the wrong word, nothing specific – about your memory lapses. I am sure she is a woman whose heart is in the right place, as we say." At this attempt to soften her impending criticisms, the Dame's face seemed to squeeze around the mouth and cheeks, becoming hollowed and pursed into an expression of concentrated concern. It looked unnatural and as if she was sucking a lemon.

"You think Brenda wants me to *leave*?"

"Well, not immediately. The time may come. I believe that is what we both feel could happen. It does with the other sisters, you know, now and then." She looked down at the desk and moved a pile of papers to one side.

"There are few who remain in this sheltered environment for years and years. Most enter rather late in life, and … we have no nursing facilities here, you realise."

Lisa clasped her hands together in her lap. Her face blanched in shock. "I am not ill," she said through gritted teeth.

"No, no, of course, my dear. But we must consider the future. There would be no shame in seeking more comfortable surroundings. Withdrawing from a rather austere life of … penance, shall we say? Intention is all, and if you wished to endorse this sanctuary for others, an endowment, say, or other financial settlement, it would be acceptable and welcome."

Bemused and angry, Lisa got to her feet. "It was a vitamin deficiency, Dame, and I am not suffering from any disease, neither mental nor physical. Now I must consider your wish to remove me." Holding back tears, she stood up and walked away, fumbling at the door handle. The Dame did not stop her and remained sitting at her desk.

****

Lisa went over the interview with the Dame repeatedly, word for word, throughout the rest of the day. She grappled with the slurs cast upon her as she saw it; living in the beguinage as an act of penance, while suffering from an illness, either mental or physical, which required specialist care. Was this Brenda's insinuation of how she saw her sister's situation? There was the idea of penance proposed to the Dame. Was that Brenda again? Attributing it to Lisa's desertion of their family all those years ago.

At their last meeting, her sister had queried whether Lisa still attended church. That startled her. Lisa noted Brenda was often unavailable on Sundays. Perhaps she was a committed churchgoer herself, a practising Roman Catholic in the faith of their childhood. Something must have induced her to tell the Dame these things.

Lisa and Brenda did not see each other every day. Recently, her sister had repeated the need to return to her job; that she had extended her leave and could not afford to continue her protracted absence. Then she spoke of Lisa's property in Cornwall and, with the fine weather they were enjoying, of how pleasant it would be to spend a few days away before she returned to work.

Lisa phoned her. With a false, cheerful air, she suggested that if Brenda was still interested; she was driving down to the house in Cornwall to check it was in order. A maintenance measure she carried out. She did not mention her conversation with the Dame, nor the threat to her staying in the beguinage. It would be sensible to first find out what Brenda said to the Dame.

There were questions Lisa wanted answering, although there never seemed to be the right moment. What had motivated Brenda to find her at this point in their lives, and what did she want from the renewal of their relationship?

They had little in common. They had taken different paths in life, were virtual strangers in reality, and no crisis, or major event, had led to the contact. When were they going to see their mother in the care home hundreds of miles away in the north of England? Lisa still did not know where it was. Brenda had asserted several times that she monitored their mother's care on a regular basis and complained of the travelling expenses, the accommodation she had to find for her overnight stays, besides the fees themselves.

Lisa's earlier emails to Madge, telling her about the reunion with her sister, spoke of her excitement. She had stopped sending news, and Madge requested further information. If it was not working, she felt some responsibility, as she had been the means of bringing the two sisters together. Concerned, Madge expressed justification for what she had done. Brenda had given her a sight of the 'proof' – Brenda's birth certificate, with the same surname, parental address, and their occupation, which Madge was familiar with regarding Lisa. More important, it seemed, the dates had all tied up. She repeated all of this in a mail.

When Lisa had not answered, Madge tried again and wanted to know if there was a problem. Was the reunion just a passing measure, a simple contact made for the sake of curiosity on Brenda's part, or was it the seed of something much more rewarding? Madge said that she could not imagine, in similar circumstances, leading a separate life from her brother Brian. Since their childhood, they had always remained close while he lived.

Chapter Twenty-Eight

The journey to Lisa's cottage in Cornwall afforded the opportunity to ask some questions. She wanted to know what passed between Brenda and the Dame, which had led to her present uneasy position in the beguinage for however long the Dame intended to allow her to stay.

When she arrived at the bungalow to collect her sister, the isolation and the anonymity of the interior of Brenda's home, with so few personal effects, struck her again. She looked around, expecting to see some changes since her first visit, but it was as bare and austere as ever. Did her sister earn so little in her present employment?

Brenda appeared relaxed, full of enthusiasm, as she stowed away a suitcase in the boot and chuckled to herself about holidays by the sea. Which was not where they were going. Lisa told her that and hoped she would not find it disappointing. In the car, she joked about Lisa's driving and warned her not to do any sudden braking because it would bring up her breakfast!

It was true Brenda used her own car when they were together and made short journeys. The one long excursion they took to London was by train. Lisa was an experienced driver of average ability and awareness, but she knew her parking skills were poor. It gave Lisa the opening to the subject, which was most on her mind, though she did not like the implication even in a joke concerning her lack of driving ability,

"I am not senile, yet, Brenda! Perfectly competent to take you to the cottage, I promise you. Although, from what you and the Dame appear to have been discussing, I will need nursing soon." She turned her head to glimpse Brenda's expression and smiled.

"It's only that I was concerned for you, dear. You're looking much better today, anyway. My company does you good. Let's not think about the future now."

"It upset me."

"We're on a little holiday, Lisa. Let's forget all about that."

If Lisa had expected an apology, none came, but Brenda patted her on the knee, which meant nothing at all, except to dismiss her conversation with the Dame.

Brenda turned on the radio. "News headlines. We could listen to those." Some music followed. She opened the window on her side a sliver. The road noise was enough to make talking difficult, but without causing a draught. "Hot flushes," Brenda said.

Lisa let the miles chalk up, watched her speed, and considered how she might put questions to her sister. There was plenty of time and Brenda was always chatty, even though about nothing of much consequence. They stopped for a coffee in a busy, noisy roadside cafe and could not hear themselves speak. Lisa felt frustrated now and, for once, intended to assert herself more than usual when they returned to the car. Brenda's asides about the scenery were banal and repetitive.

"Brenda, there are a few things I want to talk about. We've got to know each other now, haven't we?" A nod of her head, but Brenda's lips tightened and her eyes narrowed. Lisa put the key in the ignition and they fixed their seatbelts.

"Before we get going again, can you tell me about the letters I sent? Have you got them or are they with mum in the care home? I *doubt* they could be," she stressed, without giving her sister time to say that they were.

Her sister sighed and opened the glove box. "Any sweets in here, by any chance, Lisa dear?" She rummaged for a few moments. "Of course, mum has some photos with her in the bedside table drawer. Quite bed-bound, you know. Your marriage to Ted, for example. All mothers keep wedding photos, I suppose. But the letters are somewhere with me, I think. Some postcards, of various places abroad too. I cleared the house when she went into the care home. And don't think there was anything of value there either that I got out of the clearance for my trouble. She rented and there were few possessions."

"I would like to see the letters sometime, Brenda. The postcards, too. Though it will be ... emotional. I can't tell you how sad it made me that no-one ever bothered to write."

Brenda sat back. "Well, you were in the dog-house, weren't you? Taking off like that. Married so young and left us alone in the house."

It was the same refrain, and it did not hurt Lisa so much; it had lost its impact through repetition.

Lisa took another tack. "Is Ted still alive, do you know?" She allowed herself a quick sidelong glance at her sister's face. Brenda's tone was often harsh, and the depth of her feeling was difficult to measure; sometimes her words were conciliatory, at others almost vindictive. There was no sisterly love, but Lisa concluded, in its absence, that lack applied to both of them, and was to be expected. Too many decades had passed.

Latterly, the relentless contact with Brenda seemed more and more inexplicable to Lisa. Her acquiescence, she realised in surprise, was because of guilt, a growing need for repentance and a duty to atone. It was these emotions which drove her willingness to still spend time with Brenda. After this brief holiday, it could all be over, and she hoped the meetings would dwindle when her sister returned to her own life.

Brenda looked bemused at the question about Ted. Her eyes were wide, and the thick mascaraed lashes fluttered. "I've no idea what happened to Ted. Why would I? He moved away, and we saw him less and less. He could be dead by now, I suppose. Why do you want to know?"

"I'm not sure. I've been thinking about him." Lisa did not admit what she felt; a need to find him and make her peace. Had he remarried? Might he have done so saying Lisa had deserted him, rather than the reality of his prolonged absence and indifference? If he had returned to the family's home – perhaps seeking news of her – in law, it could stand as desertion and sufficient grounds for a divorce.

Although, it could only have been a civil marriage if he took a second wife. Their own church wedding was binding for life. But what if he had abandoned his faith? Lapsed, like me, she thought. She wanted to find out more.

"It's been lovely to see you, Brenda. To be reunited, I mean. I just wondered what made you do it now?" She slowed for an overtaking car and changed lanes. I had better keep my eyes on the road after that slur on my driving; Lisa thought. "Of course, I understand you may not have wanted to see me for a long time because you are so angry with me for leaving home." She could not avoid the sourness of her tone.

"Well, I needed to track you down. That wasn't easy. In fact, very expensive. The letters you sent had detailed names and addresses, especially the later ones. I flew on holiday to Spain for a cheap package trip. It was lucky because your friend still lived there in that hamlet in the hills. I preferred the coast myself, by the way. Sea and sun. Still, quite a lot of English living in that rural backwater of yours. Maybe not your sort now."

Lisa frowned in confusion. Brenda was more expansive, but what did she mean by 'your sort'?

"When I was in Spain, Madge told me you were in France. She looked out the address. You were on retreat there, she said, because of your illness."

Lisa nodded. This much they had shared. "And Marianne, the young French woman, gave you my email address?"

"That's right. Thank goodness for modern communication." Brenda sighed and unwrapped another toffee.

"So, why did you choose this time, Brenda?"

She pointed to her mouth and chewed the sweet, swallowing it down with difficulty before she answered. "Our mother having to go into a care home, of course. You needed to know that, I suppose. Have you any idea how expensive those homes are? I can't go on any longer paying out money. She would be better off in a private place than in a state-run home. I top things up as far as I can, make it better for her, but she rented that house we lived in as children and possessed no savings to speak of."

"Then we must pay her a visit," said Lisa.

****

On arrival in Cornwall, when they got out of the car, stiff and sticky, Brenda stretched and lingered to take in the picturesque view of the frontage of the Cornish cottage. Stone-built and traditional, but with modernised windows, a porch and a small conservatory, she expressed her admiration of every feature. The front garden had, if not recently, received some attention; enough to ensure that someone cut the grass to a reasonable level. Brenda took her phone out of her bag and took several photos.

"You like it that much?" Lisa laughed. "You look like an estate agent, or first-time viewer." For her, it was all so familiar. She had not thought how strong Brenda's reaction might be.

Lisa's neighbour had stocked the fridge with the basics. A fresh loaf, still in its bakery cellophane, rested on the four-square kitchen table, around which were wooden benches. Rustic, perhaps, in contrast to the smooth line of the cupboards and appliances. Brenda's eyes widened in delight as Lisa showed her into the dining room. This was in Georgian style, with a mahogany banded dining table and a set of elegant chairs. Sconces enabled real beeswax candles to complement the modern lighting.

There were two internal staircases. Brenda exclaimed that the cottage was much bigger than she expected. The bedrooms were all furnished in cottage fashion with chintzes, but two were en suite, and an enormous bathroom with a Victorian enamel bath on legs led to further cries of approval. Brenda chose her bedroom straight away. It had a double aspect. She gazed at the view from one window, facing to the back, across a field to a wooded copse on the horizon.

"You *have* done very well for yourself here, Lisa. And there's other property you own. I remember reading about the London apartment which you invited our mum to visit. Have you still got that, by the way? I wonder what you did to gain all of this." She waved her hand around the sitting room in which they now stood.

Lisa sensed growing envy mixed with the genuine compliments. The enthusiasm and smiles of delight made her happy, and she enjoyed presenting each room to her sister, but that last comment sounded cutting, and she dreaded what lay behind it.

What else had Brenda gleaned from those letters and postcards she sent? Lisa could not remember what she had written, but knew they were like a journal, rather than an account of her travels. Perhaps because there was never a response, she had included some intimate and heartfelt details. It had been akin to an unburdening.

The weather was kind and to please her sister, Lisa took her to the nearest coastal resort on the following day. They walked along sandy beaches, sniffing the brine, paddling for a few minutes while the sun was strongest and the breeze cooling. Wriggling their toes, pulling back in mock alarm as the rippling water drew closer, and laughing. For a while, they were like two children at play. Lisa took her phone and captured some animated pictures of Brenda, though she retreated from a close up and appeared impatient. .

"At our age, Lisa, we only look good in poor light, or at a distance. I only allow a photo when I have got ready for it!" She grimaced, making an ugly face, and danced away.

They had already eaten lunch by the sea. A fresh catch of seafood and flat white fish for their main course. The restaurant also offered a wide range of wines to choose from, and while Lisa was sparing with her glass because she was driving, Brenda wanted to be indulged and said so.

Their evening supper in the cottage suited them both in its simplicity. Lisa regretted her selfishness earlier. Why would she be looking forward to Brenda leaving, to be rid of her sister, when they had only reunited for such a short period?

Chapter Twenty-Nine

Brenda was red-eyed, but calm. The company she worked for had made her redundant, and she had already cleared her desk and signed papers for a small severance sum. She arrived on the doorstep of Lisa's home in the beguinage early one morning soon after their holiday, having, she said, cried enough tears. Life was treating her abysmally. What had she done to deserve it?

Lisa almost gave her a hug, but drew back. She offered a hot beverage instead, or something stronger, and prepared coffee to go with it. If it was my daughter, she thought, I would not have hesitated to hug her. Flesh and blood needing comfort.

"I've been with them for two years, you know. I will get an excellent reference. That's why I moved south – to find work. I tried to find the better paid jobs down here, although it isn't easy as you age." Brenda put down the mug of coffee on the only available surface she could see, which was on the narrow stone windowsill of the cottage in the beguinage. With a helpless sigh, she looked out and around the empty cobbled courtyard. "Not that you would understand that. Never having to work." She mumbled the latter, but Lisa heard it.

"I will soon have to give up the bungalow, too. I have little in the way of savings to pay the rent for much longer. A widow with one modest income; how could I?"

"Who is this company you worked for, Brenda? And what sort of office work did you do? You have never said."

"What's the point now? Personal Assistant. I told you about that. General secretarial was what I trained for, although the job is much wider these days and more demanding. They thought highly of me, of course, but the entire section in Human Resources is under threat. I registered with an agency for long-term temporary work, and that is my strength; my flexibility in outlook. Or it was. They have nothing to suggest at the moment. Nothing on their books."

Lisa sat on the edge of her bed in the tiny beguinage cottage. Brenda had taken the only chair, but now she moved away from the window and circled the room, which did not take long. "Look at how you're living!" she exclaimed, waving her arms around. "You have that beautiful cottage in Cornwall, an apartment in London – not central, but a decent post code in the suburbs – and you waste your life shut away in this tiny room. That's all it is!"

Lisa curled a strand of hair around her finger and wondered what to say. Brenda's face was flushed, and she paced the floor, thumping her shoes on the tiles and pausing only to glare at her sister.

"Sit down, Brenda, for goodness' sake. I'm trying to think."

"You could let me live in the apartment in London. Why not? It would be easier to get temporary work in the city."

"I can't. It's let out. I have tenants in there."

"Well, that must bring in a good *wodge*. How lucky you are!" Brenda's accusatory expression frightened Lisa, as though she had done something wrong. She felt another pang of guilt. These days it seemed to centre in the pit of her stomach like indigestion.

She folded her hands in her lap and sighed. The origins of my wealth don't bear too much scrutiny; she thought. She could not dismiss the image of the safe deposit boxes in the bank in Bern; their contents enabled her independent, privileged lifestyle, all the travel she enjoyed as a young woman, and all for as long as she had wanted.

"I deny you nothing, Brenda, and I am thinking of the best way to help you. Give me time."

Brenda sat down, legs crossed and straight-backed, and waited, looking stormy, and licking her lips as if to speak, but then remained silent.

"I will pay the rent," Lisa said, nodding her head, as if agreeing with herself. "That would be a start, wouldn't it? I can set up a direct debit if you give me some bank details."

Brenda looked up, but kept the glum expression, her mouth down-turned. "Just for a couple of months would help. I expect I will move on." She seemed more responsive and less hostile. "What about the utility bills? Some are quarterly ... others, well, I'm not sure where I am with those. Why not just give me a cheque to cover the lot for a few months?"

After a few minutes of mild haggling, Lisa found her cheque book.

****

Brenda's visit that day triggered old memories and raised unresolved issues for Lisa. She saw nothing of Brenda afterwards, but received a text the next day saying she was job hunting and would contact her soon. For the rest of that week, there were no more texts, and she appeared to have switched off her phone. Or had she blocked calls for a while? Surely, cutting off communication was not a good idea if her sister was making applications for work?

Lisa decided she must do something about her increasing desire to tell someone about what had happened in the past. The weight of it was too heavy. This has been coming on for years; she thought.

She rambled around the countryside by car to enjoy the drive. The aimlessness was soothing. She stopped in an unfamiliar linear village to wander on foot along the main street and came to the Catholic church at the centre. It was a quiet week day with not a soul in sight. Lisa stopped to read the times for Mass displayed on a printed sheet, faded by sunlight, inside a glass covered notice board. She could just make out the typed words.

From the outside, the church appeared centuries old, as did several buildings on either side of it; the worn stonework pitted by weather, the tip of the church's spire looking askew. But when she lifted the latch, the heavy creak of the door and the sight of the stations of the cross on the walls of the nave moved her to tears, and she felt the years slip away.

Lisa had visited many famous places of worship during her early adult life when touring Europe with Ray in her twenties. Her interest in and appreciation of the architecture, beauty and history of those buildings had overcome any tingle of fear at her sinful life. Besides, she was young and content, absorbed with her husband and her child, so it was easy to overlook the fleeting feeling of guilt.

As she entered this ancient village church, pleasant childhood memories of regular church attendance with her mother and siblings came to the fore and over-whelmed her. It had been a period of innocence, before faith had withered, and her adult actions had caused the guilt which she damped down and ignored. Entering a church had once given her a sense of welcome and belonging, whatever was happening in her life outside.

Even now, some sense of coming home seemed present again. The smell of incense lingered, familiar, aromatic and sweet, and she guessed that some special celebration must have occurred in the village church that day. She had lost track of the Saints' days and all but the most important days of obligation. She recalled her mother's dedication to the blessing of the Holy Sacrament at Benediction in late afternoons. Her mother had turned to it in times of especial need while Lisa looked after Brenda and Ryan. When her mother returned from church, her expression was calm, her brow smoothed and her voice soft and measured.

Lisa listened in the intense surrounding silence of this church, which was unknown to her but fundamentally the same, with growing confidence. Perhaps, because there was no-one to see, she continued up the nave and genuflected by the altar rail, then sat with her head bowed in a muddled attempt at prayer.

The silence was broken and her prayers cut short as she heard footsteps behind her pacing up the nave. Interrupted, she turned to see who it was and rose to her feet, ready to leave because it was a priest.

"Don't let me disturb you," he said.

"My prayers are from long ago, and it was too hard, anyway." She surprised herself by admitting.

"I am Father Johannes. Perhaps you would like to tell me your Christian name. That of your baptism."

She noted his accent, but could not identify its origin. "Lisa," she said. "I am a penitent, Father, and my name is Lisa."

****

Father Johannes took his time. They toured the church, and he told her the history of it and that soon settled her. Afterwards, he asked her about her penitent status, which she had given in introduction, and which he thought required something from him, meaning the church. He did not resort to platitudes about everyone being a sinner, nor query her careful replies to his questions. They both knew she was holding back.

Lisa could not fashion the words she needed to say. Foremost in her mind was her bigamous marriage. Convinced it must be a mortal sin, she did not dare to mention it.

He gave her some leaflets. These were to help prepare for confession, which she made clear was what she sought. He insisted she could see him at any time.

Afterwards, long after their first encounter, she found the preparation in the leaflet drawn out and arduous, but followed it through in the isolation of the beguinage.

She sat in a pew at the back during the services she later attended at various local churches. Throughout this time, she struggled not to be drawn into a local church community. How could she explain to new acquaintances that she was living in the beguinage? She could not take the Eucharist and parishioners would know that something was amiss by that alone. And she did not want to lie any more. So she remained anonymous, visiting different churches in the area and taking part in as few conversations as possible.

Father Johannes welcomed her, but was not pressing each time she arrived in his church. He asked her if she was sick, or feared she was terminally ill. Perhaps he thought she dreaded dying; the reason for this long delayed need. It was not the case, although when she had been in the forest in France, and awaiting her last results, it had crossed her mind. Childhood teaching about reconciliation with God and achieving a state of grace had come to the fore, and its absence had depressed her in the worst moments when living there.

One afternoon, spending the day with her daughter, she sat in

Sophie's kitchen. The dishwasher had arrived and a young man had installed it.

"You are a strange woman, mum," Sophie had said, when advised of its delivery, and she had hugged her mother for the thought. Now she asked about Lisa's religious interest. "All this church going, mum, isn't it enough that you remain in the beguinage?"

"Well, I am getting older and these things matter more for some of us."

"You're only sixty! Decades left." Sophie sliced a cake she had baked that morning and slid one piece onto her mother's plate. "You look better with a little more weight, but ... why so pale? and ... you're quite grey under the eyes. Are you sleeping?"

"I admit I have got a lot on my mind. There are things you don't know about the past."

Sophie thought this was an opening, but she was not telepathic. How could she ask questions now, probing her mother, after a lifetime of being careful to stay clear of her proscribed limits?

"Weekends are important for you, Sophie, when you're working for a living. I know you are under pressure. I shouldn't take too much of your free time. Where's David? Has he gone somewhere to get out of the way?"

"That's nonsense and you know it. I make my own hours of work and choose to take days off as I please. David's seeing an old friend, but he's a potential client, so not only for the sake of friendship." Sophie leaned forward, propped her elbows on the table, and rested her chin on her hands.

"You're not thinking about giving all your money away, or something like that, are you? I worried at first that Alice – *the Dame,* to you, I suppose – was angling for financial input to support the place. Before you raise your hand in protest, I am not questioning her motives. She believes in the set-up and the respite it gives to you all, or a lifestyle you can try."

"No, nothing to worry about. I am not intimidated by anyone, least of all the Dame." Lisa laughed at the idea. "In fact, I will not stay there for much longer. I'm not often there as it is."

"What's wrong, mum? Is it Brenda, then? You haven't seen her for a while, have you?"

Chapter Thirty

Lisa returned to Father Johannes. She made her confession, but not of the most important matters. They used the formulaic process and the traditional words. She asked for forgiveness for sins she could not remember and, restraining tears, only thought about the terrible ones, which she remembered well, but for which she was still not contrite. The priest granted her absolution.

Only God knew the extent of a sinner's confession, not he, he told her. Though she repeated the prayers he gave as penance, she did not believe it was enough, nor that the absolution could apply to what she had avoided telling him. It would require more than prayers as penance. Therefore, had she received absolution at all?

Her only alternative was to seek further knowledge of the consequences of the unconfessed mortal sin of her second marriage and, beyond that, the crime she had committed in civil law. All of her relationships after Ted were adulterous fornication in the eyes of the church. Such sins required something more than prayers and good works. Hadn't she been ignoring it, refusing to acknowledge it, for all her life?

Ray was dead. The crux of the matter was whether Ted still lived. She had no way of finding out what happened to Ted, since Brenda did not know his whereabouts, and why would anyone else? Repeated questions to Brenda about the possibility of Ted's death; whether he was a well, fit man and in good circumstances when she last saw him, however long ago, brought hostility.

One morning, Brenda arrived at the bequinage with receipts for what she called 'essentials'. She had been shopping, and her bank account was overdrawn. Lisa's careful reaction when she looked through the slips of paper, instead of just writing a cheque, showed how unconvinced she was. Lisa had already stopped giving Brenda cash, as it disappeared in no time. Her sister had suggested that if Lisa gave her a bank card, it would mean that the regular trip to a cash point, disrupting Lisa's daily life and prayers, would be unnecessary. These tactics had alarmed Lisa.

"Don't you trust me?" Brenda asked, with a tear in her eye. Lisa found her purse and emptied it out into her sister's hands. She did not want to tell her the truth that giving her a bank card would be disastrous in view of her rash expenditure. Though she could not deny her what she had in her purse.

"You need to show me what you are spending it on, Brenda, and this does not appear to be essentials." She finished leafing through the receipts which Brenda had presented. "I am sorry, Brenda, but I have already paid your rent and all the utilities. That is all I am prepared to do for now. How is your search for work going?"

Brenda shook her head. Her morose and dejected expression at the need to have the receipts checked changed to anger at Lisa's refusal to go any further. She leapt to her feet, flushed and threatening, jabbing her finger at Lisa's face, coming closer and closer. She backed Lisa away to the window, in the confines of the small room, until the ledge of the sill pressed into her back and Lisa gave a cry of pain.

"Listen to me," Brenda spat. "You are a rich woman and a wicked one. All this prayer and church going when you are a *criminal*. I could tell anyone what you did! Your daughter doesn't know, I'm willing to bet."

Lisa was unprepared for such an attack, and her breath caught in her throat in panic. What did Brenda mean?

"You married Ray, your fancy man, who gave you the wealth and the lifestyle to go with it. Had a child with him, too. Your lovely Sophie." Her voice rose in volume to a snake like hiss. You were still married to Ted, weren't you? That's bigamy, a crime. People can go to prison for years for bigamy."

"How did you find it out?" Despite her fear, Lisa's immediate response was the only thing that came into her head.

"Those letters, of course, and the postcards and wedding photos outside the church with Ray. How much you wrote of the wonder and excitement of the travelling with Ray and then living in Spain! I am not stupid, and the dates gave it all away. Besides, you were not divorced from Ted. There was not enough time, even without considering the teachings of the church: marriage is for life."

It all tumbled out, then Brenda drew breath before another thought came to her. "That's probably why our mother was so against answering those letters. She must have realised, too. Or perhaps she discussed it with Ted. I would ask her, but she's frail, and I expect she doesn't want to think about that fact that her granddaughter, Sophie, must be illegitimate."

This last outburst frightened Lisa the most. It isn't long since I first told Sophie that her father, Ray, was my second husband; Lisa thought. What must *she* believe? It's true, what Brenda says. My child is not legitimate.

She pushed back against Brenda as her knees gave way, stumbled to the bed, and fell upon it.

Brenda stood looming above her. "This sudden taking up of religion again. You think I don't know how you've been going in and out of churches? What you've done is a mortal sin. Your soul is in danger, too, and you know it."

She paused and grew calmer, taking long, even breaths and giving Lisa time to recover or prepare for more. What was it to be?

Brenda's last words were icy. "In many ways, I'm ashamed of our relationship to each other."

Lisa got up from the bed and steadied herself. "Wait a minute."

Without another word, she found her bank book and filled in a cheque for a large amount. She gave it to Brenda, who folded it, as always, and tucked it away.

Before she opened the front door, Brenda turned back to face her. "Reparation to me for abandoning our family, in helping me out with this overdue money, makes *me* the one who does *you* a favour."

She didn't glance back at Lisa and strode away down the cobblestone path, her head held high.

****

The Dame had slipped, perhaps not in person, an informative and disquieting letter through the letter boxes of each cottage. Lisa picked up her letter and was relieved to see that the Dame had sent it to the entire community. It heralded a fundamental change. For the future, the members would have to agree to remain for three years and make an annual advance payment. It was not clear if you left within the extended tenure whether some reimbursement would follow, but Lisa was certain the Dame would ensure that the payment still had to be made in full, otherwise what could be the purpose or benefit? Present members had three months to consider signing a contract to this effect or to leave the beguinage.

The explanation was brief but sound. Expenses continued to rise and the numbers of sisters fluctuated so much from month to month that it was impossible to stabilise the finances of the enterprise. Dame Alice wanted a guaranteed income for the community and the prospect of planning for a minimum of three years ahead.

Lisa sat down, unnerved. Everything she had relied on for her security was disappearing. Brenda had questioned her ability to keep her past secrets from others, and Lisa was having to come to terms with both exposure and the demands of her faith. Gone was any future avoidance; the time had come to deal with it.

Lost in thought, she noticed dusk had fallen and drew the curtains over the main window. Her body felt numb and cold. A sharp knock at the door forced her to make a move. "Come in. Is it time for supper?"

Jeanette stepped over the threshold. With a furrowed brow, she glanced around and made a low tutting sound.

"Sister, have you been asleep? Vespers was over an hour ago and our supper was only a cold collation. Although I am sure I could get you some soup, if you would like it."

Lisa shook her head. Jeanette gave a wan, sympathetic half-smile, her head tilted to one side. She watched Lisa sit down again on the bed, but she had seen the abandoned letter on the top of the prie-dieu, and her gaze sharpened in curiosity.

"You have been praying for guidance?" Jeanette picked up the letter and replaced it after a swift scan of the contents.

It took Lisa a few moments to gather her thoughts. "So, we are to be turned out?"

"Or we have to make a firmer commitment. It's a different way of looking at things, I suppose. What will you do?"

"I do not know yet. It isn't clear about the finances, is it? Do we lose the money we have paid for our accommodation etc., if we leave within those three years?"

"I'm sure the Dame will make everything … transparent, was the word I was looking for." Though she did not appear happy about the prospect, and her tone was low and gloomy.

Lisa noted again that no trace of the nun's apparel – in particular the habit and veil – remained to identify Jeanette's religiosity, nor the enthusiasm first apparent when she had arrived in the complex. It had long gone.

"Anyway, we have three months to decide what to do, and I was considering moving on." Lisa stretched out her legs. I am only sixty; she reflected with a sigh.

"Do you expect that many of the sisters will accept and stay?" Jeanette took the only chair and positioned herself on the edge, her back straight and hands clasped in her lap, shoes flat on the floor, despite the height of the heels, and legs close together.

Very nun-like in posture still; Lisa thought. "If they don't stay, the Dame will have to think again, won't she? If she only retains a few people, then the beguinage could be worse off than ever." Lisa wondered what Jeanette was thinking. From the viewpoint of how she carried herself; the modest and strict posture modelled on that of a nun; she fitted the role to perfection, but the Dame had said there was no religion in her at all. The abandoning of the 'garb', Lisa decided, was a sign of greater sincerity, more inner depth. Although, in coming to see her, Jeanette seemed undecided and seeking reassurance about whether to continue at the beguinage.

They sat for a few minutes more in silence until bells rang out in the distance. "Ah, Compline." Jeanette got up. "Are you coming?"

Lisa shook her head, smiling, but unconvinced by the nonsense of it. The beguinage was nothing like a nunnery, and the 'offices'; regular, if inaccurate, marked out times of devotion were almost farcical.

Jeanette tutted, but smiled and tottered off in her high heels. Lisa watched her unfurl a chiffon scarf and tie it in place on her head before she entered the building across the courtyard. She has no compunction for the artificiality of the life, and it comforts her, while I, in comparison, am weary and confused. Perhaps the Dame is *wrong* about her complete shallowness, and Jeanette will stay.

The week had been difficult, and Lisa felt worn down. She could find nothing to uplift her; tears made her chest ache, and that wretchedness never resulted in easing her concerns.

Although she had not even looked at it for months, she remembered where she had stored it away and groped around in the back of the highest cupboard in the kitchenette for the bottle. She dusted off a tumbler and measured out a generous brandy. It was almost too evocative, the fiery slide of the liquor in her throat, the familiar warmth in her chest, but it would do her more good than the tears she wept at night.

Chapter Thirty-One

Lisa had no contact with Brenda for several weeks. She sent her text messages, which were ignored. Sometimes she hoped that the 'reunion' period had run its course, but she maintained the direct debts and payments into Brenda's bank account.

She attended Mass at various churches and gained some relief from her participation, although she avoided Father Johannes in his church, preferring anonymity. It became easier to blend into each small congregation; they did not approach her because they did not see her again for a few weeks.

It was nearing the time when she needed to inform the Dame of her decision whether or not to continue living at the beguinage. She had always led an isolated life. Now she seemed to have more need of company than ever before, and the community proved unobtrusive. If pressed, she could only have named a few of her neighbours. Although she did not intend to sign a contract which would tie her down for three years, she hoped that with sufficient extra funding from her own purse towards the Dame's project, she could come to some interim arrangement with her. There were too many other areas of her life to consider, too strong a sense of jeopardy, and she needed a base. This might have to be it for a while longer.

The only perceptible positive she saw in her life now was the increased pleasure and sense of stability which she found in Sophie, who was not far away and kept almost in daily contact. They had never been so close.

One weekend, they met for lunch and to attend a matinee at the local theatre afterwards. Sophie insisted her mother stay with her overnight.

Lisa winced at the pain in her head at breakfast the next morning and asked Sophie for painkillers. "I drank a bit too much wine last night," she admitted.

Sophie offered a blister pack and a glass of water. "Drink that as well, mum, coffee is dehydrating."

After she swallowed the pills, she went back to bed for an hour. The coffee was appealing, but she had only eaten a piece of dry toast. Later, after a hot shower, she dressed and felt revived. She applied make-up and took extra care of her appearance.

She found Sophie in the sitting room, looking at a magazine on childcare. With no thought or expectation, Lisa joked, "Am I going to be a grandmother, then?"

Sophie looked up. "Actually, you are."

It surprised Lisa because of Sophie's age. It was late for motherhood. But she congratulated her and David, and after the initial excited talk and plans, she asked if they were going to get married now. Sophie said they might later on. Neither of them were particularly concerned. She swept aside any further discussion on that question.

She was sure that in the end Sophie and David would marry, even if Sophie was unconcerned now about the religious aspect of living together, which she always appeared to be. Lisa's first consideration, an automatic one because of her own background, was for the legitimacy of Sophie's child. Perhaps a disclosure about her daughter's own illegitimate status now seemed possible and would produce little reaction. But when to do it? She had avoided revelations for so many years. The opportunity to return to the subject disappeared because Sophie posed some urgent questions of her own.

She wanted to know about Brenda. Had her mother seen her lately, and if as she suspected the answer was no, then why not? She remarked on the fact that Lisa's life revolved around their reunion, and commented on how much she noticed the difference in her mother, especially her moods.

"You often smell of alcohol, mum and you're losing weight again. What's worrying you?"

Lisa told her about the need for a decision on remaining at the beguinage and how the condition had changed. It was a sop, she knew, and not at the heart of her anxiety and depressed spirits. Nor did it answer the question about her drinking. Yet, something impelled her to reveal more. Her present obsession with sin and confession? Or was it the idea of becoming a grandmother?

"You remember I told you I had been married before your father?"

Sophie nodded and sat back, arms crossed and patient, waiting. Lisa gave her some details of her early life in the drab town of the mid-seventies, which she had never mentioned before. The volatile situation between her mother and father, her own responsibilities in bringing up her siblings. The marriage to Ted and pretending to be pregnant to enable her to leave home. Then Ted's desertion and how lonely and unfulfilled she was.

It led to more questions from Sophie. Where did Lisa go to school and what was it like in the street, or neighbourhood, where they all lived as a family? Why had she hated it so and what employment had she found?

Lisa warmed to the telling of her story. Perhaps Sophie would understand and not condemn her.

"Everything happened so quickly after that. There was Ray and you suddenly coming along. It gave me no chance to think about what I was doing. I loved him so much." At that point, she struggled to continue; it was too hard and complicated.

Sophie reached the most important issue on her own, but she still looked puzzled. "I realised you hadn't been with Ted for long. So you lived with Ted and married Ray. Or the other way around? Does it matter? Is that why you are so concerned about David and me getting married? For the baby's sake?"

Lisa opened her mouth to attempt an answer, but floundered with the words. She nodded her head instead.

Sophie thought for a moment, frowning as she worked through the disclosures. "I often wondered why your passport was in your maiden name."

Ray's idea, Lisa thought, to protect me. How quick and discerning he always was beneath that charm. I will not lie to Sophie, but neither did she clarify what had happened. It was too soon and her daughter seemed prepared to accept she might be illegitimate. She had proposed an alternative version herself to how that might have happened. A much better one than a bigamous marriage.

Sophie gave her a hug, but she had not finished yet. "Another thing, mum. I know almost nothing about your sister, and I have only met her to talk to at the meal on your birthday. I suppose you have caught up on your childhood together with her? It must be strange. Does she have lots of photos and souvenirs from those times? I just wondered, that's all. It would be lovely to see you as children." She unfolded her arms and leaned closer to her mother than before, watching her expression.

"Have you given Brenda a lot of money? Her circumstances are vague from the little you have told me about her. Those jewels, that dress on your sixtieth birthday, for example. Have you quarrelled now?"

"She's unemployed. Made redundant, but with good references and looking for work. I have helped her out a lot, I admit. I meant us to go together to see our mother soon, in the care home. She hasn't talked about that for a while. Brenda said it might be too much of a shock just now. It could be that she had gone to see her without me. But, yes, we have had an upset."

"Is that the reason for all the alcohol, mum? Even in the mornings, I have sometimes smelled it on your breath. Not brandy for breakfast, I hope!"

Lisa smiled, but the thought that Lisa did not know how close she was to the truth made her stomach, still delicate from the previous evening, churn.

****

Jeanette was the last one to leave the Prayer Room that day after Compline and strolled back to her cottage in the golden evening sunshine. She had lingered behind until the room was empty in order to take some photographs. Reflecting on her recent decision, she stopped to take another look around the cobbled square. This had been home. She had not left the beguinage yet, and there would be time to take more photographs and in different lights to complete a visual record she had been compiling for several days. She had so many fleeting emotions and memories to store and associate with them. Would others be doing that, and how many of us will regret this? She wondered.

Jeanette thought of knocking on Lisa's front door after Compline, but she wondered if Lisa had gone to bed. She would try again in the morning and confirm what her neighbour intended to do. In a way, she already anticipated that Lisa was leaving, and Jeanette felt sad about the loss of her companionship.

The Dame had always encouraged her to keep a kindly watch on her neighbour. She described it as a sisterly bonding. Jeanette recalled her involvement in the medical appointments at the Dame's request. In the initial period of tests, Jeanette had the responsibility of making sure that Lisa did not miss them, forget to attend, and had accompanied Lisa. Later, there were the daily and then weekly vitamin injections to supervise.

None of that had been necessary for some time now. The Dame had changed her opinion of Lisa's health, satisfied that Lisa did not need a carer because the suspected ageing, mental health and memory problems had come to nothing. The tests proved it and she had informed Jeanette of the results in strict confidence.

It was still a habit, though, for Jeanette to note when and if Lisa came to the various prayer meetings and communal meals. She would miss the caring role.

Perhaps she would just say goodnight to Lisa. She tapped on her door and listened. It was quiet and after several repeated raps, she pushed at the door. It was open. Calling out Lisa's name, she stepped inside. A strong smell of alcohol permeated the room and her foot hit a bottle, which rolled away into a corner.

In the shadowy darkness of the interior, with curtains still drawn but the door wide open, she saw dishevelled bedclothes tumbled down to the floor. Huddled within them, the distinct shape of a body. As she bent down, she already knew what she would find, but sent up a fervent plea to whatever deity might listen that Lisa was not dead.

She took her phone out of her pocket and called for an ambulance before alerting the Dame.

Chapter Thirty-Two

Lisa opened her eyes and remembered where she was. What had she dreamt? Something about hellfire probably; she thought, with the beginnings of a smile at her own gallows humour. Then she felt the pain and winced as she hauled herself into a sitting position. The slight cracks in the ceiling's paintwork drew her attention before she refocused on the view from the window. She gazed into the distance at the light drizzle on bleak, far-away hills, with a rainbow just discernible in the east. The rainbow is promising, she thought, and reached for the water jug and glass. Something still hurt inside and her left hip was sore. She hoped it was only the bruising. Her mind seemed to be in a fog.

The absence of any covered dishes or cutlery meant that it was not a mealtime, and the clock on the opposite wall confirmed it as mid-afternoon. Not long before Sophie's arrival. She had almost closed her eyes again and relaxed into sleep, when the door, ajar, but not by much, opened wide and a nurse announced a visitor. He had promised he would not stay long. Lisa wished she was still asleep when she saw who it was.

"How are you, Lisa? I hope you don't see me as an unwelcome visitor." Father Johannes stood at the end of the bed.

"I did nothing deliberate, Father," she said. It was an automatic reaction. Despair was a sin, too. "How did you know I was here?"

"Your daughter tracked me down. You will have to ask her about how she did that."

It did not alarm or anger her as it might have done, although she was curious about what Sophie was doing.

"They say you will be out of the clinic soon. I am just here to ...

remind you of my availability and to wish you well. I was looking out for you in the other parishes, where I know you have been going to Mass."

He held a rolled up bundle of a few magazines, which he placed on the wheeled table. "My housekeeper chose them. She's good at that. They are not new."

He was fortunate in his housekeeper; she thought. But from the first, he had never seemed as traditional and severe as the priests from her younger days, and she was not a member of his parish, so it was kind of him to see her and to bring them.

She thanked him and surprised herself by telling him that despite what it looked like – her self-inflicted presence in a hospital bed – their conversations had helped her to clarify her thinking and her obligations in her faith.

"Well, perhaps when you recover fully we can recommence. No pressure!" He held a hand aloft in a gesture of emphasis, and it turned into a blessing before he left.

She picked up the magazines, which were indeed a good choice as one was about world-wide travel, and slipped the tracts tucked inside, verses from Scripture, underneath her pillows.

****

Sophie brought her favourite chocolates. "There's nothing you may not eat, mum. You used to like these." So far, they had not spoken of anything troublesome. Sophie cried when she saw her mother the first time, still linked to various machines. Alcoholic poisoning mixed with some tablets because she could not sleep. The hospital was now much more relaxed about her because Lisa was out of danger and recovering.

Sophie still felt guilty since they had only exchanged brief texts during the recent busy period in her work. Lisa kept repeating it made no difference, and it was all her own fault.

Since Father Johannes's visit, Lisa had been waiting for the moment to clear the air on one issue. She queried how Sophie found out about the priest and sent him to see her. Seated close to the bed, Sophie drew a deep breath and gripped the ends of the arm rests on the visitor's chair.

"Don't get annoyed. I found your journal … and before you say *anything,* I only read the last few pages from your stay at the beguinage."

That she had discovered the journal was not unexpected because the Dame, after the emergency hospitalisation of her mother, had requested Lisa's removal from the beguinage. She knew Sophie cleared the cottage and collected the few possessions found there. Reading the journal was another matter, but she restrained herself from commenting. At least, she would wait until she heard what Sophie had learned from it.

"Have you heard from Brenda? Is she blackmailing you in some evil fashion?"

Lisa took several gulps from a glass of water. The clinic was overheated. These places often were.

Sophie's concern did not surprise her. She had questioned before the presents, cheques and other payments which Lisa, if not acknowledging giving, neither had she denied. The idea of blackmail had occurred to Lisa, too, after that last cold, accusatory parting by Brenda.

"Everything I have given her, I gave freely."

"Mum, there's something I have to tell you about Brenda," Sophie began. She paused, twiddling with her hair. "She's not your sister."

"Yes, I know."

"What?" Sophie spluttered, grasped her own bottled water and tipped it all over her lap.

"Take that towel on the rack by the shower room door."

Lisa did not wait for Sophie to finish dabbing at her skirt before she explained. "I didn't know at the beginning. It was gradual. Of course, we didn't have any facial resemblance, but how would it be otherwise? I had not seen her since she was about fourteen. There were little things after that. Facts she got wrong about when we were young, and they were not something I could dismiss as memory lapses. Important things, which I knew well.

"Then there was the bungalow she lives in. So impersonal, never any family photos. Not that she wanted me there. Rented, she said, and I wondered for how long? It looked so temporary, as if for a purpose. I was the one who left home, deserted them, not her. She was a widow, but no photos of her marriage either, nor her deceased husband. Why not? All these things built up.

"I then noticed she was asking me questions about details, irrelevancies, that she would use later, throw them back at me as if we both shared that background and the same history."

Sophie said nothing. She sipped at the rest of the water with greater care. A nurse tapped on the door and reminded Lisa about a hip X-Ray. She pointed to the wall clock. In fifteen minutes. They would wheel her down and she must make sure she was ready.

"Ready means go to the toilet beforehand," Lisa said, laughing. Sophie helped her out of the bed. "How did you find out about Brenda? Tell me about that when I have finished in there." She pointed to the adjoining shower room.

On her return, Sophie referred to the discussion they had when she announced she was pregnant and Lisa would be a grandmother. She had done some research using that information; surnames, dates, where the family lived. With David's suggestion, they gained help from a genealogist because, she admitted, it limited their time, with both of them working hard.

"I must reimburse you for that," Lisa interrupted, but Sophie waved her hand in dismissal.

"I'll be gone when you get back from the X-Ray, mum, but there's a lot more to reveal from what you repeated to me that Brenda had told you about the family. A lot of it was simple fabrication; complete lies more than evasions due to lack of actual knowledge."

She gave her mother a kiss. "Nothing to worry about." She put on her jacket and turned back from the door. "By the way, her name is Alison. I saw that on her mail, but that's another story. She's moved and is having it forwarded now."

****

After forceful persuasion from them both, when Lisa left the clinic, she went to Sophie and David's apartment. He was solicitous for her comfort and, as Sophie put it, discreetly kept out of the way. It impressed Lisa. They established a routine and one week later, all three sat down to decide what to do next.

Sophie had already informed her mother with regret that Lisa's mother had died two years ago. She did not want to break this news and, perhaps because of the forthcoming birth of her child, was affected herself. She would never meet her grandmother. Of Ted, she found no trace after their church wedding.

Lisa wanted to see her mother's grave, and Sophie promised they would go together to do that. Perhaps, Sophie suggested, they could also go to Spain and see Ray's place of burial? Lisa explained Ray was cremated and, although she did not take care of the ashes herself for various reasons, after his sudden death, Madge had done everything and they could consult her.

"We had better make it quick, though, because Madge must be in her eighties."

They did not discuss the dreaded question of how Lisa married Ray when she had so recently parted from her first husband, Ted. It seemed to be an understanding that they reserved it for another day.

"Now some good news," Sophie said. She looked excited. "How about these?" She gave Lisa a photograph. "That's the real Brenda, and that is your brother, Ryan. Not the ex-con, jailbird, Ryan, which is according to … that woman, Alison. Almost everything she told you about your family was a lie!"

"Where are the two of them? It looks … is that the Sydney Opera House in the distance?"

"Exactly. They both emigrated to Australia in their early twenties. I haven't made much contact yet, but we soon will. They are looking forward to meeting us."

Lisa felt overwhelmed.

.

Chapter Thirty-Three

They agreed Lisa must confront Alison. David did not wish to get involved with the details of the discussions between mother and daughter on that point. He warned them to be careful, whatever they planned. The woman was malicious. She was after as much money as possible, and might be violent. Lisa must not see her face to face on her own.

Sophie could not understand why Lisa had continued to make financial payments to Alison when she knew, or at least suspected, that she was not her long-lost sister, Brenda. Had Alison threatened her mother with blackmail and, if that was the case, what basis did she have for it? With reluctance, Lisa had admitted that she was still making payments to Alison for her rent and bills. If the woman had moved, these were no longer necessary.

"Even if they were, mum, they are extortion. She is receiving them by fraud, impersonation, and you must put a stop to any direct debits made on her behalf at the bank. Promise me you will do it." Lisa nodded her head.

"Do it today!"

"I kept up the pretence because she was needy, I suppose, and I *wanted* it to be true. Do you remember I said to you at the beginning, Sophie, that I worried she might be angry and resentful, before I even thought of meeting her? So there were no surprises, and however often she rebuked me, or called me to account, it seemed I had earned that treatment.

Whenever she wished for anything, I got used to paying out. There were other pressures as well. Going through the past, trying to come to terms with my marriage to Ray ….”

“Mum, I *have* worked it out.” She took Lisa's hand. “From the dates: the parish church records for you and Ted, the photographs of you and my father outside that church where you married, my birth soon afterwards. Did he know? That it was bigamous?”

Lisa grabbed the box of tissues. “No, never. I am certain of that. He was so happy from the start that I was a Catholic. Whatever else he did and however he gained his wealth, which I never found out with any certainty, his faith was important to him.”

“Let's talk about something else now.” Sophie sat back on the sofa, her hand under her chin in a typical thoughtful gesture. “I think you should send Alison a text. Ask to meet and … offer a carrot. You're sorry you haven't been getting along so well and have been thinking about it a lot. Now you want to make some solid financial settlement for her future. We can work out something along those lines.”

“Yes. That sounds possible. We could talk over a lunch, and with other people around she could not hurt me. I don't think I want to do it on my own, though. Will you come with me?”

“Of course. David, too, if you …”

“No, a man's presence might put her off, make her wary. I want to find out how she discovered everything she did about me and my family. I will make that a condition. It is something I have considered, and I know her better than you. For a while, I wondered whether she was some sort of … con artist? Does she do this for a living? I don't think so for a moment. I think she saw an opportunity, and her circumstances are meagre, her prospects poor. It was too good a chance to miss, and this is a one-off.”

“I hope you're right, mum. You seem to have weighed it up.”

"Thank you, Sophie, for getting Father Johannes to visit me in the clinic. I meant to say that to you before now. I am going to continue to talk to him. Although, I don't want you reading my journal ever again. That's private!" They both laughed, but Lisa felt the need to explain her resolve.

"I know you don't have a faith at the moment. That could change. I lapsed for so long, and they brought me up in the church, my mother and the school, remember? I want to put things right, and I know this priest will help me."

****

Lisa did not delay. She saw Father Johannes for counselling. She had read the penitential tracts he gave her in the clinic, which he placed inside the roll of magazines with such forethought, and felt prepared to confess. In fact, she was eager to do everything necessary to atone and engage again in the church.

First, he advised her to seek professional advice concerning the criminal act of bigamy she committed when she married Ray. It was beyond his capability as a priest to help her in the legal aspect, but the marriage was a mortal sin and that was within his function. He had discussed the matter, in principle, with a higher authority in the church.

She did not discuss the religious side with Sophie. It was personal to herself. I am a product of my childhood and my time, she thought, as she probed for an inner truth. So much has changed within the church. I am getting older and I am contrite. Sophie is not in the same position and, although she is compassionate, she does not understand and might make my need to undertake penance even harder.

The priest could offer one consolation regarding Ray, which had worried her. When she married Ray, *she* was very young, but in full knowledge of what she was doing. That had to be accepted. In contrast, whatever else her husband had weighing on his conscience at the time of his death; when his car ploughed into a tree in Spain; he did not know Lisa had not been free to marry him, either under civil law, or the tenets of the church. He would pray for Ray's soul, and for Lisa's forgiveness.

"See a lawyer, mum." Sophie insisted; practical as ever. "You would only get a fine. Doesn't someone have to bring a case against you? Who could do that?"

They arranged a meeting with Alison. She hovered in the bistro's doorway, holding open the door, and looking around for them before she stepped inside. She saw only Lisa and her daughter and came to the table, her face expressionless. Lisa suggested they eat and then discuss matters over coffee. She hoped that a good meal and some wine might soften what came next for Alison, and that Sophie would keep in the background. They had discussed tactics beforehand.

"Let me unfold it piecemeal, and there must be no aggression from us," she told Sophie. "I don't want her running off in a huff, or in fear of prosecution. No-one is going to appear and insist on arresting her!"

Sophie had smiled at the idea. "All right, mum. You play it your way. Just warn her off for good."

Though Alison's interest in the meeting could only be in the 'settlement'; how much and in what form it would take, she was straight away in guarded retreat. Her hands shook, and she required a strong drink, as soon as Lisa announced her name, *Alison,* in a cold, formal word of greeting, before the impostor could sit down. Alison looked as though she was in a state of shock for most of what had followed.

Alison had worked in a care home as an administrative assistant. She was neither a Personal Assistant or a secretary, nor in any form of well-paid work. She had always appeared older than the younger sister, whom she impersonated. On that day of the meeting, with less attention to cosmetics, perhaps to engender more sympathy, she looked her age.

She had spent some time with the residents in the care home at which she worked and bonded with one in particular: Ted. This was her means of acquiring information. Ted was in excellent form mentally, but deteriorating fast physically from an industrial disease. Compensation had been late in coming and inadequate for his needs. He spoke with sarcasm of his position, but he kept a strong sense of humour. He talked about his past. She liked him.

It hurt Ted that his wife Lisa led a wonderful life of money, leisure and travel; staying in the best hotels, visiting foreign cities; compared to his dull, ordinary one, which was now cut short. Not only that, she had got married again, and without a divorce. He knew about it all because he had got letters and postcards written by his wife to her mother. A woman who had been living in poverty in the family home. *She* was an honourable person, Ted insisted, and he said it disgusted him what Lisa wrote of her lifestyle.

Brenda had paused in the telling, her mouth dry and her face flushed with malice. She related that Lisa's mother had hoped one day for a 'comeuppance'. But Ted thought she was 'a bit of a 'softie'. He said that Lisa's mother still valued the news of her daughter, though Ted disapproved of it.

Ted had returned after years away (he admitted it, Lisa noted) and the letters, photographs, and postcards were passed on to him. He should have them, Lisa's mother said, because he was her errant daughter's husband, and Lisa had wronged him by leaving their home.

They gathered that by this time, Lisa's mother was ill herself and soon entered sheltered housing, then a residential home.

It was the substance of Alison's story that day, and envy coloured it while she ignored her own recent duplicity. There would not be an apology and to go further, Lisa thought, would only result in greater venom. She had no way of knowing how accurate it all was.

Sophie had emptied the coffee pot and was going to reorder. Alison sat back and seemed recovered from her initial fright, having received no opposition. She requested an Irish coffee with a separate liqueur.

"I must just visit the ladies first. I'll sort out the coffee for you after that," Sophie said. Whatever was she thinking? Lisa imagined her daughter was holding back, keeping an admirable restraint.

Lisa leaned forward and seized the fortuitous break. "Have you still got all the letters and everything?"

Alison's expression changed again; she smiled for the first time. "At a price. I will not get a 'settlement', I suspect."

"Have you got them with you?"

"Yes." She bent down to extract a large manilla folder from her bag, which she had placed on the floor between her feet. Lisa had guessed that its position meant the contents must be important and of value. Though she was not her sister, Lisa felt she had judged her character well in the time they had spent together.

Lisa gazed in amazement at the letters. When she saw the photographs, she restrained tears.

Alison spotted Sophie returning to the bar area to order the promised coffee and alcohol. She nudged Lisa and pointed to her standing at the bar at the other end of the restaurant. "We need to hurry if you want them. He gave them to me."

"I'll write you a cheque now."

And put a stop on it, as you did with my other payments?

"Well, we can go to your bank, and I could make a transfer."

"Some cash would be better. Get rid of Sophie, send her home."

She could have avoided it, but Lisa was content to pay. She asked Sophie to meet her in the car park. Clutching the manilla folder, with the deed done, when she returned, she did not lie. Although Sophie shook her head at the generosity, and said her mother should not mention the payment to David, she agreed they would drop the matter and not speak of it again.

"I wish there had been the opportunity to make my peace with Ted," Lisa said later that evening. *I never reconciled with either of them, Ted or my mother.*

"You only lived with Ted for a few months. It makes the possibility of a legal case very unlikely, since both your husbands are dead. It isn't your fault that your mother had nothing further to do with you. She was a hard woman."

She comforted Lisa with the thought that Ted was the one who had deserted her. If there had been time, her mother could have gained a divorce, even if Lisa could not have remarried in church.

Lisa had already decided, with Father Johannes's knowledge, that part of her atonement was to take a solemn vow. For the rest of her life, she would never again have a relationship unless it was platonic. She was only sixty, which no-one seemed to consider as too old for a widow to form another partnership, if she was fortunate enough to do so, but this was her decision. It seemed appropriate.

The next two weeks were exciting. They all spoke via Zoom to

Brenda, Ryan, and other members of her two siblings' families in Australia. Sophie showed her delight with all these new relations.

They discussed arrangements for the families' reunions. Lisa would make the first journey to be reunited with her brother and sister. She expected David and Sophie to come to Australia to meet the family after her grandchild was born.

Lisa reflected on how much she had travelled, touring Europe and elsewhere. She had delighted in learning about other societies and cultures in very different circumstances. She would soon be on another learning journey.

Distance and the unfolding of events meant she did not see her grandchild in the flesh for a long time. Although, from her sister's home in Australia, she listened to the baby gurgling and watched her wriggling on a Zoom screen.

By then, Covid 19 had arrived in Europe, and Australia had closed her borders. Lisa must wait to meet her grandchild until her own eventual return home to Sophie and David in England was possible.

THE END

About the author

I live in a village bordering the moors in Cornwall and the location is inspiring: wonderful walking country, ever-changing skies and seascapes. My origins and those of my husband are south-east England. In between, we spent over a decade living in rural France, before returning to the UK. That is when I got down to serious writing!

The three books in the Victorian saga series are followed by two Historical Mysteries. Both are time-split novels. *To Nail A Witch* is set in the 12th century and the contemporary period, and *Monsieur Bertheau's Collection* is set in the Jazz Age of 1920s France and the contemporary period.

'Dark Clouds Breaking' is the third book in the Victorian series. I also write contemporary fiction and some of my short stories and novellas have French settings. I am drawn to different cultures, whether modern or historical and enjoy researching them.

The Victorian Saga

By Mary D Curd

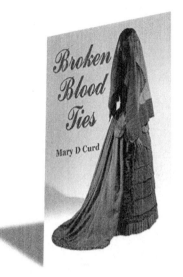

Broken Blood Ties

18th Nov, 2017

Paperback: 242 pages

Publisher: Amazon KDP Independent Publishing Platform

Language: English

ISBN-10: 9781979839525

ISBN-13: 978-1979839525

ASIN: 1979839522

Genre: Historical Fiction

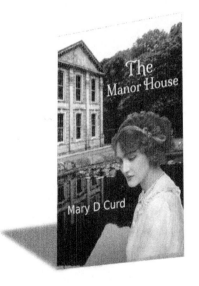

The Manor House

23rd Apr, 2018

Paperback: 290 pages

Publisher: Amazon KDP Independent Publishing Platform

Language: English

ISBN-10: 1717334458

ISBN-13: 978-1717334459

Genre: Historical Fiction

All available online at Amazon

Dark Clouds Breaking

8th Dec, 2019
Paperback: 307 pages
Publisher: Amazon KDP
Independent Publishing Platform
Language: English
ISBN-10: 171257650X
ISBN-13: 978-1712576502
Genre: Historical Fiction

To Nail a Witch

9th Feb, 2021
Paperback: 361 pages
Publisher: Amazon KDP
Independent Publishing Platform
Language: English
ISBN-13: 979-8703848104
Genre: Historical Thriller

Monsieur Bertheau's Collection

11th Nov, 2021

Paperback: 263 pages

Publisher: Amazon KDP

Independent Publishing Platform

Language: English

ISBN: 9798766247869

Genre: Historical Fiction

All available online at Amazon.co.uk

Printed in Great Britain
by Amazon

21414772R00149